FURIOUS
THING

FURIOUS THING

Jenny Downham

David Fickling Books

Scholastic Inc. / New York

Library of Congress Cataloging-in-Publication Data available
ISBN 978-1-338-54065-9

10 9 8 7 6 5 4 3 2 1   20 21 22 23 24

Printed in the U.S.A.   23
First edition, January 2020
Book design by Baily Crawford

For my sister, Tina

A Tale of Love and Death

ONCE, THERE WAS A girl who grew up wicked. She threw things and slammed things and swore. She was clumsy and rude and had no friends. Her teachers thought her half-witted. Her family despaired.

"Why can't you be well-behaved and calm like other girls?" they cried. "Why are you so freaking difficult day after day?"

The girl didn't know the answer.

Her family tapped their feet and shook their heads disapprovingly, trying to work her out.

"I'll change," the girl said. "I'll be good from now on, I promise."

She wanted it to be true.

She wanted her family to love her.

But fury sat in her belly like a vicious snake. And some promises are hard to keep.

One

I RAN INTO THE yard to hide. I'd been there for over ten minutes and thought I was going to get away with it, when Mom came
out of the apartment and down the steps. I tried my best to be invisible, but when she walked across the lawn, she saw me.

She said, "Get down from the tree and come and apologize
right now."

"Is he angry?"

"We both are."

"Is he going to ground me?"

"I don't know. But you can't speak to people like that and think
nothing's going to happen."

"I didn't mean to. The words just fell out."

"Is that right?" She held out her hand to tick them off. "You
hope tonight's going to be a disaster. You hope the guests get food
poisoning. You have no intention of coming to the party and we can
all piss off. Those words just fell out of you, did they?"

I spread my fingers to touch a black-velvet leaf bud. If I were a
leaf, nothing would be expected of me.

Mom said, "Pretty hurtful, wouldn't you say?"

I peered down through the branches to look at her. She was wearing yoga pants and a T-shirt. She had an apron tied round her waist and her face was flushed. I melted looking at her. I'd promised to help get things ready and all I'd done was cause trouble. "I'm sorry, Mom."

She smiled wearily up at me. "I know you're disappointed Kass isn't coming, but you can still have fun without him. Think of all the delicious food and how amazing the yard's going to look with the lights and everyone dancing."

But the only person I wanted to dance with was Kass. I hadn't seen him since he went back to college after Christmas. That was sixty-five whole days ago.

Mom said, "Come on—down you get. The sooner you apologize to John, the less painful it will be."

I climbed down slowly. I hoped I looked graceful.

"I've had an idea about tonight," she said when I finally stood next to her on the grass. "I know you find social events hard and I'm sorry your brother can't be here."

"He's not my brother."

"You know what I mean. If Kass was here, you'd find everything easier. But he's not coming, so there we are. So, how about you hand hors d'oeuvres around at the beginning? What do you think? It'll give you the chance to socialize without pressure."

I saw where this was going and felt a pinprick of panic. "I can't speak to people."

"Having a task might help."

What would she do if I turned round and climbed the tree again? Would she grab my ankles? If I scrambled up quickly enough, maybe she'd walk back across the lawn and tell John I'd disappeared? They'd have to celebrate their engagement without me. But as moments kept slipping by, it was obvious we weren't going in that direction. I shoved my hands in my pockets and waited.

"Lex?" she said eventually.

"Surely, the whole point of a buffet is that people help themselves?"

"They help themselves to the main course, but it's usual to offer appetizers as guests arrive."

"Please don't make me. Get Iris to do it instead."

"Iris is a little young." She linked her arm with mine and squeezed. "This is a fresh start for us. I want you involved."

She was excited. I could feel it through her fingers. She'd waited years for John's divorce to come through, and now she could finally be his wife, she didn't need me messing things up.

"I'll collect empty glasses if you like. I'll look after coats."

"That doesn't get you mingling, Lex."

"Honestly, Mom, me walking around with trays of food is going to be a disaster. You know it is."

"I don't know anything of the sort."

I'd trip. I'd spill stuff. I'd forget the names of the hors d'oeuvres. "What's this?" people would ask, pointing at something on my tray, and they'd expect a sensible answer and I'd stand there mumbling nonsense and they'd look at me weirdly and I'd get so mad I'd fling the tray on the grass and stomp off. John's glossy coworkers would discover what he already knew—that I was an idiot with a terrible temper. Someone was bound to ask him, "Is this girl anything to do with you?" And then there'd be that awful disappointed look on his face as he said, "Alexandra is going to be my stepdaughter."

Mom kissed the top of my head. I don't know why. Maybe she was wishing me luck or maybe she was letting me know that even though I was a nightmare, she still loved me.

I said, "I'm angry with Kass."

Mom nodded. "I know."

I'd texted him from my bedroom earlier:

U AWAKE?

He took thirty-seven minutes to text back.

AM NOW.

STILL NOT CMING?

He said no. He said sorry and that he'd make it up to me. I wanted to ask how he planned on doing that, but I didn't. I switched my phone off instead.

Mom took my hand as we walked back to the apartment. "You'll get used to him being gone one day, Lex."

She didn't get it at all.

✳

I was eight when I first met Kass and he was nearly eleven. Mom was already pregnant with Iris, so making a new family was a fait accompli, which means you get no choice.

Kass was told to look after me in the yard while the adults talked. I decided to ignore him. I was eight and didn't need looking after. Also, it was *my* yard. I decided if I didn't speak to him or look at him that he'd go away. But he didn't. The first thing he did was sit on a step of the fire escape and say, "If there really was a fire, these stairs would be useless." He pointed out that they led directly into a walled yard from which there was no escape and that once everyone from the apartment building had collected there, it would be hell— with bits of burning building falling on our heads and no way out. "You should get a rope with knots in it," he said, "and tie it to your bed or the window frame and go out the front."

I liked it that he could think about terrible things in such a calm way. I also liked it that he wanted to save me. In "Hansel and Gretel," it was the girl who did the saving, but the other way around might be fun.

"My mom's going to go nuts when she knows I've been here," he said next. He picked up a handful of gravel from the steps and threw each little stone one by one onto the grass. "Your mom's the other woman. Did you know?"

I shook my head.

"That's why my mom's going to go nuts. She went ballistic when she found out. She thought my dad was busy at work, not going on dates."

"He's been seeing my mom for ages," I said.

"Exactly," Kass said.

He told me his mom threw his dad out, but she let him back when he promised to change. He said his dad was great at apologies, but they were usually bullshit and he wished his parents would stop being morons.

"Then my mom found out about the baby." He looked right at me and something sad in his eyes made my heart leap.

"What did she do?" I whispered.

"Yelled a lot. Chucked stuff. The funniest thing she threw was a cup of tea at my dad's head."

He laughed, so I laughed too. "Did it hit him?"

"He ducked, and it smashed on the wall, but he got soaked anyway."

I kept looking in his eyes. "What else did she throw?"

"The biggest thing was the TV, which she flung down the stairwell."

We cracked up at that. I thought his mom must be very strong, but he told me it was a portable TV, so it wasn't that impressive. Also, that his mom wanted to get a new one anyway, so it wasn't much of a loss.

Kass said, "My mom thinks my dad's got this amazing new life with a new place to live and a new woman and a ready-made daughter."

"She knows about me?"

"Of course."

The idea that the grown-ups had been talking about me, and a total stranger was jealous of my life, made me gloriously happy.

I showed Kass my special way of climbing the tree and which branch to use to drop down to the wall. He said I clearly already knew what to do if there was a fire and could've rescued myself all along. From the top branch, I showed him which apartment was mine, and we searched the windows looking for my mom or his dad, but the sun was glaring, so we just got bright reflections back. Then we looked at other people's windows to see if we could see anyone naked, but we couldn't. We played silly games—the craziest curtains, the most things on a window ledge, the dirtiest glass, the ugliest plant. We agreed on loads. And we laughed a lot. I was ridiculously glad that I could make him laugh.

But nothing was as good as the moment when he asked about my dad.

"I never met him," I said. "He dumped my mom when she got pregnant with me."

Until then, I hadn't felt the smallest bit pleased about never having known my dad. But saying it out loud was like giving Kass an important gift.

He whistled low and long. Then he took my hand and squeezed it.

"Adults really piss me off," he said.

It was like we'd cut our fingers with knives and become bound.

Two

INSIDE, THE APARTMENT WAS like a TV commercial—full of sunshine and cooking smells. Iris sat at the coffee table with her coloring things, John was in his chair with the Saturday newspapers spread across the carpet at his feet. I wondered if he was going to give me the silent treatment, but he looked up as I walked in. "Calmed down?"

"Sorry."

"Is that it?"

"Sorry I said the things I did. I didn't mean them. I hope your party is a huge success and I won't lose my temper ever again."

"Well, now you just sound sarcastic."

He went back to his paper. I breathed easier.

Iris flicked me a smile. "Come and look at my picture." She'd drawn a fairy-tale castle made of glass and mirrors, erupting into a blue sky. "It's our new house," she said. "The one Daddy's going to build when we're rich. This is a turret"—she pointed at the smallest tower—"and these are called crenellations."

"Good girl," John said. "You want me to teach you a bastion next?"

"No, thank you." She sucked the end of her pen. "I'm going to do direction posters for the party now so everyone knows to come upstairs for the bathroom."

I kissed the top of her head. She smelled of cookies. "That's sounds like a lot of work."

She nodded. "I have infinite patience."

I often doubted we were related. Not just the amount of words she knew for a six-year-old, but how talented she was at everything. Also, she was insanely pretty. It was like she was from a different species. It was John and Mom's genes mixed together. I was an ogre compared to the rest of them.

John flapped his paper. "Uninhibited," he said. "Eight letters, second letter is *m*."

I wished more than anything I knew. I wanted to stun him with sudden intelligence.

"I thought it might be *immoral*," John said, "but that's not enough letters."

Was he really wanting help? I plonked myself on the sofa opposite him. "You want me to look it up on my phone?"

"No, because that would be cheating." Definitely not wanting help. He tapped his pen on the paper. "You know tonight's smart casual, right?"

I looked down at my jeans. They had a hole in one knee and mud round both hems. I'd been wearing them yesterday and had dragged them back on this morning.

"I'm planning on wearing a dress."

"Great. Have I seen it?"

"It's new. I'll show you later. Mom's got jobs for me first."

I could hear her out in the kitchen clunking stuff around. John's colleagues were used to catered parties, but John said he wanted theirs to be authentic, which meant everything home-made.

I slunk down into the sofa, suddenly full of dread. All those architects from John's work would be smart and polished like him. I was going to spend the evening feeling like such a loser.

John folded his paper and picked up his cigarettes. "Iris, I'm going to smoke. Can you leave the room for ten minutes?"

"But I'm doing something."

"Take a break and come back." He smiled at her. "Bedroom or kitchen—your choice."

She put down a felt-tip pen and picked up a new color. "I choose to stay."

"No, sweetheart—I don't want your lungs full of smoke and tar."

She snapped the lid off the pen. "I don't want your lungs full of that either."

He laughed. "Come on, give me a break here."

"Smoking's very bad for you, Daddy."

He held his hands up in surrender. "All right, you win. How about making me some tea instead?"

She frowned, suspicious. "So you can smoke when I'm gone?"

He waggled the cigarette at her. "I promise if you make some tea and bring me a slice of shortbread, I will never smoke this."

She hopped off her chair and held out her hand. "Give it to me, then." He passed it over and she patted his head. "Good boy."

He was never obedient like that with me. I wish I could make him sit, lie down, beg, come to heel . . .

"So," John said, and I realized too late that he'd sent Iris away on purpose. "I understand you pestered Kass about joining us tonight?"

My heart scudded. "He told you that?"

He pulled a fresh cigarette from the packet and lit it. "I believe you told your mother."

I knew I was blushing. I sighed as if everything about Kass was boring and slid down the sofa some more. "I happened to text him. I happened to mention it."

"And his answer was . . . ?"

"He's still busy." I checked out my nails.

"And that brought on your tantrum?" He leaned forward, smoke coiling between us. "We talked about this, didn't we? I don't want him thinking he has to rush down from Manchester at the drop of a hat."

I checked my cuticles, the dry patch on my palm.

John said, "He's got exams coming up. No one expected him to come tonight and now he feels guilty."

"I wasn't trying to make him feel guilty."

He frowned. Beat, beat went our hearts.

"What were you trying to make him feel, Alexandra?"

If I had to sum up, I'd say: *a crushing desire to spend the rest of his life with me*. But I wasn't going to admit that out loud. Not until I'd proved to John that I was good enough for his son.

"Give the boy a break," John said.

"I thought you'd like him at your party."

"He'll be back after exams, OK?" He gave me a tight smile. "Although, if you keep hassling him, he might prefer to stay away."

The furious thing inside me came roaring up, but I swallowed it. "I'm not hassling him. I'm communicating."

"Well, communicate less."

"Yes, John." I used my robot voice.

"Now, about tonight. I don't want any more outbursts, so best behavior—OK?"

"I'm going to help. I'm going to hand out hors d'oeuvres."

"Seriously? Is that a good idea?"

"Don't worry. I won't drop anything."

"How about you just keep your temper in check?" He tapped his cigarette on the edge of the ashtray. "Be polite, that's all I ask—be nice to my friends and super nice to my boss."

"Why? You after a raise?"

He laughed. "Think you can get that for me?"

There's a valley in Norway where the sun hardly ever shines, and the people are shivering and gloomy for half the year. Then, one day, someone had the brilliant idea to put giant mirrors at the top of the mountain to reflect the sun down and they put benches around the town square, so people could sit and lift their faces to the light. Living in the shade makes you afraid to dream of the sun and then, when you feel it at last, it's thrilling.

"Best behavior," I said. "I promise. By the end of the night, you'll be proud to know me."

He nodded, and for a moment he looked as if he believed it might be possible.

Three

THE FIRST TIME I met John, I was seven and Mom had invited him round to the apartment. I was wearing my sequin dress and Mom was wearing her favorite skirt with the lace at the bottom and a new pink blouse that was see-through, but she said that didn't matter because she was wearing a fancy bra. She'd tidied up and vacuumed and sprayed air freshener. She'd bought a case of beer and put it in the fridge.

While we waited for him to arrive, we looked at the website for the architects' office where he worked. We pressed the button called About Us, and pictures of everyone who worked there appeared.

"That's him," Mom said. "Hasn't he got a lovely smile?"

There weren't any pictures of houses he'd built because he wasn't a partner, so we came off the projects page and looked at his photo again. Then Mom checked the time on her phone and went to the window to look out. "It probably looks different in daylight," she said. "All the other times, it's been dark when he's come here. I hope he hasn't walked straight past."

"All the other times?" I said.

"Oh," she said, waving a hand. "When you were asleep."

She called her friend Meryam. "Has he forgotten? Has he got cold feet? Has he had an accident?" She took the phone out to the kitchen, but I could hear her anyway. "You think he's playing hard to get? You think this is because of Lex? He wanted me to send her to her grandfather for the weekend—you think I should have done it?"

I twirled in my dress so I wouldn't have to listen. The skirt spun around me.

"I just got a text," Mom said, coming back into the living room. "He's running late but he's still coming, so that's a relief."

I pirouetted for her and the skirt danced.

"You've messed up your hair," she said.

She sat me on the stool in the living room and brushed me neat again. She decided I needed shoes, even though we were indoors, and went off to find them. She changed her earrings and reapplied lipstick. She said my hair had a mind of its own and she'd braid it while we waited. I liked the feel of her fingers in my hair. She hadn't braided it for weeks. "He's here!" Mom squealed suddenly. She nudged me from the stool and threw the brush on the bookshelf. She pulled me away from the window. "Don't let him see you looking!"

She stood in the center of the room with her hand flat on her belly. "Breathe," she told herself.

I'd never seen her like this. It was as if she wasn't in charge anymore.

She walked very slowly to the door when the intercom buzzed. She stood there not answering and I watched her count, her lips moving from one to ten, and then she pressed the button and said,

"Hello?" and she managed to make herself sound casual, as if she barely cared. "Oh, hi," she said. "Just push the door and come up."

She winked at me as we listened to his footsteps coming up the stairs.

"Lexi, this is John," Mom said as he walked through the door and into the hallway, and she waved at me and then she did an odd little bow to him like he was a king. "And this is my daughter, Lexi."

He held out his hand and I shook it. "Hello," he said. "Nice to meet you."

"Thank you," I said. I had no other words for him and we stood there looking at each other. His smile was like being warmed under a lamp.

Four

GO DOWN THE STAIRS, I told myself. *You've got this.*

But standing on the top of the fire escape looking down at all the swanky people in the yard made me feel like Cinderella. No—her ugly sister, the one who cut her toes off to make the glass slipper fit. My feet looked massive in Mom's dainty shoes, my hands were clumsy paws sticking out from the sleeves of her dress. She'd wrapped it round me, pulled the belt so tight that my hips and breasts were squashed flat, and then told me I looked lovely.

When I'd put on the dress I'd *wanted* to wear, the material had followed my curves like the website suggested: *Show off your best features and offer a flattering silhouette.* I did look lovely then. But when I'd gone into the living room to twirl for John, he'd shouted, "No, no!" and called for Mom. He'd pointed at me. "It's way too revealing. She can't wear that. Did you buy that for her?"

Mom told him she'd never seen the dress before and I had to confess I'd secretly used her Amazon account and bought it online. John told Mom she really needed to keep a better eye on me and I said I was sorry and promised (again) to be on my best behavior.

Mom put an arm around me and led me away. "Come on, babe. Let's find something else."

She took me to her bedroom and riffled through the hangers in her wardrobe, plucking out dresses and holding them against me, then frowning and putting them back. Finally, she pulled out a black dress covered in dry cleaner's plastic.

"This one," she said. "It's a wraparound. I bought it for Granddad's funeral."

"Well, that's cheery."

"It was very expensive. You'll look sophisticated."

"I'll look like I'm in mourning. It's the exact opposite of a party outfit."

She laughed. "Your idea of a party outfit was a little risqué."

"Well, I'm only agreeing if I can wear the necklace with it." It was the one thing Mom had inherited—a gift from her dad to her mom on their fortieth wedding anniversary and concrete proof that love could last a lifetime. "Granddad said we could share it when I turned sixteen."

"That's weeks away."

"Today's a special occasion and it's a waste keeping it shut in a box all the time."

But Mom said it was too precious, and if I lost it, it'd break her heart.

Once I was sealed into the dress, she brushed my hair. "You don't know this," she said, "but when we first moved here, I wasn't speaking to Granddad. He thought I was foolish getting pregnant so young. And he was ashamed your dad wanted nothing to do with me."

"That wasn't your fault."

"I should have made better choices, apparently. I shouldn't have thrown my future away." She smiled at me in the mirror. "I let him pay for the apartment, but nothing else. I wanted to prove I could manage. I was eighteen years old with a new baby and I didn't know a single person in London. I had no job, no friends, and hardly any money."

"You had me."

"Yes, I had you. And you were beautiful." She wrapped a band round my hair and pulled it tight. "But I'd go days without speaking to anyone. I'd sit in the park and watch couples with their kids and it felt like I came from a different planet. Even after I met Meryam and made a few friends, it was tough. I didn't go on a date for years. I began to think I'd never be loved that way by a man again."

"Mom, that's gross!"

She laughed as she twisted my hair into a knot. "You'll understand when you're older. What I'm trying to tell you is that when John came along it was like my lights switched back on."

"That's gross too!"

"It's important to me that you two get along."

"So you keep saying."

"Especially now that we're getting married."

"OK. I get it."

"Good. And talking of Meryam—she's coming tonight, so you'll know someone."

"Meryam's *your* friend."

"But you've known her all your life, so you can chat to her. And she might bring Ben."

"What did you invite him for? I see him every day at school, so that's just weird." I tried to read the look that flickered across Mom's face. "Are you secretly thinking I've got no friends?"

She sighed. "No, I'm secretly thinking we've got precisely twenty minutes before people start to arrive." She snapped a hair clip into place at the top of my head. "You're done."

But I was wrong in so many places. Even my hair misbehaved and had to be tucked away. I wanted something to be right. So, after she went off to get Iris ready, I snuck open Mom's jewelry box and took the necklace. It was like something a queen would wear—a solid gold chain with eight rubies set along it. The stones held fire.

Standing at the top of the stairs now, I lifted the necklace to the light. "Granddad," I whispered. "Help me nail this."

If you want a favor from the dead, you have to offer them something back—like leaving them food or doing a special job or keeping their secrets. Whenever I asked my granddad for help, I promised never to forget him.

Iris was wearing her fairy outfit. She whirled on the lawn, her hair tumbling loose and her wings sparkling. She saw me and waved. "Lexi!" I waved back, and she ran up the stairs to me. I picked her up and she wrapped her legs around my waist and I spun her.

John was watching, and he called, "Careful on those steps, Alexandra."

I set Iris gently down. "Wish me luck with the hors d'oeuvres."

"You want me to help?"

"I promised I'd do it. I'm supposed to mingle."

"We could do it together. Then you're already mingling."

I took her hand. "Will you do the talking?"

"And you hold the tray?"

"Exactly. Like a sister double act. You're the clever one and I'm the strong one."

She was brilliant at it. I held the tray and tried not to drop anything, and Iris was my angelic assistant.

"Crostini?" she said. "Or we have filo tartlets, vol-au-vents, or breaded prawns. I've tried them all and they're delicious."

People loved her. People radiated warmth just looking at her.

"Look at the little one, isn't she adorable?"

"Gorgeous."

"Not surprising, given her father . . ."

"That man gets more handsome each week, I swear."

"What about the older girl?"

"She's not his."

Not yet I wasn't. But after the wedding I would be.

I pulled Iris close. "What do you do," I asked, "to make everyone love you?"

"I smile a lot."

"Doesn't that make your jaw ache? Don't you get sick of it?"

She glared at me. "It takes more muscles to frown."

Which made me laugh. Which made her laugh too.

We gave out two whole trays of starters and had nearly finished the third, when we saw Meryam. Iris ran over and hugged her.

Meryam held her arms out to me. "Lexi," she said. "I haven't seen you for ages."

I couldn't hug her properly because of the tray, so I leaned in and she stroked me on the back.

"How are you?" she said.

I shrugged. "OK, thanks."

"She doesn't like people she doesn't know," Iris told her. "And she thinks smiling makes your jaw ache."

Meryam laughed. "You have my sympathy, Lex. It's tough to be smiley with strangers—especially such stylish ones. I find it helps to imagine them on the toilet."

Iris giggled so much that people looked over. I liked it that we looked as if we were having more fun than them. It made it easy to tell Meryam about the red dress I'd originally been wearing and how John had a meltdown when he saw it. "It was funky," I said. "Much nicer than this one." Meryam stroked my arm and said that no dress could hide my youthful beauty.

We talked about the surprise of John's marriage proposal after all these years, and I said it was because Kass's mom wouldn't sign the divorce papers, and Iris said she probably still loved him and I said it was because she was badass and we all started giggling again. Then Meryam said, "I'm sorry, girls, but I've finally seen someone I know. Do you mind if I wander off and talk to them?"

Iris gave her an electric smile. "I'm going first." And she skipped away, her fairy wings bouncing. Me and Meryam watched her go. We seemed less without her.

Meryam said, "Come with me if you want, Lex."

I knew it was because she felt sorry for me and I jiggled my tray. "I've got to hand these out."

"Let me call Ben over to help you. He's by the bar—look."

He was taking a swig from a bottle of beer. He was the same age as me, so how come he was allowed to break the rules? He didn't seem to have to follow the dress code either and was wearing jeans and a hoodie.

Meryam nudged me. "Why not go over and say hello?"

"I will in a minute. I'll get rid of these hors d'oeuvres first."

She gave me a gentle rub on the back and walked off. I pretended to be Iris as I took the tray round the yard again. I tried to look friendly and normal. "Crostini? Filo tartlet?"

Mom and John were talking by the fence, so I went over and held out my tray. "Vol-au-vent?"

Mom gave me a small smile. "Not now, Lex."

"What's up?"

"Nothing, babe, it's OK."

But John looked hassled and Mom was all tense, so something was going on.

"It's a party," John said to her. "I'm allowed to talk to people, surely?"

"I don't have a problem with you talking, John. That's not what I meant."

I took a piece of cucumber from the tray and shoved it in my mouth. It wasn't as nice as it looked. It tasted of water and fridges.

John wiped an arm across his face and it made him look tired, and maybe Mom felt guilty about whatever she'd said because she took a big breath. "Forget I said anything."

"Bit late for that."

I took another piece of cucumber and chomped it down at top volume.

John blinked at me. "What're you doing?"

I smiled up at him. "Nothing."

"Aren't you supposed to be handing food around instead of eating it yourself?"

"It's only cucumber."

"What, you think that doesn't count?"

"It's got like zero calories."

"I'm talking about the fact that you're not leaving any for anyone else."

I took a vol-au-vent instead and ate it while staring at him.

"Are you not going to stop her?" he said to Mom. "It was your idea to have her helping and now she's guzzling everything."

Mom smiled soothingly at him. "Let me deal with Lexi. You get back to the guests."

He huffed through his nose, like that's what he'd wanted all along. "Speech in ten minutes?" he said. His voice had lost some of its edge.

"Sure," Mom said.

He kissed her on the cheek. "I love you. Never forget it."

We watched him walk away.

I waited for Mom to yell at me about the hors d'oeuvres, but she'd noticed the necklace and was frowning.

"Oh, Lex, what did I tell you?"

I skimmed my hand along the chain. "It'll be fine. I won't lose it."

"Does nothing I say to you make any difference?"

"I'll be careful. It's helping me feel brave."

She shook her head. "Please. You promised best behavior tonight."

I hated that disappointed look in her eyes. "OK, OK, I'll take it off."

"Not here. Finish handing out the hors d'oeuvres. I've got to bring the main buffet down in a minute. Then straight upstairs and put it back in my jewelry box."

I quickly did another tour of the lawn, offloading most of what was left, and then took the almost-empty tray over to a couple standing by one of the outdoor heaters. He was gray-haired and expensive-looking; she was pretty and much younger than him. I gave them my best attempt at a smile. "Breaded prawn?"

The woman shook her head politely. "No, thank you."

The guy looked me up and down. "Any chance you could get me another glass of Chablis?"

I balanced the tray on one arm and helped myself to a crostini and stuffed it in my mouth.

He stared at me. The woman stared at me too.

"I don't work here," I said. "I'm one of the daughters."

I picked up a vol-au-vent to prove it, but as I brought it to my mouth, it collapsed and slid out of my hand. The woman gave a little yelp as it landed on her foot.

"Shit," I said. "I'm really sorry."

John came bounding over. "What happened?"

27

"An accident," the woman said, waving a hand. "No harm done."

"Right on your shoe! Oh, Alexandra—butterfingers . . ."

"I didn't do it on purpose," I said quietly.

"Run and get some tissues, quickly."

The guy handed me his napkin. "Use this."

I knelt on the grass and scooped the biggest lump from the woman's shoe. My face burned as I folded it into the cloth and dabbed at what was left. I felt all three of them looking down at me.

"Can't get the staff," John said.

"Ha ha," said the man.

I'd smeared everything and made it worse—the shoe looked cloudy and damp.

"Never mind," the woman said. "Really, it doesn't matter."

"It does," John said. "Send me the bill if it needs a specialist clean, Monika. Honestly, I mean it."

I stood up and held the man's napkin out to him, but John waved me away. "I think the trash can, don't you?"

I walked two circumferences of the yard. I thought about camouflaging myself as a bush. I thought about lying on the ground and pretending to be dead. I thought about creeping up the stairs and going to my room.

Instead, I found a dark place under my tree and sat there.

"Hey, Lex!"

I snapped my eyes open, convinced for one amazing second it was Kass—but no: Ben was standing grinning in front of me.

"Why are you sitting by yourself?" he said.

"Because I hate parties."

He laughed. "Are you hatching a plan to wreck it?"

I stared at him. "Why would I do that? You think I'm crazy?"

I sounded furious and he looked embarrassed. His feelings were always right there on the surface for anyone to see.

I said, "Did your mom tell you to talk to me?"

He shook his head.

"Because I don't need a friend. So, feel free to go away."

"Jesus," he said. "I only came over to say hi."

I should be kind to him. Our moms had been friends for years and we'd played together as kids. But I just sat there not saying anything and he stood in front of me shuffling from foot to foot.

"Can I have some of your beer?" I said eventually.

He handed it over and watched as I knocked it back. He didn't even look as if he minded.

"You're very generous," I said. I meant it, although it came out sounding sarcastic.

He said, "So, where's Kass tonight?"

"He couldn't come. He's studying."

I sounded bored of the whole deal. My boring stepbrother and his dull life. I liked how ordinary I sounded.

Ben said, "Have you started studying for exams yet?"

"Of course not."

"They're coming up soon, Lex, and they'll chuck you out of school if you don't pass. Don't you want to stay on at sixth form?"

Was he teasing me? "You need to get averages of five or above."

"And won't you?"

"Not unless a miracle happens."

He shrugged. "You'll do fantastic in drama."

"That's one GCSE exam. I need to pass at least four others to stay on. My only other good subject is media and I haven't even started my project yet."

"There's still time. Come on, Lex—you can do it. You're not bad at English, are you? You'll get a five for that, easily."

Some nights I lay in bed in a sweat because of everything I didn't know. Once, I looked at an old science paper on my laptop and it was like reading a foreign language. It showed how far we'd grown apart if Ben thought opening a few books was going to sort my life out. I stared at him so he'd stop talking about school. He had freckles and, even though Meryam was dark-haired, Ben's hair was chestnut red, but you couldn't tell those things in the dark.

"Don't give up, Lex," he said. "It'd be terrible if you got thrown out of school. You'll end up retaking the tests at some crappy college or being enrolled on an apprenticeship somewhere. You don't want to be a plumber, do you? Or a hairdresser? That's what they'll have you doing if you fail—something vocational. I bet you can pass five exams easily if you put your mind to it."

I was going to tell him to please talk about something else when we were interrupted by the clinking of a glass from across the lawn and people shouting, "Speech, speech!"

"Here we go," Ben said.

John was standing on the steps and Mom was next to him. As I watched, Iris ran over and John picked her up and she wrapped an arm round his shoulder and he cradled her close.

He turned to the crowd and smiled his golden smile. "Thank you so much for coming tonight," he said. "I'd like to say a few words if you'll indulge me . . ."

He talked about meeting Mom and how, from the minute he saw her, he knew she was "the one." "Well, look at her," he said. She laughed and did a shy little curtsy. "Just as well she stole my heart," he said, "because she was pregnant within five minutes." He lifted Iris to the crowd and everyone cooed. He talked about moving into the apartment when his ex-wife claimed his assets—should people laugh at that?—and pointed out the lines of new bricks where he'd eventually bought the apartment above and converted them into one. "But," he said, "my real dream house is on a roll of white tracing paper in my desk and, as many of you are aware, finding building plots in London is not the simplest task." The crowd lapped it up. They were mostly architects, so I guess it was interesting to them.

"I would like to propose a toast to my fiancée," John said. "Georgia, you're beautiful and patient and everything I could hope for in a woman. Just as soon as I'm made partner and can afford it"—more laughter—"I promise to build you the home you deserve." He accepted the kiss she planted on his cheek and waved his hand to acknowledge cheers from the crowd.

"Seriously," he said, "thank you for taking time out of your busy lives to celebrate with us. Please enjoy the buffet and the bar and don't forget to throw some shapes on the dance floor." He raised his glass. "To the future."

"What?" Ben said as all the adults raised their glasses and echoed John's words. "No PowerPoint presentation?"

I shot him a look. "What are you talking about?"

"Nothing."

"Why did you say it, then?"

He shrugged. "He just sounds a tiny bit of a prick, that's all."

"That's extremely rude of you."

He gazed at me for a minute, then nodded. "I'm going to get a drink."

He walked away, and I went in the opposite direction. I helped myself to a plate of food and sat back under my tree. I watched the party grow and swell as more people arrived and the ones who were there got louder. Empty plates were gathered up. The cakes were brought out. More lights came on and the yard glittered. The morning felt like years ago.

I scanned the lawn for Iris. She'd taken her ballet slippers off and hung them in a bush, their silky ribbons trailing to the ground. She looked like a painting of a girl sitting exhausted on the grass beneath them with her hair spilling around her shoulders. If I offered to take her in and put her to bed, it might get me back in everyone's good books.

A man sidled up as I walked into the light. "Hello again." It was the guy from earlier. He held out his hand for me to shake. "Sorry about before. I had no idea you were John's girl. I'm Roger."

His handshake was firm and made me feel grown-up. And I liked being John's girl. "Hello," I said.

I had no idea beyond that—what was supposed to happen next.

"And you're Alexandra, I believe?"

I nodded. He nodded back at me.

"So," he said. "No longer gainfully employed handing out food?"

"I got sacked."

He chuckled. "Because of Monika's shoe?"

"I pretty much ruined it."

He chuckled some more and nodded over to her. She was standing with John by the stairs. "I wouldn't worry," Roger said. "She's only the intern. I doubt she has expensive shoes."

"You work with her?"

"I guess you could say so. I'm senior partner."

Be super nice to my boss.

It was weird standing with Roger—both of us gazing across the grass. John must've said something funny because Monika was tipping her face up with laughter. I could see the long length of her throat. I looked for Mom and saw her over by the buffet table, scraping plates.

"I better go," I said. "If I help my mom, she'll be free to dance with John."

Roger turned to smile at me. "I've got a better idea."

I noticed for the first time the pale mustache on his lip. I also noticed that his eyes seemed out of focus as he looked at me.

He held out his arms. "You're going to dance with me."

"I can't. Honestly, I'm not very good at it."

"Nonsense." He came closer and wrapped his arms around me, and even though he was old and drunk, I felt a tiny bit proud. John had told me to be super nice to his boss and here I was about to dance with him.

He made little sounds as we began to move to the music—a sort of breathy humming mixed with the slosh of faraway liquid. I imagined bubbles from the champagne fizzing inside him.

"This all right for you?" he said.

"Sure."

He nodded. "Excellent."

I wanted John to see, but he was still chatting to Monika. I wanted Ben to see too—wanted him to know that I attracted older men who knew about the world. But the only person looking was Mom and I didn't want her making another scene if she noticed I was still wearing the necklace, so I gave her a cheery wave as Roger whisked me off.

His hand gripped my waist more firmly as we whirled into a darker part of the yard. Before, he'd kept a distance, but now he pressed himself closer. I tried to steer us back toward the lights, but I wasn't in charge of steering.

"I like a girl with curves," he said, and I caught a whiff of seafood on his breath. "Too many girls are like sticks these days."

I was in a crowd, with my family, in my own yard. Around me, people were chatting and laughing. I was stupid to mind Roger's hot fingers gripping my waist.

Roger said, "Well, this is a treat I wasn't anticipating."

Where was Mom now? Still over by the buffet table, clattering plates onto trays. Where was John? Still talking to Monika. He had his hand on the small of her back as if he was about to lead her away up the stairs.

Roger held me more tightly. His fingers had sunk below my waist and were almost on my butt.

I stalled on the grass. "I really should go and help my mom."

Roger pulled me closer and the hand that was almost on my butt slid farther down and my heart went speedy and my breath went raggedy and I could see myself outside, like I was watching TV and going, "Lex, this man is touching your butt!"

His creepy hand was on me and his stinky breath was mixing with mine and my blood was pounding in my ears. And the furious thing came roaring. *Stamp on his foot, Lex. Elbow him in the face. Knee him in the nuts. Yank him over to the tree and stab a twig in his eye.*

And suddenly I had gallons of oxygen and decibels of voice and tons of energy and they grew inside me like I'd explode if I didn't use them.

I pulled my arms free and shoved him hard. "Get the hell off me."

He staggered slightly backward. "What on earth's wrong with you?"

"You touched me."

"Don't be ridiculous."

"You just groped me."

"What sort of accusation is that to throw at someone?"

"Look, I don't want to dance, so just fuck off, will you?"

The yard went quiet. People looked over. And maybe Roger felt bad groping a fifteen-year-old in public, because he slapped a hand to his chest as if he'd been suddenly shot.

From across the lawn, a guy yelled, "You all right, boss?"

Roger hunched into himself and took several rapid breaths. "No," he said. "No, I don't think I am."

I knew they'd blame me. I thought, Well, I'm going to have to brazen it out. I gave Monika a death stare as she came trotting over with John. *Stupid shoe woman. Idiot intern.*

She said, "What happened?"

"Nothing to do with me."

She put a hand on my arm. "What was the shouting about?"

I shrugged her off.

We both looked at Roger, bent double, gasping like a fish. I had a brief vision of John grabbing him round the neck and shaking, shaking him. I wanted him to yell, *What did you do to my girl to make her swear at you like that?* But of course, he didn't. Instead, he put a steadying arm round Roger. "Something's brought on an asthma attack."

"Probably all the booze," I said.

He turned to glare at me. "I suggest you keep quiet."

Monika fetched a chair and Roger sank into it. John patted down Roger's jacket and discovered an inhaler. Someone brought over a glass of water and soon there was a small crowd. A woman removed her shawl and laid it tenderly over Roger's shoulders. And he sat there with his eyes shut, innocently wheezing.

Mom scurried over. "What's going on?"

"He's faking," I said.

"He's severely asthmatic," John said, his voice like ice.

The gaze of the entire group was on me. This is how it feels to be hunted down by a mob, I thought.

"Do you want to all stop gawping?" I said. "I didn't freaking do anything."

John said, "Language, Alexandra."

Mom looked at Roger rasping in his chair. "So, what's all this about?"

"He's a creep," I said, "and I'm being blamed."

Roger took a huge puff on his inhaler for dramatic effect and people fussed around him again. Was he cold? Did he want a blanket? Should they call a doctor? Roger shook his head and whispered he was fine, and please could everyone stop worrying? John gave him a manly slap on the shoulder before turning to the crowd and smiling. "I should've warned my soon-to-be stepdaughter about some of you charming older men. I should've advised her you're less robust than you look." There was polite laughter. "I think in her youthful enthusiasm, she's overexerted you, Roger?"

Roger waved his inhaler in agreement and I felt something claw at my gut.

"And perhaps," John said, turning to me, "she's been a little too eager at the bar?"

I stared at him. "That's total crap. I haven't been anywhere near the bar."

"Never mind. No harm done. Time for bed, do you think, Alexandra?"

"You can't send me to bed! I'm not a kid."

John sighed. "I think the jury might be out on that."

"Better go," Mom said. "We'll talk about this tomorrow."

Iris appeared and slipped her hand into mine, but John took her other hand and pulled her away. "Alexandra, I mean it. Off you go."

"Fuck you," I mouthed. Then a bit louder. "Fuck you!"

I could hear how it sounded. I knew what they'd all think. I watched everyone shake their heads in disbelief.

"I'm sorry, guys," John told them. "It's been a long day."

I told him to fuck himself one more time before I stomped across the lawn to the stairs.

Five

"IT HAPPENED AGAIN," I whispered to Kass when I called him from the safety of my bed.

"It's what we all love about you," Kass said. "All that drama . . ."

"I've probably ruined your dad's career. Everyone was staring."

"Screw them. Who cares what they think?"

Kass had laughed when I'd told him about Roger. But that was because I'd made myself out to be a badass who'd shoved a drunken guy halfway across the yard. I couldn't keep that version of the story up anymore. It was late, and I was tired.

"Your dad's never going to like me," I whispered.

"Of course he likes you."

"We're supposed to get along better now they're engaged, and I'm not supposed to get angry anymore."

"You're wicked and wild, Lex. You can't help who you are."

"I've got worse since you left. If you don't come back, I'll probably kill someone."

"I can't come back. It's the middle of the semester."

"Just for a weekend? Think about it at least."

I looked down at my legs in their pajamas and breathed. I could hear Kass breathing too. I pulled the zipper on his jacket more firmly up toward my throat so I could smell the leather. I always imagined the smell would run out, but it never did. "I'm wearing your jacket," I said.

"Cool."

I imagined him lying on his bed in his dorm room. He'd be on his back with the phone nestled against his ear. If I closed my eyes, I could imagine myself there, our heads sharing a pillow.

"What am I going to do without you?" I'd said when Kass announced he'd got into college.

He'd shrugged off his jacket. "You're going to wear this."

"But it's yours."

"Anarchist gift. Everything I have is yours, Lex."

"Everything?"

"Sure. Why not?"

There had been a silence so deep I could hear it.

Now I pulled the jacket tighter and the leather creaked against my skin. The zipper pressed onto my belly and I knew there'd be a mark, a red stipple from my belly button down.

"Does bad stuff happen when I'm around, Kass?"

"Who told you that?"

"Your dad. Years ago."

"Why did he say that? What bad stuff?"

I stayed silent, because I didn't want to remind him how my granddad died.

Kass said, "Are you talking about Iris and her accident?"

"And my dad leaving."

"You weren't even born when that happened."

"He knew I'd be a disaster."

"Don't be silly, Lex. Do you know how defeatist you sound right now? I guarantee if your dad had bothered to meet you, he'd think his daughter was awesome."

That was a nice thing to say. I sat with it for a second. "I wish your dad thought that. Then I could be part of the whole golden family thing."

"Golden family?"

"Iris and my mom being so pretty and you studying architecture and now the fairy-tale wedding. What's golden about me? Your dad can't work at home when I'm here, did you know that? I sap his creative energy."

"He's just winding you up."

"You totally need to come back and save me."

He laughed. "You don't need saving. You're indestructible."

"What, like a cockroach?"

"No, like the planet itself. Like rocks or the wind."

I let the words sink into me. I imagined myself a goddess with long, silky hair holding up the sky with her bare hands.

"Just stay out of his way," Kass said. "Isn't that the best plan?"

The goddess dissolved. "How do I do that? We live in the same apartment and I'm about to be grounded for months."

"Keep your head down. Nod in the right places. You're more than a match for him, Lex."

"I'm fifteen. How can you say that?"

"His bark's worse than his bite."

"You never go against him—that's why you never get in trouble. What makes you think it's easy for me?"

"I'm not saying it's easy."

"And to be honest, I think his bite's about to get worse than his bark. He keeps looking at me weird."

"That's because you're gorgeous."

"He doesn't look at me in that way! Don't say that about him. I mean he watches me like he's planning something. Like the way a lion watches an antelope."

Kass sighed. "I should probably go."

I was making him uncomfortable. Or maybe he had stuff to do. Maybe he was going to the student union to watch a band or had plans to go to a club. He was a great dancer— confident but not too serious. All the girls at the club would stare at him and their thoughts would heat up their bodies until they felt on fire.

Kass's phone pinged and he said he had to look and then he said, "I really do have to go."

I wanted to ask who'd texted, but I didn't want to make him claustrophobic, so I asked a polite question about the only girl whose name I knew. "How's Cerys?"

"She's cool."

"Has she been to visit?"

"Not yet."

The *yet* gave me hope, because it might never happen. It was tough keeping relationships going with miles between you. One hundred and ninety-eight miles, to be exact. Kass was joined to me by family, and I'd always have access to him. But girlfriends came and went.

Six

CERYS CHECKED OUT MY gray school skirt and socks, my blue shirt and flat black shoes. "I admire you," she said. "Not caring what people think is a gift."

We were in her bedroom. I was cross-legged on the carpet staring up at her and she was perched on the window ledge. Sixth formers didn't have a uniform and she was wearing a denim minidress. I could see the white lace of her bra when she lifted her arm to suck on her vape.

"What are you talking about?" I said. "Of course I care what people think."

"Do you? You don't seem to." She blew sweet-smelling vapor across the room. "You just seem to go about not giving a crap about anything."

"I didn't mean to wreck the party. It was an accident."

She nodded, and we sat with that for a bit. I'd come straight from school because I couldn't face going home and I couldn't think where else to go. The last few days had been a nightmare and I wanted to be with someone who knew about my world, and who better than

Kass's girlfriend? I also wanted to be with someone who could give me advice and Cerys was one of the most popular girls at school.

She'd looked a bit surprised to see me when she opened the door. Her face sort of fell. But when I told her I was just passing and wouldn't stay long, she invited me in.

"What would you have done," I said, "if you thought some drunk guy was groping you?"

"I'd have walked away." She blinked at me. "Or told my dad."

I think life is very different for girls like Cerys. If I could wake up in the morning and be someone else for twenty-four hours, I'd be her. I'd kiss my loving father goodbye, then shimmy down the street making plans with friends on group chat. When I got to school, I'd hand in my perfect assignments to smiling teachers and I'd think, Ah, this is how it feels to absolutely know that the rest of your life is going to be a breeze.

She took another long drag on her vape. From outside appearances, she looked like someone who didn't give a damn. But Kass said she was very ambitious and often got anxious, so maybe vaping helped her focus. I'd never tried any kind of nicotine. I didn't want to die before I'd been properly happy.

"I used to feel you were judging me," Cerys said. "When I first started going out with Kass, I mean. I didn't think you liked me at all. You have this particularly intense way of looking at people sometimes."

"Do I?"

"It's not a bad thing. You're doing it right now and it's fine. It doesn't freak me out anymore."

"I freak you out?"

"You used to. Don't get upset. Being intense is a good thing. It means you're deep."

I didn't know if she was being sincere or not. It was difficult to tell with Cerys. She had the most beautiful fake smile I'd ever seen. I guess it helped her get popular. She snapped her bag open and put the vape away. "Now," she said. "Tell me everything. I'll get it all from Kass at some point, but I want your side first."

Did me and Kass have different sides? I chewed the end of my hair for a bit. I wondered if I should tell Cerys that, when John grounded me the morning after the party, he'd also written a list. In capital letters at the top he wrote: *ZERO TOLERANCE*, which meant he'd put up with me for years and had finally had enough. Underneath, he wrote: *I will not lie or swear. I will control my temper. I won't take things without asking.* He watched me sign it, then stuck it on the fridge. He made me write apology letters to Roger and Monika, and then he locked Mom's necklace in his safe so I wouldn't be tempted to steal it again.

"Well," I said eventually, "John hates me, and I was wondering if you had any advice?"

"Your stepfather does *not* hate you."

"He thinks I'm out of control."

"And are you?"

"I don't know, but I want him to think I'm awesome."

I could tell by her face she was up for the challenge. Pretty girls often wanted to get their hands on those of us who were less than perfect. "We need to find something you're good at that he can admire you for," she said. "It shouldn't be something he does himself. Like, if he's great at soccer, you should pick a different sport. Otherwise, it'll look like you're competing or making fun of him."

"John doesn't play soccer."

"Drawing, then. He's an architect, isn't he? So, don't choose art."

"I'm terrible at art."

"OK, well, what skills do you have? Let's make a list." She pulled a notebook and pen from her bag and settled herself against the window.

But I couldn't think of a thing. Loving Iris and Kass? When I was a kid I used to be good at loads. On a Saturday, I'd have a whole timetable for Mom—reading stories, writing new ones, cobbling costumes together, and putting on a show. Where had that all gone?

"I like walking around looking at people," I said. "You know, imagining who they are and what they're thinking."

"I'll put psychology down," she said.

"When I was young, my granddad did loads of stuff with me—he taught me about knots and how to climb trees and everything I know about nature."

Cerys sighed. "Yeah, that's all very 1950s, but what about now? Any current hobbies? Anything you like doing with friends?"

"Nothing. Honestly, there really isn't anything."

"There's a confidence issue going on here." She eyed me steadily. "What are your favorite subjects at school?"

Brightly and neatly she steered away from the obvious fact that I had no hobbies or friends. I told her that I enjoyed media and drama. My voice was beginning to sound whispery.

"Kass said you were great in your drama project," she said. "So, I'm going to put acting down. It takes guts to get onstage and pretend to be someone else." She drummed the end of her pen on the paper. "What about your other subjects? Any chance of good exam results?"

Her face was upbeat and eager. I felt a stab of frustration. "Why does everyone keep going on about exams? I'm not smart like Kass and Iris. I need something else."

"Well, that's why we're making a list. You don't have to do it all."

"Why can't John just like me?"

"Mm," Cerys said. "I wonder if you might be a teensy bit jealous?"

It was true that when I wanted to comfort myself, I imagined myself as brilliant and beautiful as the rest of them.

"I'm taking your silence as a yes." Cerys hunched over the paper. "Jealousy isn't helpful when trying to impress someone, so I'm writing the word 'empathy' on your list. Do you know what that means?"

"Not being jealous?"

"It's the ability to understand and share the feelings of another. John's the only one with a job, right? That means he's supporting everyone, paying for everything. He wants to relax when he comes home, not get hassled. Think about it from his perspective, that's all I'm saying."

There it was—right there, the advice I'd come for. *Put John first.*

"Kass told me his dad gets easily stressed," Cerys said. "And planning a wedding is right up there with death and redundancy.

Did you know that? Do some nice things for him—make him cups of tea, offer to help around the apartment."

Be nicer. Practice empathy.

"Why not surprise everyone with a homemade meal?" she said. "Tell them sorry about the party and promise next time you get angry, you'll count to ten and calm down. Treat it like an experiment, you know?"

Be nicer. Practice empathy. Be sorry. Calm down.

Cerys said, "Combine all that with a new hobby and a bit of studying and we'll have a whole new you." She gave me a dazzling smile. "How's that sound? Can you manage that?"

A Whole New Me

INSTEAD OF KEEPING SILENT at the supper table and letting John do the talking, I decided to show some interest in his world. I'd googled "being an architect" and discovered that the work was hard, the hours long, the clients annoying, and the pay was less than people thought.

I also looked up "how to be made partner," because John couldn't build his dream house without money and, even though I didn't want to move, I was trying to be empathetic.

I repeated three pre-prepared questions in my head several times and then, when there was a window of silence, I asked John if he found dealing with builders, manufacturers, and suppliers stressful?

He said, "I've had a long day, Alexandra."

"I also wondered if you realized that the best way of becoming a partner at your firm is having a sense of ownership and acting as mentor for the team?"

"Enough," he said. "I can't be dealing with you right now."

I took myself away, because I was clearly getting something wrong. A whole new me? Maybe I should start with my appearance?

Cerys always made loads of effort. And Mom often said looking good was part of her commitment to John.

I watched some videos about the best methods of disguising myself. I used Mom's special foundation to even out my skin tone, and for dramatic eyes, I used brown, silver, and green eye shadow. I tamed my hair with some of Mom's expensive serum. My torn jeans were a bit casual, so I jazzed them up with Mom's diamanté belt and black top. It was elasticated, so stretched to accommodate me and had a secret internal bra that gave my breasts loads of lift. I barely recognized myself when I stood in front of the full-length mirror. If I'd been a boy, I'd definitely be interested in me. But when I went into the living room and spun for them, Mom said, "Is that my top you're wearing?"

She told me to take it off before I stretched it out of shape. I reminded her that the top didn't fit her since she'd got so skinny and John looked up from his phone and told me to stop being confrontational and go and do some homework.

"I haven't got any."

"You've got exams coming up, so I'd say you probably do."

Mom frowned at me. I knew what that look meant. She followed me to my bedroom. "Stop winding him up, Lex."

"I'm not. I'm getting him to like me."

She sighed and sank down onto the bed. "Ah, so that's what this is about."

"No need to sound sad about it."

She studied me for a long time. She didn't say anything.

I said, "Why are you looking at me like that?"

51

"Because if you behaved, there wouldn't be a problem."

"That's what I'm trying to do. I just told you. I'm going to make him a coffee next."

She nodded. "He likes it from the espresso maker. You want me to show you?"

After scrubbing my face, we got straight on to John's caffeine hit. He'd gone up to his study to finish some important work and Mom showed me how to measure the coffee and how to use the milk frother to make foam and how to sprinkle chocolate powder on top like they do in cafés. We used his favorite cup and put some of the new shortbreads on a plate and put it all on a tray.

"Attagirl," Mom said. "He'll love it."

I went up the stairs and stood in the doorway of his study until he noticed me and invited me in. He looked pleased. He fancied a coffee, he said. I must be a mind reader. He took several sips and then he ate two cookies one after the other. I stood there watching him, wondering if I should leave, or if he expected me to take everything away on the tray when he'd finished. I figured he'd tell me what to do, so I stood there breathing and waiting and trying not to be annoying.

Eventually he said, "You're still grounded for one more week."

"I know."

"I'm still furious about the party."

"Yes."

"Asking random questions at supper and making me coffee doesn't make up for anything."

"Of course not."

He drained his cup and passed it to me. "Now get out of here. I've got work to do."

"Would you like anything else?"

"I'll have a tea next time. In about an hour. Oh, and tell your mom to get those shortbreads again—they were delicious."

Be nicer. Be sorry. Calm down.

It was easier than I'd ever imagined.

Me and Mom washed up the coffee things. I helped put Iris to bed. We sat together in the living room waiting for John to finish work and come and join us. I thought the three of us might watch a movie, but when John appeared he said he was going out.

"It's a bit late for the bar," Mom said.

"I'm seeing a client."

"At this time?"

He frowned. "Don't start."

He went out to the hallway and put his shoes on and Mom took his jacket from the hook and held it tight to her chest and said, "You'll come back?"

"Can I have my jacket?"

"Is that a yes or a no?"

"For Christ's sake."

Please, I thought. *Please don't.*

"I was looking forward to spending time with you," Mom said.

"Jacket," he said, holding out his hand.

"John, I don't want to argue."

"Well, you're doing a great job of it. I'm going to be late for my client now. How do you think that's going to look?"

There was a thudding in my head and a sick bright feeling behind my eyes as my knee slammed into the coffee table and the crystal fruit bowl smashed to the floor and oranges and apples rolled across the carpet before settling themselves among splinters of glass.

John dashed in from the hallway and surveyed every glittering shard.

I said, "Whoops."

He stared at me and it was like some kind of liquid washed from him into me. It made my heart thunder.

"Get out of my sight," he said.

From my bedroom, I heard Mom sweep up the mess and John cancel his client before opening a bottle of wine. I heard him say, "We can't go on like this," and Mom say, "I'll talk to her tomorrow," and him say, "Talking doesn't cut it anymore."

The TV was switched on and I couldn't hear them after that. They were probably cuddled together on the sofa. He'd be telling her work was stressful and he was exhausted, and she'd be comforting him. He'd tell her he was sorry for being short-tempered earlier and he loved her. Did she know that—how much he loved her?

Seven

I WAS SURPRISED TO find myself walking toward the drama studio after school. I never did extracurricular activities, but when I saw the poster—*Auditions today*—it felt like an instruction. Cerys said I needed to do something that everyone could admire, and for nearly a week, I'd found nothing to fit that category. But drama had always been my favorite subject. For one thing, I liked other people's lives more than my own. Also, it was the only class where teachers ever looked at me with that secret smile on their face that girls like Cerys probably got every lesson. A smile that meant—you are a joy to teach.

If I got a role in *The Tempest*, John would definitely think I was awesome. Everyone knew you had to be smart to understand Shakespeare, and it would also count as studying, since it was one of the main texts for English. We'd seen the film version in class, where a woman played Prospero, and I liked how powerful she was. It'd be great to march around waving a magic staff to change the weather and control everyone. But Prospero had so many lines that

I wasn't sure I'd remember them all, so I thought I'd try for the role of the daughter instead. A girl stuck on an island all her life, knowing nothing about the world, was a great chance to practice being nicer. Also, she got to tumble around with a handsome prince who got shipwrecked.

"I'm proud of you," John would say when I shared the news that I was playing Miranda. "I forgive you for breaking the fruit bowl and I'm going to reinstate your allowance."

"I love you so much," Mom would say. "I always knew you were exceptional."

Iris would sit on my lap and plant kisses all over my face because her older sister was finally someone to be proud of.

As for Kass—he'd come down from Manchester to watch every show and, on the last night, Mom and John would take us out for dinner and John would say, "Why aren't you two boyfriend and girlfriend? You're made for each other . . ." And Kass would smile and ask me out and I'd pretend to think about it and then we'd all laugh as I said yes, and my life would be perfect from then on.

There were about thirty kids waiting outside the theater in the lobby of the drama block. A few turned to look as the door shut behind me. I slipped my rucksack off and slung it over my shoulder to give at least one hand something to do.

Usually, I'd pretend not to care if people were looking. I'd stare back, giving the evil eye to anyone who didn't look away. But today, I was trying to stick to the Cerys Instruction List. *Be nicer.*

A girl from my drama class named Jamila was standing near the stairs. I waved at her. She waved back and looked friendly enough, so I walked over.

"Hi," I said. "What part are you going for?"

"Miranda."

"Me too."

"Oh," she said. "Are you sure?"

"Why wouldn't I be sure?"

She shrugged. "I don't know. She's pretty quiet, I guess."

Was that an insult? She thought I was too disruptive? I frowned at her, but then remembered I was trying to be nicer.

"You'd be great as Miranda," I said.

We were silent for a bit. A few more kids came in and stood behind us. I was glad not to be standing by myself anymore.

"So many people here," Jamila said, looking around. Her cheeks were flushed, and I thought maybe she was panicky. Mom had that look about her sometimes.

"You're better than any of them," I said.

Jamila used to go to my primary school. I was invited to her tenth birthday party. This was the first time we'd spoken in ages. I wasn't sure why. A teacher once said that making friends meant you had to *do* something, because "make" is an active verb. I knew that. I'd always known it. I was just out of practice.

I was about to ask Jamila a string of friendly questions when the drama studio door opened, and Ben stood there grinning. "You can all come in now."

What was he doing dishing out instructions? Who put him in charge? I tried to ignore him as we all shuffled in, but he said, "Lex, are you auditioning?"

I held up my hands as if he'd accused me of doing something illegal. "Do I need your permission?"

He shook his head, laughing. "Lovely to see you too."

Mr. Darby, my drama teacher, was inside the room. "Come and take a seat, everyone."

I liked him—he was young and sometimes funny and once, at parents' evening, he'd told Mom I was the best kind of trouble. I think that was a compliment.

He raised an eyebrow as I walked past. "A surprise to see you here, Lexi."

"A surprise to be here, sir."

I don't know why I said that. It made me sound like an idiot. I lost Jamila as kids spread out into the auditorium, so I sat by myself. There were spotlights aimed at the stage. And a camera. Were they going to film us?

When we were all sitting down, Mr. Darby gave us a talk about teamwork and commitment and how being in a play was a challenging and enriching experience that would promote personal development and creative ambition. "For your information," he said, "Ben Osman's going to be filming auditions for his media project. If anyone objects, say so now. Otherwise, let's get on with it."

Ben leaped onstage and fiddled with the camera and lights. He looked like Bambi rushing about with his long legs, skinny black trousers, and red hair.

Mr. Darby pointed to five bowls on a table at the side of the stage. They were each labeled with a character's name and contained lines from one of their speeches. We were to go up alphabetically and take a piece of paper from the bowl that represented the role we wanted, look at the line, and then just "be" the character onstage for one minute. We could explore the imaginary island, sit on the sand, look out to sea, walk about, whatever helped us find our motivation. Then he wanted us to say something approximating our line in plain English, then say the actual written line.

"Clear as mud?" he said. "OK, first up is Josh Abraham."

The poor boy looked terrified. He was tiny and reminded me of Iris with his sweet face and long hair. He chose a line from the Ferdinand bowl, silently read it, and walked onstage. He paused as if listening and then his face lit up as if he could hear something wonderful. He started following the imaginary sound, running around in different directions, and then stopping to listen again.

Eventually he said, "Is this music even real or is it in my head?" Then he read the written line. *"Where should this music be? In the air or the earth?"*

He was good—but too young to be the prince. Ferdinand needed to be sexy, not cute. Some chunky kid I'd never seen before went next and he was like a professional Prospero, summoning a thunderstorm above our heads. Three boys in a row tried out for Caliban but they were horrible. The actor playing the role in the movie said, *I am subject to a tyrant*, as if he was sharing a terrible secret. Those boys wasted the words.

A girl with pink hair wanted to be Miranda but was way too shy. Miranda had never seen a boy before. She had to be lusty. She had to fancy the pants off the prince.

"Now," Mr. Darby said, "let's see what you've got to offer, Lexi Robinson."

I tried to get my pulse under control as I made my way to the stage. I avoided Ben's eyes as I took a scrap of paper from the Miranda bowl, read it, and slowly walked into the bright space under the lights. They were hot and made a ticking sound, but it helped me imagine a blazing sun. I blocked out the audience and imagined myself alone on the shore of an island. I imagined the churning sea, the cry of birds, and the vast blue sky. It was beautiful. Suddenly, I saw the shipwrecked prince, gathering firewood ahead of me on the beach. He had Kass's gorgeous face and I wanted two things at the exact same time—to watch him forever without him noticing and to run over and touch him so he'd know I loved him. I put a hand out in longing. I pulled it back, trying to resist. He turned. He smiled. I dared to smile back.

I said, "I've waited years for you to show up. And now you're here, you're way better than I imagined. I'm probably never going to like another boy my whole life." And then I read the actual line: "*I would not wish any companion in the world but you, nor can imagination form a shape, besides yourself, to like of.*"

I knew I was good. I could feel a hush in the air, like the audience had stopped breathing. I'd felt it before in drama class—like I was a hook that people got snagged on before I hauled them in.

"I wonder," Mr. Darby said as I walked offstage, "if I could I have a word with you, Lexi?"

He hadn't asked anyone else to go and talk to him. It reminded me of *The X Factor*, when the judges asked someone to sing a second song. It was a good sign. Everyone watched me walk over to him, but I was buzzing with adrenaline and didn't care.

He said. "Would you try a different part for me, just to see?"

Prospero, I thought. Jamila had been right—Miranda was too quiet a role for me. Mr. Darby had seen my command of the stage. Maybe Jamila would be Miranda, and I'd be Prospero, and we'd be friends again.

"Sure," I said. "Why not?"

"Great. I'd like you to try Caliban."

I blinked at him. "Is this a joke?"

He gave me a curious smile. "Not a joke."

"I don't want to."

"Just try it for me, Lexi. I think it'll be interesting."

Interesting? I looked around the room. People were quiet, watching us. Ben was sitting on the edge of the stage, trying to hear.

I leaned closer to Mr. Darby. "Caliban's a boy's part."

"There's only one female part in the whole play, so we're going to have to cross-cast."

Caliban was also a monster. It said so at the front of the play. It said: *Caliban, a strange and deformed slave.*

I was blushing, I could feel it. "I want to be Miranda."

"I know and I'm considering you for that, but humor me here. Caliban's a great role. He has a strong ego and a healthy appetite and just wants what he wants. You can relate to that, surely? Everyone can."

"It's not a girl's role."

Why was I repeating myself? I sounded stupid and childish.

"Actually," Mr. Darby said, "there have been several all-female productions."

"I don't want to be Caliban."

"All right, but give me a better reason than gender."

My whole face felt on fire. "I don't want to be a monster."

There, I'd said it.

Mr. Darby said, "That's just the identity others attribute to Caliban. It's not how he sees himself." He smiled. "This is a compliment, Lexi. I'm only asking you because you're good enough to do the part justice."

That was slightly comforting. It was also cheering to see the faces of the three boys who'd already tried out for him. They were scowling at me.

"Well?" said Mr. Darby.

This had gone on too long. I'd look more ridiculous refusing than accepting. I wished I was wearing Granddad's necklace. I wanted to thread its coolness through my fingers. Caliban wanted things he couldn't have too. "All right. Whatever you say."

Mr. Darby grinned. "Excellent."

I changed my body as I walked back to the stage. I built rock inside it—brittle rock, that could break into shards. Caliban had his island stolen and was punished and insulted every day. Miranda called him a villain and said she couldn't bear to look at him. Prospero called him a poisonous slave and cursed him with cramps.

I walked to the bowls and took a Caliban speech. I read it and walked onstage. Again, the ticking and humming of the lights helped me imagine the heat and sapphire sky of the island.

Caliban was the child of a witch and a devil. I let him walk about the stage with the shame of having looked in a mirror. I covered my face as if I was hideous; then I let him peer through his fingers, craving to be king of the island again.

How was he when he was alone? He was beautiful and sensitive and vulnerable. I walked him along the shore. But he heard a noise and cowered. When others looked at him, he was clumsy and gross and smelled of fish. They saw he was disfigured and were disgusted.

But alone?

I lay on the stage and breathed as him. He was a sleeping child, curled in, hugging his own belly. He was content, dreaming of his mother. But then another noise came, and he woke up yelping—he was a lonely dog who Prospero wanted to imprison and punish.

I stood up and wailed. Everything on the island had been ripped from him. All that was good about him had gone. His mother had died. He knew silence so deep it broke his heart. He was precious, and no one knew. His voice was a secret, even to himself.

He could only get comfort through fury.

I gave him all this. I scuttled across the stage imagining my own stink, my own loss. I crawled out of my cave to be faced with Prospero. I begged him not to curse me again, appalled at my own groveling, disgusted at being forced to be a slave. I wanted to rip out Prospero's eyes, drag away his staff, and impale him.

I howled at him, "This was my home. Mine! My island. I lived here with my mother; then you came and pretended to be kind and I believed you. I loved you like a father. I showed you everything I cared about, and you stole it from me."

Like a bolt of steel running through my spine. Like something to grab hold of in a storm. Anger was something to believe in when the world let you down.

I roared with it. *"Cursed be I that did so! All the charms of Sycorax, toads, beetles, bats, light on you! For I am all the subjects that you have, which first was mine own king: and here you sty me in this hard rock, whiles you do keep from me the rest o' the island."*

Coming out of it was like waking from a dream. There was absolute silence as I blinked into the lights and back into my own body. I couldn't see anyone, but I knew every person in the room was staring at me.

Time slowed down. I noticed the skylight was open. I noticed that outside it was beginning to get gloomy.

You are not here, I thought. You're alone in the yard surrounded by rustling leaves and the sound of birds going to bed.

"Actually," I blurted, "I'm not interested in being in a play. I'm busy. I just remembered."

I heard laughter. Of course. What insanity to think I could join a group, make friends, be nicer, learn empathy.

I scrunched up Caliban's lines and let the paper fall. My throat tightened as I walked offstage. I collected my bag and coat, my face burning. I didn't look at anyone. I shut all my doors, put up all my barricades.

"Lexi," Mr. Darby said. Then, "Alexia." Finally, "Alexandra."

Fuck you, I thought, as I marched to the door and yanked it open. You're as bad as the rest of them.

He came after me. I jogged, and he ran. I ran faster, but he caught up with me in the foyer and grabbed my arm. "Lexi, don't run away."

"Don't touch me!"

I jerked my arm free and he sighed. Like he was so well-behaved and good and me being upset was nothing to do with him.

I said, "Leave me the fuck alone."

The principal appeared from nowhere. She said, "Alexandra Robinson, don't you dare talk to a member of my staff that way."

"It's OK," Mr. Darby said. "I've got this."

"No," said the principal. "*I've* got this."

I was an object. A thing to be fought over. And they could argue about me over the top of my head.

"You apologize to Mr. Darby—right now, Alexandra."

I tried to push the anger down, because it would make things worse and they'd see, and it would hurt my throat and make me cry.

But there wasn't any stopping it.

Like a bolt of steel running through me. Like something to grab hold of in a storm.

And the principal stood in front of me, her eyes full of opinions. I was wrong and bad and out of control. I was wasting her time and testing her patience. I was nothing and she was everything and she had a million better things to be doing than dealing with me.

And I swallowed, swallowed, but the fury came louder.

She said, "You hear me, Alexandra? I'm waiting . . ."

Like fingernails down chalkboards, like forks on plates, like all my bones screaming.

"Put that chair down right now, Alexandra."

Like the reddest, hottest feeling. Like I'd burst if I didn't.

"Don't you walk away from me!"

And I said to myself, *Just do it.*

"I mean it, Alexandra. Put that chair down immediately."

I said to myself, *What's there to lose?*

"Put it down—you hear me?"

You already think I'm bad.

"You will be in a great deal of trouble if you throw that chair anywhere near that window."

Do what you like to me. I don't care.

"Listen to me, Alexandra."

No. No. No.

The glass exploded. Like hailstones. Like splinters of ice.

Eight

MOM SAT ON THE window ledge in the living room and helped herself to one of John's cigarette butts from the ashtray.

I said, "I'm sorry, Mom."

"So you keep saying."

"Why don't you believe me?"

She lit the stub and blew smoke at the ceiling. "Do you have any idea how horrible it was getting a call from your principal telling me you threw a chair through a window? I said there must be a mistake, that she was calling the wrong parent, had the wrong kid. But deep down, I knew it was you." She glared at me. "Why did I know? Why wasn't I surprised?"

"Mom, why are you smoking?"

"Because I'm stressed!"

I stared at the curve of her back as she turned from me and opened the window. She inhaled hard. She kept the smoke in her lungs for ages. "You'll have to pay for replacement glass. That's the very least they're going to make you do."

"You think I'll get expelled?"

"I'd say that's a possibility."

"John's going to go nuts."

She turned to look at me. "Do you blame him?"

I wanted her to beckon me over. I wanted her to hold me close and tell me she loved me. But she just kept sitting there frowning like she didn't know me at all.

I said, "I know the wedding's supposed to be a new start. I know I'm not supposed to get angry anymore."

"So, why does it happen day after day? What on earth possesses you?"

"Well," I said. "It varies. But today, I wanted to be Miranda in the school play and Mr. Darby didn't cast me."

"That's it?"

"Isn't that enough?"

"So, it's Mr. Darby's fault?" She tossed what was left of the butt out the window and slid herself to the floor. "We're going to have such a horrible evening now."

* * *

I wasn't always wicked.

There was that time, right at the start, when I was having breakfast in the kitchen and Mom said, "I think I hear someone up," and I hadn't even known John had stayed over. She hopped from the stool and went to the kitchen door. She stood there all curves and smiles. "Hey," she said to him, "want a coffee?"

"I want you," he said.

She put her finger to her lips. "Lex is here."

"Morning, Alexandra," he called, and then in a quieter voice, "I thought she was going on a playdate?"

But Meryam wasn't free, so I got to spend the day with them.

We went on a picnic to Hampstead Heath. John bought loads of stuff from a fancy deli and Mom said she'd never heard of half the things and he said he wanted to widen her horizons and this was just the beginning.

We parked the car and John and Mom held hands as we walked up a hill. When we got to the top, we sat on a bench and looked down on London and John pointed out all the different landmarks and a man with a dog winked at me and said, "You've got a clever dad there."

I was an angel child that day. Mom and John both said so.

Another time, John took us on a tour of the Docklands to look at a building he'd helped design, and we ended up in a restaurant by the river and Mom said it was too expensive and he said it was his treat and we could order whatever we wanted. My shoes bumped his under the table and his gently bumped mine back.

"Isn't this fun?" Mom said when he went outside to smoke. "Isn't he lovely?"

I told Mom he was like a prince from a story, and when he came back she told him, and he laughed and said that made me and Mom a pair of princesses.

Mom started cooking amazing meals. She said dinner was called supper now and the living room was the sitting room. She learned how to mix cocktails and started buying organic. John came round most days after work and we sat at the kitchen table (now called the dining table) like a proper family. I saved things up to tell him—the merit sticker I'd earned, the assembly I'd been in, the birthday party I'd been invited to. I told him jokes and he laughed, and it made the apartment full of life.

Mom told him her plans—she was writing her CV, she was applying for jobs, she was thinking about college. Now that John was in our lives, all things were possible. Happiness suited her, he said, but she shouldn't worry about money or work because he was going to look after us.

It was wonderful giving him the details of our lives. His smiles kept us warm. He'd drink the cocktails Mom made and listen to our stories and then he'd kick off his shoes and say, "So, ladies, you want to hear about my day?"

He told Mom to come off benefits and he opened a bank account and put money in it every week.

He took her out to buy new clothes.

He introduced her to his friends. They went to wine bars and fancy clubs.

He couldn't believe what a sheltered life she'd had—pregnant straight out of school and never been to college or done any traveling. He bought tickets to take her to Paris for the weekend. He asked if I'd be a sweetheart and stay with Granddad by myself? "Give me the chance to spoil your mom, eh?"

I was an angel. A princess. A sweetheart.

One day, after John officially moved in with us, he sent Mom a text saying he wouldn't be home.

I said, "So, where do you think he is?"

And Mom said, "I don't know, Lex. He didn't say."

"But you must have an idea? Like, do you think he's with friends, or is it a work thing?"

"It's not a work thing. I called the reception."

"You asked if they knew where your boyfriend was?"

"No, of course not. I didn't even tell them it was me, just asked to be put through and they said he left hours ago."

I suggested some places he could be that were so silly they could never be true. I said he was probably in Russia on a spy mission or he'd been sent to the moon because he was a secret astronaut. I said maybe he'd bumped his head and forgotten who he was or he'd been stolen by aliens and experimented on. Mom laughed so much she cried. I hugged her, and we stood there holding one another up in the kitchen.

"Precious girl," she said.

She called John up and left messages. Then she called his friends and asked if they knew where he was. John came back the next day and called her hysterical. He said she was raving, and he'd had enough. He went in the bedroom and locked the door and Mom stood outside and banged and banged.

For days after that, he wouldn't speak to her. He wouldn't look at her either. He walked out of the room if she walked in. He cooked alone, ate alone, and even bought himself a mini fridge to keep his stuff in.

"What did I do?" Mom kept saying.

When he eventually told her, he had a whole list. She was trying to trap him. She was small-town stupid. She could barely hold a conversation. She had no original thoughts. She was a millstone dragging him down. She was driving him crazy with her irrational jealousy.

We made him an apology snack—blueberries and orange slices in the shape of a face, with chocolate fingers for hair. We brewed a pot of tea and put everything on a tray and took it up to his study, pretending we were servants.

"Good girl," Mom said as we crept back down the stairs.

The next day he came home from work clutching twelve long-stemmed roses. One for each day he'd hurt her. He was sorry. He didn't know what he'd been thinking. He was a fool and didn't deserve her. All week he bought her gifts—scarves and perfume and lingerie. When the roses died, he filled the sitting room with lilies and we had to open the window because the scent was so strong we could taste it.

He bought tickets for a cruise. She was the love of his life and he wanted to take her away. I'd be bored on a boat, he told me, so why didn't I stay with Granddad again? He knew he could depend on me.

I was precious. A good girl. Dependable.

Nine

"SO, THE SCHOOL PUT me on probation."

"Well," Cerys said from her place on the window ledge, "you can hardly blame them."

"And John grounded me for a month and is making me pay for the broken glass. To be honest, I don't know why the principal even told him. She could have punished me privately, or just told my mom, but no—she insisted on a family meeting. She even offered them parenting classes. I hate her. Next time, I'll throw *her* out the window."

"I wouldn't do that—you'd hate jail more." Cerys raised her arms behind her head and yawned, her mouth as pink and clean as a cat's.

"You told me to get a hobby."

"Hey, this isn't my fault! I didn't tell you to swear at your drama teacher or chuck chairs around."

"Mr. Darby deserved it. He wanted me to read for the part of a strange and deformed slave."

"That *was* a bit insensitive." Cerys picked up her phone and swiped the screen open. "Speaking of which—I haven't heard from your brother for over a week. You'd think he'd have made contact over the Easter break, wouldn't you? Do you have any idea what's going on with him?"

"He's not my brother."

"Thanks, that's helpful." She clicked her phone off and slapped it back on the ledge. Then she opened her bag and took out her vape. She took five long puffs without looking at me once.

"Want to hear my idea?" I said.

"Do I have a choice?"

"I'm going to stay away from home as much as possible. John will like me better if I'm never there."

Cerys looked down at me from her perch. "I thought you were grounded?"

"I'm ignoring that."

"That'll piss him off more. You can't just not go home." She sucked on her vape again and exhaled a cloud of diamond-colored mist. "Have you actually apologized? You don't have to mean it. Damage limitation, you know?"

"I've said sorry a million times. It doesn't make a difference."

"Do something to show you're going to change, then. Hey, why not start studying?"

She smiled at me so prettily I almost considered it. Then I remembered why I'd come to see her in the first place. It wasn't for study advice. No, I was here for the kind of practical help that was only available from a girl as popular as her.

"There's a party tonight," I said. "Kass is coming back for it."

It was as if I'd poked her with an electric stick. Everything about her came to attention. "Whose party?"

"Someone he was at school with."

"Who exactly?"

"He never said."

"Well, what *did* he say?"

"Just there was a party and he was going."

"He's not due back until after exams."

"He's coming down for the weekend, because of everything that's been going on."

"Why didn't he tell me?"

I shrugged. I hadn't a clue. But I hoped it was because things were cooling between them. He was coming home to see *me*.

Cerys reached for her phone and scrolled through. She obviously had no new messages. "*When* did he tell you about this party?"

"A few days ago. I was in the principal's office listening to John go on about how crap the school is. Instead of offering parenting classes, he said, why didn't they adopt traditional teaching methods—tough discipline, silent corridors, all that . . . ?"

"What's this got to do with Kass?"

"I asked to go to the bathroom and, since that's a human right, they had to say yes. I called Kass and asked him to come home."

"And he told you about the party?"

"No, he didn't pick up. I had to go back to the stupid meeting and sit through John's lecture on tiger teaching."

"What the hell's that?"

"It's like private school—housemasters and endless lessons and corporal punishment. Anyway, the principal told John that hitting children is illegal, and he said he was aware of that, but I needed a more structured program. So she asked me if I enjoyed learning and I told her I hated it. Then John said I should be ashamed of myself and education was a privilege, so I said if he loved learning that much, why didn't he play the role of a deformed monster in the school play? Then Mom said not to talk to John like that and it kind of kicked off from there."

Cerys laughed. A genuine one. I joined in. I hadn't laughed for days. It sounded strange, like it came from a soundtrack and didn't have anything to do with my life.

I didn't tell Cerys about John saying I was beyond redemption, or Mom shaking her head in despair or me running out of the room. I didn't tell her that the empty playground looked sullen in the rain, like it was angry too. And I didn't tell her that when, like a miracle, Kass rang, I closed my eyes as we talked and imagined him next to me.

"You have to call him, Cerys."

She shut her vape away in her bag. "Why do I have to do that?"

"To find out where the party is."

"If he wanted me there, he would've told me about it."

"He's not in charge, is he? It's not his party."

"Why don't *you* call him?"

"He's not going to give me the address when he knows I'm grounded. He says he'll see me tomorrow, but I can't wait that long."

"I don't feel comfortable about this, Lexi. If I tell you where the party is and you get into trouble, it'll be *my* fault."

"Loads of people are going. Hundreds, probably. Anyone could've told me. Surely you want to see Kass, don't you? It's been weeks."

She frowned down at me. "Why do you care?"

I could've said, *Because you're my only way of getting into the party and I can't stand another minute without him.*

But instead, I said, "I know how much you've missed him."

Cerys looked unsure, but not totally against it. "I suppose we could go for an hour."

"Great, so now we need to find out the address and get ourselves on the guest list. There's a Facebook group, but it's closed."

She sighed and picked up her phone. "And let me guess—you don't have an account?"

"I don't like the stuff everyone puts up—all their friends and pictures of what they're doing. It's depressing. It makes other people feel left out."

"They *are* left out," Cerys said. "But that's because they're not on Facebook."

She insisted on making me an account. She put a raffia sun hat on my head (I insisted on a disguise) and stood me by the window to take a profile picture.

"I look like a gnome."

"You look cute."

"I want to look passionate."

"Do you? Why?"

I smiled so she wouldn't know I was a threat. She added me as her friend.

She messaged a couple of people about the party and asked someone who was invited to get her included in the group. I liked watching her tapping away on her phone all slick and certain. She reminded me of a bank robber I'd seen in a film, spinning dials on a safe.

"Sorted." She clicked her phone off and sat with it in her lap. "I still don't know if this is a good idea . . ."

"It's the best idea ever. Now could you be my alibi when I call John? He'll hunt me down otherwise."

She closed her eyes as if she was exhausted. She wanted Kass and instead she had me like a splinter in her side. "I do *not* want your stepdad blaming me."

"It won't be like that, I promise. I've got a plan. Just pretend your name's Jamila, OK?"

She didn't look happy about it, but she nodded. While I dialed John, she took out her vape again. Her addiction to fruit-flavored nicotine was pretty excessive.

John picked up on the first ring. I put the phone to speaker. "Hi," I said. "Sorry to bug you at work, but I wanted to tell you the school let me leave detention early because I wasn't feeling well, and on the way home I bumped into my friend Jamila."

"And this is relevant why?"

"She's looking after me. We were right by her house when I began to feel worse, so I'm resting."

Cerys looked at me wide-eyed, then shook her head in that new weary way.

"Well," John said, "since you're grounded, I suggest you get up from lying down and go home. I'm surprised your mother hasn't let me know you're not back yet."

"She'll be at ballet class with Iris, so you can't blame her."

Cerys raised an eyebrow. *"Be nice,"* she mouthed.

"Straight home after school," John said. "That was the agreement."

"But I've got stomach cramps. I almost fainted earlier. I think it might be an ovary or something."

Cerys laughed. It made me laugh right back at her. I had to turn it into a groan to avoid suspicion.

"I'm bleeding quite a lot too. Down there, you know . . . I really think I need to stay with someone female."

"Alexandra Robinson, I do not need you pulling any new stunts. I want you to go home immediately, please."

"I can barely walk."

"You have twenty minutes to get there, or I add another week to the grounding."

So I played the only card I had left. It was unfair to Cerys, but I was running out of options.

"All right, John. I'm sorry to hassle you. Would you be able to have a quick word with Jamila's mom first, though? It's just that she's quite worried about me."

He was quiet then. He'd hate talking to some strange woman about female stuff. But he'd look heartless if he refused. What if I died on the way home?

Cerys was mouthing, "No, no!" and waving at me in horror.

"Please," I silently begged her.

She hopped off the ledge and walked to the door, shaking her head.

"All right," John said. "Let me talk to the damn woman. As if I haven't got better things to do."

His voice was raspy over the speaker. He sounded like a furious machine. It changed something in Cerys. She turned from the door and sat on the bed and put one hand on my arm, like she was saying she was on my team. I handed her the phone.

"Hello." She deepened her voice. She sounded cold and very certain. "Is this Lexi's father?"

"Not exactly, but you can talk to me. What's the problem?"

Cerys crossed her fingers and bit her lip. She was so well-behaved usually. This was like drawing her into a forbidden kingdom. "I don't think she's up to walking home."

"Seriously?"

"Her cramps are quite severe. I'd drop her off myself, but I think she needs to rest. She's very welcome to stay until she's feeling better."

I heard him sigh. But her kind of charm could swing anything, and I could tell he was faltering. "OK. I'll get her mom to call later. Thanks for looking out for her."

Cerys laughed as she switched my phone off. I thought she'd be angry that I forced her into it, but she wasn't at all. "That was fun!"

I loved her in that moment. I was breathless with freedom.

"Right," I said, "next step—can I borrow something to wear?"

Ten

WHEN I WAS ELEVEN and Kass was fourteen, he picked me up at the apartment and walked with me on my first day of secondary school.

At the gate, he said, "Will you be all right?"

"You're leaving me?"

He looked longingly over at the Astroturf where a whole crowd of kids was playing soccer and a whole crowd of other kids was standing around watching. I could see what he wanted, and I knew it'd be bad for his reputation to be seen with me. The trouble was, it'd be excellent for mine.

He said, "I'll see you at break. The new kids have their own playground, so I'll come and say hello. And I'll probably see you in the corridors and stuff. But if anyone thumps you or shoves you in a trash can or whatever, come and find me, OK? I'll sort them out."

At that moment, a group of boys came out of the school building and shouted to Kass. He pretended not to hear them. They shouted again, and he tensed as they came sauntering over. It was like magnets—him repelling them, but them being attracted to him. As they got closer, they clocked my fresh school uniform and my unscuffed shoes and the bright white headband that was trying to stop my hair doing its untamed thing and one of them put his arm around Kass and said, "Chatting up the newbies, bro?"

"She's my stepsister."

The boy looked me up and down before his eyes landed on my chest. "So, you're related?"

"I just told you," Kass said.

"But stepsister means you're not blood-related, right?"

He had a mocking smile and I had no clue what his words meant or why the other boys were laughing. But I knew Kass understood and was embarrassed. For the first time I felt I had something. Not the Iris something: not all that beauty and innocence, but something else—something to do with wild hair and budding breasts and the monstrous thoughts I had simmering behind my eyes. And that "something" was embarrassing Kass.

My heart was slamming as I stepped toward the boy. I said, "Are you an idiot?"

The boy laughed and clicked his fingers at me.

I said, "Don't laugh."

They all laughed then. I looked at them, one by one, and they all thought I was hilarious. My face rushed with blood. I could feel it burning and I was ashamed. I thought I'd humiliated Kass, that I'd got it all wrong.

"Fuck off," I said. "You're a bunch of meatheads and you can all fuck off."

Their laughter turned to high fives. They included Kass and he responded. He was laughing too now, and they stood around and looked at me some more and one of them asked some normal questions—like what my name was and what tutor group I was in.

Before he walked off with them, Kass nudged me and whispered, "Attagirl."

It was one of Mom's expressions. She used it when I'd done well against the odds. It meant I'd be fine. It meant I didn't have to worry about kids shoving me in trash cans after all. It meant I could look after myself.

Kass never did come to the playground to say hello and I never expected him to. Not long after that, his dad moved him to an academy school with an excellent education program.

It was only on alternate weekends, when his mom let him stay at ours, that we let down our guard and he was mine again. We'd camp on the sofa with our feet together in the middle, like sharing a bath. We'd get blankets and snacks and watch crap TV and talk about nothing and laugh at everything. Sometimes we'd let Iris join us, but mostly we wouldn't.

"They're like a couple of puppies in a basket," Mom once said to John.

He flicked us a look. "He should be studying."

When Kass stayed over, he slept in my room and I bunked in with Iris, and one time, after we'd gone to bed, I crept back down the hallway. I thought he'd be awake and we could talk, but he was asleep. I stood just inside the door watching him and then he opened his eyes, as if he hadn't been sleeping at all, just waiting for me to turn up, and he never said a word as he opened the duvet like an envelope and I slipped in beside him. He said I could stay until my feet got warm, but John saw the door ajar and told me to leave his son alone.

Another time, me and Kass babysat Iris together. After we put her to bed, we watched two movies and drank four beers and then we fell asleep, cuddled together on the sofa. We woke to John staring down at us. He banned us from ever babysitting together again and sent Kass home in a cab. He said I was a bad influence.

I was a bad influence on Cerys too. Well, that's what she told me as we trotted down the road—me in borrowed boots and a floral jumpsuit (Cerys had never worn it because it was too full-on) and her in Zara satin heels and a delicate white dress.

"A lot of house parties have someone on the door," she said. "If we're not on the guest list and we get turned away, there's not much we can do."

"I'll just throw a chair through the window," I said.

Cerys laughed. "Don't you dare."

I liked making her laugh.

She went on to tell me that I probably wouldn't know anyone, but she'd look out for me. She said if Kass didn't turn up, we'd only stay a while, because she had a long exam-studying weekend planned and didn't want to start it off exhausted. She said I'd better get a cab home with her so it could drop me off afterward and we could keep up the pretense of me having been unwell.

She said, "I've got money on me, so we'll save that for the taxi."

"Do you ever get exhausted being so organized?" I asked.

She shook her head. "No detail should be too small to escape attention, Lex. That's one of the first principles of getting good grades."

She was quite the killjoy. But I didn't want to hurt her by saying so out loud.

Of course, we got in. We were like a pair of show ponies in Cerys's pretty clothes. We approached the house with our heels clicking and our manes swinging and the guys on the door just waved us through.

Inside smelled different from any place I'd ever been—a mixture of sweat and smoke and something sweet like burned sugar. I thought it might be pheromones, but Cerys told me that was ridiculous. It was louder than any place I'd ever been as well—a throbbing bass from a sound system that vibrated through the soles of my boots and made my legs buzz.

There was a tension as we pushed our way through the jammed hallway—like all the people squashed together were hoping for someone or something, and they looked us up and down as we squeezed past to see if we were it. I wondered what they saw in me. If any of them hoped for anything from me. They were mostly looking at Cerys.

"Stick together," she yelled as she steered me into a room at the back of the house. It was heaving with people—a lot were dancing, but most leaned on walls or sat in groups at the edge. I stood there breathing in the perfume of other lives, the warmth of many bodies as the music pounded through my chest and into my blood.

"Not here," Cerys mouthed, and steered me back out.

We checked the stairs, the landing, and all the bedrooms. Cerys saw some girls she knew and went over to ask if they'd seen Kass. I stood by the door while she pointed at me, and they all turned to look. I wondered what they saw. A kid in a flowery jumpsuit, or Cerys's intriguing new friend?

"No one's seen him," Cerys said, coming back to me. "Are you absolutely sure he said he'd be here?"

We went downstairs and walked the length of the yard. I had a low, sad feeling in my belly, as if I might never see Kass again. Maybe I'd imagined our conversation? Maybe he wasn't coming home for the weekend at all? I took my phone out to check for messages, but there was only a missed call from Mom.

"Nothing?" Cerys said.

She looked so doubtful that it made me believe again. Someone had to. "He'll turn up," I said. "Let's get a drink."

"Some kids chipped in to run a bar, so drinks aren't free."

"But you've got money. If you lend me ten pounds, I'll buy you a drink and pay you back."

Cerys sighed. I was annoying her now. She'd rather be at home with her books. I felt for her, but one of us needed to stay focused.

Behind a trestle table in the kitchen, a girl with shaved hair and several piercings was serving cocktails from jugs. There was a gin and cranberry, a margarita, and some mango concoction. They were only two pounds each, but Cerys refused to let me buy one. She said the money was technically still hers, even though I'd borrowed it, and she was supposed to be looking after me. She agreed I could buy two small beers because they were only three percent alcohol by volume and she didn't want me going home drunk when I was supposed to be ill at Jamila's house. I kept forgetting that's where I was supposed to be.

We moved out of the kitchen and back to the dance room. We stood against a wall. There was a crowd in the corner, all holding balloons like they were at a kid's party. Purple, green, and blue balloons being sucked like pacifiers by teenagers. They nipped the balloons shut while they laughed. They yelled at each other not to waste it. They were mesmerizing.

"Nitrous oxide," Cerys whispered. "Very bad for you."

I thought Cerys would be more out there than she was, that she'd know people or want to get drunk, but I was beginning to understand what Kass meant about her being anxious. It was probably hard work being popular, pretty, and smart all at once. She seemed uneasy and restless, as if something was ratcheting up inside her. Her vape had run out of juice and she was biting her nails.

I had a strange idea that if we stopped looking for Kass, he'd come. That if we danced, we'd summon him. I took several quick gulps of beer, then grabbed Cerys and pulled her reluctantly to the dance floor. She shook her head, but I didn't let go of her hand until she started to move. Someone had to show her how to loosen up.

I closed my eyes and let the music fill me—let it thump inside my boots and up my legs. I imagined the sound as blocks of flashing color. I thought of Kass's beautiful smile and the way his hair fell over one eye so he looked like a pirate. I thought of all the years I'd known him—all the seasons and weather and moods of him.

Come to me, I thought. Come to me, Kass.

I let the power of the music bring him. All of us dancers dancing. We were one throbbing beat. We pulsated together.

The music ended, and I opened my eyes. Cerys had gone. Cerys had stopped dancing.

Because she'd found Kass.

I watched them from a distance. They were talking together in the hallway. I couldn't see his face, only the back of his head as he bent it to hers and she spoke directly into his ear. I wondered what she was saying. *Can you keep your mad sister away from my house? Do you still love me? Why didn't you tell me you were coming back this weekend?*

As I approached, Kass pulled away and saw me. Cerys had clearly told him I was with her, because he didn't look shocked to see me, but he did do a great double take when he saw what I was wearing. He looked me up and down like boys had looked at Cerys earlier. It was thrilling. I bet he imagined I'd be in school uniform or jeans like always. He had no idea I brushed up so nicely. I had makeup on. I was wearing fancy clothes. My hair was loose and flowing. I had a new smooth rhythm.

He shook his head at me—half-disapproving, half-amused. "What the fuck are you doing here, Lex?"

I fell into him and breathed in the wonderful Kass-ness of him. "Having fun."

He held me at arm's length and looked at me in that deep serious way he sometimes had. "Does my dad know you're here?"

Cerys laughed. "I'm her alibi. Don't worry—it'll be fine."

Kass ignored her. "Has there been another fight? I thought you were grounded."

I didn't want him to be like this. I wanted him to be pleased to see me, to tell me I looked beautiful. To ask me to dance. "It doesn't matter."

He reached up and touched my cheek. A shiver ran through me. "I'd say it probably does."

I shook him off. "I need a drink."

"No, Lex. You need to go home."

But he wasn't the king of me. I didn't need his permission. "Oh, please," I said. "You sound like your dad."

I marched back to the trestle table and asked for a gin-and-cranberry cocktail. My voice sounded different, which pissed me off. The shaven-haired girl smiled as she passed me the drink and I handed over more of Cerys's money.

"Enjoy," she said.

I liked her. She didn't judge me at all.

I moved from the kitchen and back to the dance room. I deliberately avoided looking at Kass, still talking to Cerys in her pretty white dress. Her legs were thin and brown and bony like a boy's. The dress shone like a light onto her face. She looked lovely with her hair caught up in a band and a silver chain around the thin curve of her neck. I imagined Kass's lips on that throat—caressing and smoothing that impossibly soft skin.

I wondered if they'd ever had sex. They must've. They both looked amazing. How could they keep their hands off each other?

I drank my cocktail. It was so sweet and delicious, I bought another one—the mango kind.

I watched the dancing while I drank it.

I walked slowly round the room.

I sat on a chair, but that looked strange because no one else was sitting down—and why was the chair even there?

I walked the length of the yard and back, pretending I was looking for someone. I spied on Cerys and Kass through the window. They were still talking, more animatedly now. Cerys was flinging her pretty hands around and Kass looked as if he was listening hard. I hoped they were talking about me. Even bad stuff. I wanted to be on his radar.

I bought another cocktail. The third kind.

Then I was ready to dance again . . .

Eleven

I IMAGINED MYSELF SLIM and lithe. I let the music surge through me. I didn't care how much room I took up. My hands rippled like underwater creatures as I moved. I was Lex—fifteen and beautiful—and that boy leaning against the wall was smiling at me. I didn't bother wondering what he might be thinking. I didn't let the fleeting thought that I looked like an idiot occupy the smallest space in my brain. I just fixed onto his smile and danced.

When the song ended, I sashayed over. "Buy me a balloon?"

He nodded. "Sure."

I was dizzy from cocktails and thought maybe I hadn't heard him right. "Serious? You will?"

"You have a color preference?"

I followed him to the corner of the room. "Purple," I told him.

While he paid, I looked about for Kass, but he'd gone. No Cerys either. They'd probably gone to a bedroom to have sex. I shook the thought away because jealousy wasn't helpful when trying to get someone to like you. Hadn't Cerys told me that?

I followed the boy into the kitchen, past the table where the girl was still serving drinks, and we sat on some steps by the back door.

We were shielded from the party, in the dark. The kitchen behind us smelled of overripe fruit. I wondered whose house this was.

"So," the boy said, holding out the purple balloon and smiling at me, "here you go."

I took it from him, keeping it pinched shut. "Will it make me feel awesome?"

His smile faded. "Haven't you done it before?"

"First time for everything, right?"

He looked me full in the face as if trying to work out what sort of person I might be. "What's your name?"

"Lex."

"What's that short for?"

"Lexi. Or Alexia. Well, Alexandra, really . . ."

"That's a lot of names." He edged closer. "You get a quick buzz, that's all. It makes you light-headed and you get to talk like Darth Vader. You'll laugh your head off."

He lost something as he inhaled his own balloon—some reserved thing. He looked like a kid suddenly thrilled with life. He leaned across the doorway and kissed me. And I let him. He put his hot tongue right inside my mouth and I let him do that too.

He pulled away from me and sucked at his balloon again. I watched the buzz hit his bloodstream, his eyes tip back in his head. He kissed me again—harder and for longer, his tongue searching inside my mouth. I thought of all the chemicals swimming in his brain, like a crack in reality opening in his skull. When it was over, he sat with the balloon limp in his hand and laughed. I laughed right along with him. Maybe the kissing had got me high? I wondered if we'd kiss some more after I'd had my own balloon and had just brought it to my mouth to inhale, when the table behind us clattered to the floor.

Drinks spilled and jugs shattered and the girl behind the counter screamed, "What the hell?" and lights went on and people scattered and suddenly there was Kass looming above me. Where did he come from? He grabbed the balloon from me and let it go; he dragged the boy from the floor by his T-shirt and hauled him upright.

"Leave her the fuck alone," he said.

The night had turned supersonic.

Kass wanted to take the boy outside. The boy wanted to stay inside. The boy kept saying, "Calm down, dude. Just calm down."

There was no blood or pounding fists. It was just Kass shaking the boy and the boy saying, "Just chill, man." And the girl with the piercings looking at the mess on the floor and saying, "My parents are going to kill me."

So, it was her house. She looked a lot less cool than she had earlier. She looked younger as well—about sixteen, instead of the mature person I'd thought she was.

"Sorry," Kass said to her. "I'd help you clean up, but she's my sister and I've got to take her home."

"I'm not his sister," I told her. "I've never seen him before in my life."

"Ignore her," Kass said.

I scowled at him. "Stop ordering me around."

He grabbed me by my arm and pulled me down the hallway and through the front door. The street was empty, and the party felt suddenly far away.

"You were taking drugs," he said.

"I was not. You didn't give me the chance!"

He kept pulling me along past other houses and toward the park. "Do you know people have died using that nitrous oxide shit?"

"I wasn't using it."

"And what was going on with that lad? Do you know him?"

I pushed him off me. "Yeah, he's my dealer. Oh, no, actually, he's my pimp."

"Funny. Well, whoever he was, I suggest you steer clear. He's a total prick."

"You'd know."

We stood there glaring at each other. Blood rushed to my head. My ears pounded. My hands were freezing.

Kass bundled me across the road toward the park. The gate was shut, but there was a bench outside.

"Sit," he said.

I crossed my arms. "I don't want to."

I hated that I was shivering, hated that my eyes stung with tears, that every bit of me was trembling with cold.

"Now tell me what you were really doing there," he said.

"It was a party."

"I know that. But what were *you* doing at it?"

He said *you* the way John sometimes said it, as if he was sickened and infuriated by me all at once.

"Me and Cerys needed a night out."

"I don't recall you being friends with Cerys."

"Well, you don't know everything about me, then, do you?"

"You need to leave her alone."

"I'm sure she can look after herself."

He looked away, biting his lip. "I should take you home and let my dad deal with you."

"Seriously? Listen to yourself."

"You can't keep fighting him all the time, Lex. Can't you just do what he says for once?"

"I'm always doing what he says, and I get it wrong anyway. I'm staying away from him as much as possible—it's my new strategy."

"Yeah? How's that working out for you?" He ran a hand through his hair, looked back at the house.

"Worried about your girlfriend?"

"Shut up, Lex."

He was slipping through my fingers. I'd felt it for months.

"I miss you," I said. "You've been gone for ages."

"I'm at college, Lex. I'm supposed to be gone."

"You hardly ever call. It's always me that contacts you. Why are you avoiding me?"

"I'm here now, aren't I?"

He sat on the bench. I crashed next to him and we stayed silent for a bit, our breath like smoke in the cold air.

"I'm sorry," he said eventually.

"What's going on?"

"It's complicated." He looked at his feet for a while. "I know it sounds really obvious, but being away—it's a relief, you know?"

"A relief?"

"To be free of family stuff."

My heart felt like it was trying to punch through my rib cage. "You can't just be free of us. You mean, all of us? You want to be free of me too?"

He shook his head. "Don't be like that. I'm only here this weekend because of you."

"So, I need to throw chairs around to get you to come home?"

Kass tensed. "I can't be dealing with this."

"With what? Me? Your dad?"

"Any of it. This family's doing my head in." He turned on the bench. "You should know my dad's been saying stuff about you."

"What stuff?"

"About you having a condition."

"What kind of condition?"

"I don't know, but he wants you to see some doctor friend of his."

"He can't make me see a doctor! He's not my parent."

"No, but your mom is, and she agrees with him apparently."

"What kind of doctor? One for crazy people?"

"I doubt it."

"Some scary bastard who uses electricity to fry people's brains?"

"Calm down, Lex. I'll talk to him. He's just annoyed about the window thing."

97

I couldn't speak, couldn't breathe. It was as if the whole world had concertinaed shut and caught me in its folds.

"Shit," Kass said. "Are you crying? You never cry."

"My mom never said anything. She must agree with him. Do you? Do you think I've got a condition?"

"No."

"What if I do? What if I've got some kind of explosive anger disorder? What if it turns out I'm a psycho?"

"You're not."

"This is why your dad doesn't like me, isn't it? He stood on those steps at the party going on about his wonderful life, and Iris was in his arms and Mom was standing next to him and I was right there, and he never mentioned me at all."

"Was this before or after you told his boss to fuck off?"

"It's not funny, Kass. He's ashamed because I'm not perfect."

Kass took my hand and held it. I knew I was disgusting, blubbing all over him. "None of us are perfect, Lex. I'm certainly not."

"Hey," I said. "Maybe you've got a condition too? Remember all the tricks we used to play on your dad? Remember all the times we hid or ran away? Most of that stuff was your idea."

"We were kids, Lex."

"What, and you're all grown up, so everything's different now?" I used my sleeve to wipe my nose and he laughed, so I hit him. "It's not funny! I don't want to be the only crazy one."

"You are so very drunk," he said.

I said, "Your dad told the principal I'm always causing trouble at home and she said it was the same at school and why did I insist on winding everyone up? And my mom sat there saying nothing. Not one word. Why does she never say anything?"

Kass shook me then. He shook me gently by the shoulders until the tears turned to something else, like banging the back of a screen when it pixelated.

"Is the doctor thing why you've been avoiding me?" I said. "You felt bad for knowing?"

He held out his hand. "Come on, let's walk some of that booze off."

"I read a story once about a girl whose dad got her kidnapped and taken to some private nuthouse in the middle of nowhere."

"That's not happening to you."

"They can do what they like to you in those places. They can beat the crap out of you and no one cares."

"I'll break you out," Kass said.

"I bet you won't."

"I will."

"It'll be illegal, and you'd need a gun and you won't have time and after a few weeks you'll forget all about me."

"Yeah, you're probably right—you're not very memorable."

I didn't laugh. I felt young and small and sad. I knew I was drunk, but it felt like the worst night of my life.

"Let's go back to the party," I said. "Have you ever tried that stuff in the balloons? Does it stop life being crap? Will it make me happy?"

He looked at me in that way he sometimes did when I went too far—as if he wanted to come with me and wanted to put the brakes on all at once. "I should take you home."

"I want to get drunk instead."

"I'd say you've already achieved that ambition."

I took his hand. "Can I come back to your place?"

"What?"

"I'm supposed to be ill. Cerys was my alibi." I blinked at him. "Where is Cerys? Is she still at the party?"

"She left."

"Why did she do that?"

"It doesn't matter. Look, it's going to be tricky you coming to my place. My mom's there."

"Then I'll go back to the party and go home with balloon boy."

He held my hand all the way to the end of the street. It was dark, and the sky was full of mist and we didn't see anyone as we walked along. I said if he didn't let me crash at his place, I'd run away. He said I was an idiot and, if I did that, I'd be in ridiculous trouble. I said I didn't care. He said he was unwilling to worry his mom or get into shit with his dad, and either I went home or he was going to call his dad to come and pick me up. I said I'd walk the streets all night rather than get in a car with his father and when I got murdered it would be his fault. He said I was very unlikely to be murdered, but I might get hypothermia or get hungry or get hassled by drunk boys. That made me smile. I don't know why.

"I can't believe your dad wants to send me to a doctor," I said. "It's not even his decision."

Kass shrugged. "It is if your mom agrees."

"Why can't she be more like your mom and throw stuff at his head?"

"My mom hasn't thrown anything for years."

"Why not?" I looked at Kass, seriously expecting an answer. I was drunk, and the night felt as if it might have some truth in it, but all he did was shrug.

"So," he said, "I guess you can come back to my place, but you have to drink two glasses of water and go straight to bed. I am *not* getting blamed for your morning hangover. I'll call my mom and tell her you can't bear to go home 'cause my dad's been a prick for some reason. I'm sure she'll be very hospitable."

I wasn't sure that was true, but I felt excited suddenly.

Kass said, "Call your mom."

I knew she'd be mad, so I offered to text her. "I'll tell her I'm staying at Jamila's for the night."

Of course, Mom rang as soon as she got the text. I refused to answer. I refused to listen to her voice mail. Kass whipped the phone from me and listened and then he sent her a new text. Apparently, she wanted an actual conversation.

"I've texted that you're nearly asleep, feeling much better, and will contact her first thing in the morning, OK?"

"I'm nearly sixteen," I said as he passed me my phone back. "When will this be over?"

Kass chuckled as we carried on walking. "You're very lucky, because I happen to know the answer to that one." He stooped down and kissed my hair. "And the answer is, by the time you're eighteen, my love, you will be free."

"You're already there," I said.

"Yep."

"You called me *my love*."

"I did." We stood in the street blinking at each other.

Twelve

I HADN'T SEEN KASS'S mom since me and Kass wheeled newborn Iris over in her stroller because he wanted his mom to meet his half sister. Sophie had been kind that day, giving us cake and lemonade and making a smiling fuss of Iris. She hadn't said a single mean thing about my mom stealing her husband.

Six years later and she didn't look so friendly as we walked into her living room. She was watching TV in the dark and paused the screen as we came through the door. She was only ten minutes into some movie, which meant she'd started watching it after Kass called her and was only pretending to be busy.

"Hey, Sophie," I said. "Long time no see."

"Hello, Alexandra. Yes, it's been a while."

"Lex," said Kass. "She prefers to be called Lex. Or Lexi."

Sophie turned the TV off and switched on a raffia lamp by her side. The wall by her head was instantly covered in dappled light. She'd put weight on since I'd last seen her and looked prettier. Her hair was a tangle of dark curls like Kass's, but she had streaks of gray in it now. She observed me warily.

"So," she said, "what's happened that you can't go home?"

"Nothing much," Kass said. "She broke a grounding and drank too many cocktails. I've squared it with Dad—don't worry." He clapped his hands. "Right—water and Advil for Lex. Tea for me. Mom, you want anything?"

His mom frowned at me. "How many cocktails have you had?"

"Mom, don't fuss," Kass said. "Everything's under control."

His mom kept frowning as she declined tea and waved a hand at me to sit opposite her. Kass went to the kitchen and I sat down. It was awkward. I didn't want her to disapprove of me. I wanted to stay the night.

"So," she said. "Tell me about the party."

Images of cocktails, balloons, and a falling table lit up my brain. But those things would make me sound debauched, so I told her instead about the people and the music and how I'd kept faith Kass would show up. "I enjoyed dancing," I said. "Which was a surprise because I usually don't. And I liked not knowing anyone. Well, except for Kass and Cerys."

"Ah, Cerys. What happened to her?"

I blinked at her. "She left without us."

She frowned again. We'd neglected Cerys and she knew it. "And you decided to break a grounding?"

Tears pricked, and I wiped them away. "I thought if I stayed away from home for a while, things might go better for everyone."

"Things aren't good at home?"

Her voice was cool. It felt like an interrogation. Had she deliberately waited for Kass to be out of the room to ask me questions?

104

"It's more that me and John don't get along. He'd like me to be charming and obedient and I can't seem to do it."

She nodded.

"I'm making an extra effort now they're getting married, though. So long as I keep out of everyone's way and avoid getting sent to a nuthouse, it should be all right."

Sophie looked shocked. "What do you mean?"

I stared back at her, embarrassed. Kass shouldn't've left us alone. Anything could fall out of me. I might tell her I was in love with her son next. I might confess I planned to creep into his bed later.

Thinking about him brought him. He came in with a tray—tea, two glasses of water, and a plate of buttered toast.

"Both waters are for you, Lex," he said. "And half the toast." He handed me two Advil and made me drink one whole glass of water.

I gave him my most dazzling smile as I handed back the glass.

"Toast next," he said. "Then the other water. Then bed."

I kept grinning. The room tilted and still I grinned. I couldn't believe I was being looked after by Kass in the apartment where he'd grown up with his mom. It felt like a dream. John would go mental if he found out.

"I like it here," I said.

They both gazed silently at me. I kept grinning.

"Toast," Kass said.

"You're incredibly bossy," I said.

He rolled his eyes. "Just eat it."

I stuck my tongue out at him to show Sophie how well I knew her son—that I could be casual with him like that. I wanted him to

105

laugh in that free way he did with me. I wanted to sit next to him and press my leg against his. But he sat on the sofa next to his mom and asked her how her evening had been.

She told him about some news program she'd watched and about the friend in the States she'd Skyped, and he asked when she was going to get her act together and get on a plane and visit the friend and she teased him about handing over some of his student loan to pay for it.

She asked him about the party. Kass didn't tell her much. He probably didn't want to get me into trouble.

I ate slowly, trying to make it last. I liked watching them together. If Kass was my boyfriend, it would always be this way.

When I finished the second glass of water, Sophie said she better change the sheets on Kass's bed for me and find some bedding for the sofa and then we should probably all get some sleep.

"I'll have the sofa," I said.

She shook her head. "You're a guest. You're having a bed."

"I don't need fresh linen, though."

"You do," she said. "I haven't changed it since last time Kass was home." She made it seem as if Kass was very dirty. She didn't realize I'd be happy breathing in his scent.

She was going, and I wanted to speak to her some more because I might not see her for another six years, but I didn't know what to say.

My chance came when Kass was washing up the cups and she went to sort out bedding. I walked silently out of the living room and found her in her bedroom. It was big with a mirrored wardrobe, a double bed, and orange curtains.

"Hello," I said.

"Oh, hello. You all right?"

I couldn't think of a single reason to have followed her to her bedroom. "Do you have a spare tampon?" I asked.

She slid one of the glass doors of the wardrobe open and passed me a box. "Take them," she said. "Use as many as you need." She slid the wardrobe shut, clearly expecting me to go.

I stood there. I was closest to the door. Kass was still clunking about in the kitchen and she was trapped.

"I want you to know," I said, "that John didn't get an amazing new life with us. He got me as part of the deal and I have a terrible temper."

"I see," she said.

"I didn't want to tell you earlier, but I threw a chair through a window the other day."

She nodded politely. She was giving nothing away.

"I was wondering if you had any anger management tips? I thought you might be a good person to ask."

A pause. A breath. In and out.

"Why did you think I might be a good person to ask?" she said.

I gazed at her. The room swayed slightly, as if I'd just stepped onto a boat. "Kass told me you used to chuck things."

For the first time, she smiled at me. It was a sad and sorry smile, but it lit up her face. "You're a sweet girl," she said. "But I really think you need to get some sleep."

"I'm not having a go at you."

107

"I know you're not." She walked over and put an arm round me and led me out of the room. I wanted to ask if John had ever threatened her with a doctor or told her she had a condition, but I didn't because she ushered me into the bathroom and, when I came out, Kass was waiting for me.

"What did you say to my mom?"

"Nothing. Why?"

"Never mind. She's gone to bed. She said to tell you good night."

He escorted me to his room. I sat on the bed and waited for him to tell me what would happen next. Maybe he wasn't going to stay on the sofa after all. Maybe he was going to shut the door behind him and climb into bed with me.

Instead, he stood in the doorway and looked at me.

I looked back at him. My heart hurt. I wanted to cry again, and I didn't know why.

"Good night, Lex."

"Why are you being weird?"

He shrugged. "It's a weird situation."

"Do you wish I wasn't here?"

"No."

"Have you had any texts?"

He checked his phone. "Not about you."

"From Cerys?"

He put his phone away. "Get some sleep, Lex."

I held out my hand. "Do you think I'll be grounded for the rest of my life?"

"They think you're at a friend's house, don't they? You'll be fine."

"And you won't tell?"

He mimed zipping his lips, then came to sit next to me on his bed. He smelled so familiar, but also different. I think he had a new aftershave.

"I kissed a boy tonight," I said.

"I noticed. Did you like him?"

"He wanted to kiss me, that's all."

"You don't have to kiss people just because they want to."

"I know."

"What did *you* want?"

"To know what it would feel like."

Kass was silent for a moment. Then, "Was that your first kiss?"

I thought it might be wrong to admit it—like it made me less wild. But I also wanted him to know that I'd been waiting for him, saving myself for him, that the boy at the party was meaningless. I turned to tell him, and he was looking right at me and I hadn't even known.

He was so beautiful and so close. Whole seconds went by with us looking at each other.

"I should go," he said.

But he didn't sound as if he meant it, so I reached out to touch his hair. I'd been wanting to do it all night. It was black and soft, and his curls were the same shape as my fingers when I crooked them, and seemed to turn blue in the light.

He whispered, "What are you doing?"

But again, he didn't stop me. I moved my hand down to stroke the skin of his neck and shoulder. I traced his tattoo and wondered if anyone but me had ever touched him there so tenderly. I thought Cerys might've, but she wasn't there to claim him, was she? She was probably the one who was ringing him, though. I could hear the dull vibration of his phone from his pocket.

"Don't answer it," I said.

He took hold of my wrist. "Lex. You have to stop."

I counted his breaths to get rid of the sound of the phone. I laid my other hand gently on his chest and counted his heartbeats.

"Lex," he said again.

"No," I said. "I don't want to stop."

I edged closer and his skin grazed mine, rough with stubble, and our lips touched, barely pressing, and I was thinking, Is this even real?

But it was. There, on his boyhood bed, I got my wish and we kissed—my mouth on his, my arms around him. Then his mouth on mine, pulling me nearer. He hauled me onto his lap and I straddled him, and he wrapped me closer still and pressed against me as we kissed some more.

It went on for ages. I was breathless with it. We stopped and couldn't look at one another. I buried my face in his shirt, his chest, his neck. He held the back of my head, his fingers threading my hair, his breath hot on the side of my face.

"Fuck," he whispered.

I could feel his heart pounding. I think it was his. It may have been mine.

I thought of the tree and how we were bound.

"What just happened?" he said.

I didn't say anything. I couldn't speak. I wanted to look at him but was scared I'd see something in his eyes that said he was sorry.

"Lex?" he said. He moved back and with one gentle hand touched my cheek so I'd look at him. "You shouldn't've done that."

I wanted to tell him that he'd done it too, but I didn't. "I love you," I said. "I always have."

"Ah, Lexi." He sounded so sad as he kissed the top of my head. "I love you too. But I'm going now. You're going to sleep here and I'm going to sleep on the sofa."

"I don't want that to happen."

"I know." He kissed the top of my head again. "Good night, Lex. Everything's going to be all right. I promise."

Thirteen

SOPHIE WOKE ME UP the next morning with a mug of tea. She said Kass had gone out to meet friends and would see me later. I've kissed your son, I thought. I wondered if I looked different—more grown-up, prettier, and more mature. I'd never kissed a boy in my life and last night I'd kissed two. The world was opening and my place in it would soon be obvious.

"How's the head?" she asked. "You need any more painkillers?"

"I'm fine."

"Ah," she said, "the recovery rate of the young . . ."

I didn't know what that meant, but it sounded like she envied me, so I smiled kindly at her. I wondered what she did all day. I wondered if she had any friends, or if she'd ever find a new man to love?

After I'd drunk the tea, I went to the kitchen to give her back the mug. She was standing looking out of the window, but turned round when I came in.

"I've thought of some advice for you," she said. "You still want it?"

I put the mug in the sink. "Sure."

"OK, it's simply this—you're allowed to be angry."

"That's it?"

"You asked for anger management tips. Well, that's my tip. Because what's the alternative? If you're not angry you become afraid—afraid to stand up against things that are wrong, afraid to speak out, afraid to act. A healthy girl *should* be furious, because it's an unfair world."

That was easy for her to say—she was an adult. Maybe my disappointment showed on my face because she walked over and gave me a hug. I was a bit surprised but hugged her back.

"I have a question for you," she said. She held me at arm's length and looked at me. "Does Kass treat you kindly?"

Did she know we'd kissed? I felt myself blush. "Of course."

She looked at me for a few moments longer. "You can be angry with him too, you know."

"Why would I be?"

She smiled. "All right. Well, that's good. Now take care of yourself."

I told her I would.

"It was lovely to meet you again," she said. And she gave me such a warm look that I almost didn't want to leave because she seemed sorry to see me go.

In the elevator on the way down, I checked my phone to see if Kass had left me any messages. He hadn't, but I did have thirteen missed calls from Mom and several voice mails. I knew it'd be hell at home, so I decided to go and see Cerys and get my clothes back. I wanted to say sorry too—not for stealing her boyfriend, I wasn't going to confess that, but for abandoning her at the party. I also thought she might know the friends Kass had gone to meet and could give me some useful information about where he might be.

She looked pale when she opened the door and didn't invite me in. "I'm studying," she said. "I have a strict timetable."

She told me she wouldn't be going out again until her exams were over. She couldn't chat for long, she said, because she should be doing two hours of studying English, but she'd talk to me for twenty puffs of her new flavor e-juice.

"That's a very unhealthy boundary," I said.

She laughed as she shut the door behind her and we sat on the doorstep. "You always cheer me up, Lex, you know that?"

She had no makeup on and looked younger and fresh-faced. She really was very pretty. I wished it was possible to have both her and Kass in my life. Maybe we'd have to wait until she found someone new before announcing our relationship together?

"What happened to you last night?" I said.

She breathed out a plume of vapor. It smelled of gingerbread. We both watched it fade into air. "I'm not blaming you for this, Lex, but going to that party was a mistake. If I'd just stayed home like I'd wanted to, I'd still be happy."

She knows about our kiss, I thought in a panic. She's going to say it out loud and accuse me of things and she might tell John and then it will end before it's even begun.

"You're not happy?" I said.

She took a long drag of the vape. "I think Kass is going to dump me."

"What makes you think that?"

114

"Something he said at the party."

That was before our kiss. That was nothing to do with me.

"He said I wasn't invited and shouldn't've gone," Cerys said. "It made him feel watched and claustrophobic. He said when people go to college they usually split with their boyfriend or girlfriend from school because it's immature not to move forward." She wiped a hand across her eyes. "You reckon he's seeing someone else?"

"I don't know." I looked across the street to the row of houses opposite and thought of all the people who lived in them getting on with their innocent lives.

"Could you find out?"

I hugged my legs with both arms and sank my head onto my knees. "We don't usually talk about stuff like that—he'd be suspicious."

"Oh, well, don't worry about it, then. We'll probably work it out." I listened to her drag on the vape a few more times. The smell reminded me of Christmas. "Hey, Lex," she said, "are you OK? Why are you hiding?"

"I've got a hangover."

"You need a coffee?"

I agreed, but only because I didn't know what else to do. I followed her through the hallway and into the kitchen. Her dad was there and that made me feel worse, because he grinned at me and said, "Who do we have here, then?"

"This is Lex," Cerys said. "Kass's sister."

"I'm not his sister," I said.

"Stepsister," Cerys said.

Not even that, I thought, but it felt stupid to say so.

Her dad reached out to shake my hand. "Lovely to meet you, whoever you are. Now, can I get you two ladies anything?"

"I'm going to make coffee," Cerys said. "Lex has a headache and I need caffeine."

"Have mine," he said. "I've just made a pot."

"We can't take yours."

"It's fine. I expect your need is greater." He tweaked the end of her nose and she laughed up at him. "You girls want hot milk? I can offer you soy, almond, or scary dairy."

I didn't want to choose, so I just said, "Whatever Cerys is having."

"Almond," she said. "Better for the brain cells."

"Your brain cells are perfect." Her dad winked at me as he filled a saucepan with milk, and me and Cerys settled ourselves on stools at the breakfast bar. He said, "I feel sorry for young people these days. Exams weren't such a big deal when I was at school. Colleges are so competitive now and they want such high grades, don't they?"

"I don't know," I said.

"I do," Cerys said. "And I'm going to get them."

He smiled lovingly at her. "I'm sure you will with your work ethic, kid. But it's fine if you don't. You know that, right?"

Everything about her relaxed as she smiled back at him. I felt like a ghost in their kitchen watching them together.

"What about you, Lex?" he said. "You got big ambitions?"

I shrugged. My only ambition was to steal Kass away from his daughter. I had to grit my teeth, sitting under his smile.

"Well, you seem very chill," he said. "That's healthy. Good for you."

He didn't ask me anything else as he poured the coffee and Cerys talked about her plans for the day. He told her to make sure she took good breaks and reminded her she should consider using his study for schoolwork and not her bedroom, because that was where she slept, and he'd been reading an article about feng shui that suggested you don't learn well in a room where you sleep.

I felt like a ghost again and had to ask for my clothes back to change the vibe. Cerys fetched them, and I went to change in the bathroom. I locked the little bolt on the door and sat on the closed toilet seat and buried my head in my hands. I was a horrible person. I should call Kass up and tell him it was over between us. He should keep going out with Cerys. She was a good person who deserved good things.

But the longer I sat there, the less guilty I felt. Cerys was popular and looked like a model. She was a straight-A student and her dad was twinkly and kind—that should be enough for her.

I changed into my own clothes and checked my phone again. Nothing from Kass. A missed call from John.

Back in the kitchen, the mood was different. Cerys's dad had gone and maybe he'd told her to get rid of me, because she was taking great swigs of coffee and not saying much. I asked if I could see her study plan and she brought it up on her phone. She was taking English, Spanish, and history. I never knew that about her.

"You're so smart," I said.

I sounded guilty, even to myself—like I was only saying nice things because I'd kissed her boyfriend.

"I'm no smarter than you," she said. "I just work harder."

"There's no way I could take essay subjects."

We both scanned her plan. Even her color code was confusing. She had to use two different shades of blue to find enough colors.

"It looks worse than it is," she said confidently. "And when I get anxious, I just tell myself that one day everything will be over."

"And what then?"

"Then," she said, "I'll be at college trying to be mature and move forward."

She was talking about Kass again. I thanked her for the coffee and pulled my jacket on.

"Will you see your brother again before he goes back?" she said.

I'd gone there hoping she'd know where he was and now she was asking me. I could barely look at her. "He's invited for supper later."

"Well," she said, "no pressure, but if you find anything out about him cheating on me, will you let me know?"

Fourteen

THEY WERE WAITING FOR me in the living room.

John said, "Sit down, Alexandra."

I told myself I was fifteen and not five. I told myself that Mom was my parent and John had no legal rights over me. But still, I sat down.

"Where were you last night?" he said.

"Jamila's house."

"Incorrect. Try again."

Everything about him was accusing—from the way he squeezed his eyes to his thin lips and folded hands.

I said, "You spoke to her mom, remember?"

"I spoke to a woman you *said* was her mother. But when you failed to respond to messages across the next few hours and then sent a text announcing you weren't coming home, your mom got hold of Jamila's landline and the woman who answered—who I assume was the *real* mother—said she hadn't seen you for years and had certainly not spoken with me earlier in the day."

"Did you call the right Jamila, Mom?"

She shook her head sadly. "Please, Lexi . . . don't make this worse."

"You're being offered an opportunity here," John said. "And I suggest you take it. This meeting will go much better if you tell the truth."

I stared at him, my blood racing. I had no idea what he knew. That I'd been at Kass's apartment? That we'd kissed?

He said, "Imagine your mother's shame having to admit to a stranger she had no idea where you were. 'Oh,' the woman said, 'why not have a word with Jamila?' and her daughter was dragged to the phone. 'Do you happen to know where Lexi is?' your mom asked. You know what Jamila told her?"

I shook my head.

"She said she was very sorry, but she hadn't spoken to you for days, had no clue who you hung around with, and absolutely no idea where you might be. Imagine how worried your mom was now?"

I looked over at her. She was chewing her lip and staring at her shoes as if reenacting the worry.

"So then," John said, "I called Kass, thinking perhaps he'd heard from you, but he didn't pick up. We didn't know where else to turn, so your mom called Meryam, thinking Ben might have seen you. He hadn't. She called Cerys, who also didn't pick up. Your poor mother left frantic messages everywhere and was just asking me if I thought we should contact the police when the phone rang. You want to guess who it was?"

Maybe Cerys had buckled under pressure? Maybe Ben had decided to provide an alibi?

"After six whole years and with barely a word passing between us, my ex-wife calls me up."

"Sophie called you?"

Mom flinched at the sound of her name. When John went back to Sophie those times, Mom said she couldn't breathe.

"Sophie, is it now?" John said. "Pals with her, are you?"

Not if she'd called him up, no. Why would she do that? Why would she get me into trouble?

"So," John said, "here's a final chance to tell the truth. Do you want to take it?"

I took a breath, tried not to let my voice wobble. "I shouldn't've fibbed about Jamila and I'm sorry. I did feel ill after school, though, and I was walking home and bumped into Kass and he said to come back to his and then I got worse and I thought you'd be mad if I was at Sophie's—"

"Stop lying!" John slapped his hand on the arm of the chair. "Do you have any idea how humiliating it was to get a call from my ex-wife telling me you'd turned up at her place drunk? Oh, she had quite the field day—why didn't I have a better relationship with you? Why was I allowing a vulnerable young person to fall under the radar?" He stabbed a finger at me. "You made me look a fool, Alexandra Robinson."

"I need to go to the bathroom," I said.

"I haven't finished with you," John said. "Not by a long way. You need to know that your mother and I have been doing some research—"

"I already know. You want to send me to your doctor friend."

121

Surprise flickered in his eyes. "You've been talking to Kass, I see. Well, Derek Leaman is a lot more than a doctor. He's a whole new start. Your mother and I found it hugely helpful to speak to someone with years of experience who understood what we're going through."

I stared at Mom. "You've met him?"

She looked tired and suddenly old. "We're worried about you."

"Exactly," John said. "We're worried that leaving you untreated might negatively affect your future."

"*Untreated?*" I whispered. "What does that mean?"

"It means we've been fools not to seek professional help sooner."

"I don't need help."

"I beg to differ."

I turned to Mom. "You agree with this?"

She could hardly look at me. "I want a new start for you."

"Your mom tells me you were bright when you were young," John said.

"Oh, and I'm an idiot now?"

"Not at all, but something's impeding your ability to learn. You've become inattentive and impulsive; you're often very challenging. What if these behaviors prevent you from ever holding down a job or maintaining a relationship?"

I wanted to tell him to shut up. I wanted to tell him he knew nothing about anything and neither did his stupid doctor friend.

"Anyway," John went on, "Derek helped us see the situation more clearly and he'd like to meet you."

"Absolutely no way."

"He said you'd say that," John said. He turned to Mom. "Didn't he say that?"

She nodded, not looking at me.

"It might comfort you to know," John said, "that you're not alone. According to Derek, ADHD affects at least five percent of children."

"I haven't got ADHD!"

"Well, of course he can't diagnose you without seeing you, but Dr. Leaman thought an attention deficit disorder was a definite possibility."

"Dr. Leaman can fuck off!"

"Language, Alexandra! You're not helping yourself one iota here."

"I broke a grounding. I went to a party. Why does that mean I need to see a doctor?"

"Because that's not the whole picture, is it? You're struggling at school. You need instructions repeated, you hardly ever sit still, you have poor peer relationships, you need a high level of adult supervision. You want me to go on? No, I didn't think so." He leaned back in his chair. "I know it's not easy to hear, but won't you feel relieved to have a diagnosis?"

I couldn't bear it. I had to latch on to John's weak things to stop myself screaming. His hair needed a wash. He had the beginnings of a zit blooming on his neck. Those two, plus a thread hanging loose from his sleeve and a patch of dry skin on the back of his wrist. Four weak things.

"I've been telling your mom for years that you need a firmer hand, and now we're getting married, it makes sense for me to be more involved. I care about this family, Alexandra, and I'm not going to let you destroy it."

I looked desperately at Mom. Stop him, I thought.

"The last few weeks have been a nightmare," he went on. "Imagine how mortified I felt facing my colleagues after the party? Imagine the shame when your teacher suggested parenting classes? And now I've got my ex-wife having a go at me." The cold in his voice was frightening. "I've done my very best for you and your mother over the years, Alexandra, and all I get back from you is abuse. Well, not anymore."

Mom wasn't going to do anything to save me. Her skin appeared yellow-tinged and she looked small beside John, who seemed enormous.

"In the first instance," John said, "the doctor suggested some small changes—some behavior modification, if you like. So I've made a new list and once again you're going to sign it, and once again it's going on the fridge where everyone can see it. But this time it's a proper *contract*. You're going to start studying, stick to your grounding, and be polite, focused, and well-behaved. If you prove you can do all that, then we'll reassess. But if you break the contract by even a hairsbreadth, you go straight to Dr. Leaman." There was something excited in the way he licked his lips, in the way he smiled at me now. "You're dangerously close to the edge, Alexandra."

Another Tale of Love and Death

ONCE, THERE WAS A woman who lived alone with her young daughter. They were very poor and often hungry, but they were happy because they loved each other. One winter, snow fell for weeks and although the mother did her best—begging for scraps from neighbors and searching the streets for firewood—the pair was soon starving. They lay huddled together under a thin blanket, telling each other stories of summer days, in the hope it would keep death away.

One night, there was a knock at the door and in walked a handsome prince. He had food with him and warm clothes and fuel for the fire and he told the mother he'd seen her wandering around and thought she looked frail and beautiful and he'd fallen in love and was here to look after her.

"What about my daughter?" she asked, pointing to the child shivering on the bed. "Will you love her too?"

"Shit," he said. "I didn't know you had a kid." He made his apologies and went away.

"That was my fault," said the child.

"No," the mother said. "The prince has a child and wife of his own. It's better not to get involved." But she took to crying. "Wouldn't it be wonderful if he could have saved us?" she said. "And he was very handsome, did you notice? And did you hear him say I was beautiful?"

"I'll save us," the daughter said. "I'll go out hunting."

But the mother said she was too young. She said it was *her* job to look after the child, not the other way round. But she didn't get out of bed to do anything about it. She seemed to have lost energy. She said she couldn't breathe properly. She got thinner and frailer.

A few days later, the prince came back. "I've had an idea," he said. He suggested he pay for the daughter to go and stay with relatives. "It'll give me and your mother a chance to get to know one another," he said, smiling at the girl.

"And what about your wife?" the mother said.

"Oh, it's over between us," the prince assured her. "It's you I love."

And so the child went to stay with her grandfather every other weekend.

For a while, everything went well. The mother blossomed in love, growing healthy and happy and more beautiful. The prince adored her. He'd never met anyone like her. He loved her more than anyone else ever would.

The girl blossomed too. She hadn't been able to visit her grandfather much before, because he lived so far away, and the fare was expensive, so it was wonderful spending time with him. He was kind and gentle to the girl and taught her many useful skills, such as how to climb trees and the names of all the birds.

The only bad thing was that when the child returned home, all the rooms smelled different—either cold and stale because her mother and the prince had been out partying, or smoky and strange because they hadn't gone out at all. The prince's smell was on her mother's skin and between the covers of the bed.

Oh, and one other bad thing was that the child's mother spent hours looking in mirrors and trying on clothes and practicing her dancing and had very little time for snuggling in blankets or telling stories. "Why would we want to do that?" the mother said. "We were starving and freezing when we did that! I want to forget about those days."

So the child let her memories grow fuzzy, like a drawing being slowly erased.

She told herself her mother was happy and that they were lucky not to be hungry anymore. And, of course, the child was glad to spend time with her granddad.

But one night a terrible thing happened.

The child was at her grandfather's house and was just getting ready for bed when the old man collapsed onto the floor.

"I'll call for a doctor," the child said.

The old man begged her not to. He hated a fuss. He said doctors killed people and he just needed to rest, and he'd be fine in the morning. So the girl fetched him a blanket and pillow and settled him where he'd fallen. She got him water and lay next to him all night holding his hand.

But when she woke in the morning her grandfather's skin was gray, and when he tried to speak, only nonsense came out of his mouth.

When the mother arrived, she said, "Why on earth didn't you fetch the doctor?"

"Grandfather told me not to."

When the doctor arrived, he said, "There's nothing I can do. It's too late for anything."

When the prince found out, he said, "The child's clearly an idiot." Then he said, "Well, that's ruined our fun."

And he went back to his wife.

For weeks after her grandfather died, the girl tried not to imagine him below the ground. She didn't like thinking he might be leaking into the soil or that worms might be living in his eyes. It was horrible to think his fingers might have their bones poking through. Her comfort was a necklace her grandfather had left for her and her mother to share. It seemed to bind the child to the dead—making them feel close, as if perhaps they were looking out for her.

"Can I wear it sometimes?" the girl asked her mother. "I think it has magical powers."

"Then ask it for a miracle," the mother said from her sick bed (she'd lost her appetite and was finding it hard to breathe again after so many weeks without seeing the prince).

"All right," said the girl, and she touched the red stones and asked for her mother to be happy again.

Less than a week later, her mother discovered she was expecting the prince's baby. She was full of smiles. She got up and got dressed and looked in a mirror.

"He'll come back now," she told the girl.

"But what about me?"

"What *about* you? We're going to be a proper family."

The child liked her saying that. But the way her mother said it made it sound like a wish, rather than something she was sure of. So the child ran the stones through her fingers and asked for one more miracle.

"Don't let him kill me," she whispered.

Fifteen

MERYAM LOOKED SURPRISED WHEN she opened the door and saw me standing on her step.

"What's happened?" she said.

"Nothing. I was passing, and it started to rain, so I thought I'd come and say hi."

Meryam looked doubtful. But she was Mom's oldest friend and she'd have to offer me shelter from the storm.

"Come in," she said. "Come and have a cup of tea."

I'd been in her house hundreds of times as a kid, but not in the last few years. I wondered if Ben was in, but I wasn't going to ask. I didn't want Meryam thinking I'd come round to see her son. It was her I wanted.

"I've got some doughnuts, if you want one?" she said.

I followed her past the shoes and bikes in the hallway and through to the kitchen. An enormous tabby lay sleeping on the sofa by the window. He was new.

"Shove him along," Meryam said. "He won't mind."

I stroked the cat, who purred like an engine while Meryam filled the kettle.

"You won't tell Mom I'm here, will you?" I said. "I'm supposed to be in the library making a study plan."

"Oh dear," Meryam said. "Test prep's a pain, isn't it? You want to talk about it?"

I didn't. It was the last thing I wanted. I'd come for something else, but I wasn't ready to say it yet. I looked around the room for something safe to fill the time. There was a corkboard by the fridge with photos and postcards stuck on it, so I stared at that—all the stages of Ben and Meryam's lives laid out.

"You do a lot of stuff together," I said.

Meryam didn't reply, just glanced fondly at the board. Perhaps it was a strange thing to say? She scurried about getting doughnuts and cups of tea together and I stared at all the beaches and picnics and birthday parties in the photos and I couldn't think of a single normal thing to say about any of it.

"You want me to ask Ben about study plans?" Meryam said as she finally plonked onto the chair opposite me. "He's out and about with his camera, but I could call him."

"Is he still filming the school play?"

"Hasn't he told you?" She leaned close, as if it was a spectacular secret. "He's making a movie called *Terrified*."

"A horror movie?"

She laughed. "That's what I thought. No, it's about the top ten things people find scary. He wants to examine human frailty, he says. That's why he filmed the auditions. And did he tell you about the trip his uncle planned?"

I shook my head. She didn't seem to mind that the conversation was one-way.

She said, "My brother, Hasan, has got a friend who designs plane engines. Fear of flying is on Ben's list, so he thought he'd get some interesting footage. You know what he came back with? A video of his uncle's friend firing a chicken gun."

I must've looked confused, because she laughed. "I had exactly that face when he told me! 'What on earth's a chicken gun?' I said. 'Well, Mom,' he said. 'It allows you to fire a dead chicken at great speed into a jet engine and at the cockpit windows to see if the plane can sustain a bird strike.'" She shook her head, chuckling, as if it was the craziest thing she'd ever heard. "All that learning, all that money spent on education, and the guy's firing dead chickens from a gun!" She took a sip of tea, still smiling. "Dead, standard-sized chickens like you'd serve for Sunday dinner. Crazy, isn't it?"

I had no idea that people took such care about things. Next time I went on a plane, I'd like knowing someone had tested the windows in case a flock of geese slammed into them or that the engines wouldn't burst into flames if a swan got sucked inside.

Ben's movie was about what people found scary, but that story made me feel safe. There were good people in the world—plane engineers, Meryam, Ben, and his uncle . . . It felt easier than to get to the point of why I'd come round.

I said, "Do you think there's something wrong with me?"

I saw something land in Meryam's eyes—maybe some understanding of why I'd knocked on her door. "Wrong in what way?"

I got my cell out and pulled up the screen grab: *Impulsivity is a hallmark symptom of ADHD. Mix it with anger, and you often get an explosion. Where other kids might quietly fume, your child might slam a door or kick the furniture. She's just not able to contain her intense feelings.*

"Sound like me?" I said.

She smiled. "Diagnosing yourself from the internet isn't the best idea, Lex."

"John thinks I've got it. He wants to send me to a doctor. And the doctor's his friend, so he'll just agree."

"I'm not sure that's how it works, Lexi."

"I've had to sign a contract." I glanced at the clock on her wall. "I'm supposed to show him a study plan tonight."

"Don't worry about that. We'll get Ben to help."

I looked away and out of her window. Her tiny yard was dripping with rain.

"It's like the yard's crying," I said.

She bent forward and patted my knee. "He might not mean any of this. It might be a tactic to get you to study. No doctor's going to diagnose you just because John says so."

"John's got money to bribe him."

"That would be against the law, Lex. What's your mom say about it? Does she think John's got your best interests at heart?"

"She just sits there in silence."

Meryam slumped back in her chair. "Oh dear."

"Do you remember that I used to go and stay with my granddad when Mom started seeing John?"

"I remember."

"I was with him that night when he fell, and all I did was put a blanket over him."

Meryam leaned forward again. "You were eight."

"You know this story?"

"Your mom told me."

I stared at her. "You think I did the wrong thing because I have a condition?"

"Of course not. You did what your granddad asked, and he told you not to call an ambulance."

I thought of him there on the floor, so peaceful through the night. I'd put a cushion under his head. It was orange and black and was made from the same material as the curtains. The blanket was bright primary squares. We'd had a picnic on it in the yard once. He'd slept so deeply. It had been so quiet. When Mom turned up in the morning, she'd been scared. I knew I'd got it wrong from the look on her face.

Meryam said, "It wasn't your fault, Lexi."

I drank my tea and stared out at the yard, and Meryam breathed and so did I and so did the cat and nothing happened, nothing happened, nothing happened.

And that was when I dared.

"Do you like John?" I said.

She blinked in surprise. "I don't really know him that well, Lex. I didn't see your mom so often after she met him."

"But when you do see him—what do you think?"

"I've never had reason not to like him."

"Do you think he's good for Mom?"

"Good in what way?"

"Do you think he makes her happy?"

She looked at me steadily and said nothing.

"You don't like me talking about him," I said. "Nobody does."

"Who else have you talked to?"

"Kass. Cerys, a bit—she's Kass's girlfriend." I didn't mention Sophie. I don't know why. Maybe I didn't want Meryam to be jealous that she wasn't the only older woman in my life.

She said, "You can talk about whatever you want, Lex."

But that wasn't the same as her talking to *me*. Adults had their codes, just like kids. Mom was her friend. I was secondary. Meryam's loyalty was to Mom.

"Will you help?" I said.

"Help how?"

"Would you tell him I don't need to see a doctor? You've known me all my life. Do I seem like I've got a condition to you?"

I crossed my fingers and stared at her. She was looking at her hands folded on her lap. Her hands were old. It must be strange for Ben having a mom who was nearly sixty. My mom was thirty-four. Meryam was old enough to be my grandmother. I'd never had one of those.

"I'm happy to talk to your mom," she said eventually. "But I don't think it's going to help if I go storming in telling John what to do. He's not the sort of person who'd take kindly to that. I think a softly-softly approach is best."

"Softly-softly?"

"Why don't we call your mom and ask her to pop round? We can discuss it together?"

*

I'd just started school when Meryam suggested Mom join a dating site. Mom was lonely and Meryam said she needed to get out more. She offered to babysit while Mom met different men. When Mom met John, it was Meryam she talked to. Adults never think kids are listening if they whisper. But whispering sounds exciting and that's when kids listen especially hard.

Mom didn't tell John I existed for weeks because she didn't want him to think she was looking for someone to provide for her child. She also wanted to avoid pedophiles. It wasn't until he confessed he had a son that Mom told him about me.

"I share responsibility for my boy," he said. "Your kid has no one but you. I never signed up for this."

He told her it was over—that she'd lied and led him on. Meryam told Mom she was better off rid of him. But Mom couldn't breathe without him. So, when John finally texted and asked if she was willing to compromise, of course she said yes. And I started spending weekends at Granddad's.

*

"Maybe it's not me," I said.

"What do you mean?"

"Maybe it's John. Maybe he's the one with the condition."

"What kind of condition might John have?"

"One that makes other people feel terrible."

It sounded ridiculous. Like something a little kid would say. But it was my strongest thought. Being in a room with John was how I imagined I might feel if someone got onto a subway train with a bomb in their bag and I saw the wires sticking out.

"You talking to Mom's not going to help," I said.

"It might."

"Not unless you persuade her not to marry him."

She looked uncomfortable. "She loves him, Lex. She's wanted this wedding for years."

"He was flirting with the office intern at the party."

"Where are you going with this?"

"You could tell Mom you saw him. Tell her to kick him out."

"Lex, what you're asking me to do isn't reasonable."

I threw my hands in the air. "So, what am I going to do?"

"You're going to let me talk to your mom."

"She does whatever he tells her. It won't make a difference. You know it won't."

She regarded me silently across the table. It had stopped raining. I'd had an idea she'd grab her coat and march round to the apartment and tell John there was nothing wrong with me and I didn't need fixing. I thought she might invite me, Mom, and Iris to live at her house. But, of course, she wasn't going to do that. She'd been intimidated at the party. She'd had to imagine John's friends on the toilet even to dare speak to anyone. She barely saw Mom anymore. What kind of friend was she anyway?

I slid my jacket back on.

"Lex," she said. "Don't go."

But if I was out too long, I'd be breaking the contract. I couldn't get sent to the doctor today because Kass was coming for supper and I wanted to kiss him again.

"Lex," she said. "I'm happy to talk to your mom. But I'm not going blazing round to have a go at John—not with the wedding coming up."

"Can I use your toilet before I leave?"

She nodded sadly. She knew as well as I did, this was over.

Ben had the same bedroom he'd always had—next to the bathroom upstairs. His door was open and there on his wall, just as I'd hoped, was his study plan. I took two photos to get it all in. He wasn't the same as Cerys—hungry for As and busy with felt-tip pens and color coding—but he took almost the same subjects as me and it was good enough to convince John I'd spent hours on it.

Next to the timetable was a poster of Ben's top-ten list of scary things for his movie. Number one was *fear itself.* He'd put a quote next to it: *What we fear most is fear.*

This was followed by being buried alive, being burned alive, being stranded on an open ocean, and being in a plane crash. Creepy animals and insects were number six.

Number seven was being lost in space, then a zombie apocalypse, followed by waking up in hell. There was nothing about being groped by drunk old men or being threatened with doctors or being told over and over there was something wrong with you.

My list would be very different.

But I took a photo of number ten: *the unknown.*

There was another quote: *Bad things happen with no warning.*

Sixteen

WHEN IRIS WAS FOUR and I was thirteen, I promised to show her a secret place. I held her hand down the stairs to the yard and when we got to the bottom I asked if she could guess where it was.

She scanned the lawn and the scrubby bushes by the shed. "Have you got a cave?"

"Better," I said. "I've got a perch in a tree."

"Is that the secret? That's crap. I already know about the tree."

"I bet you don't know it's an ash tree. Or that people think ash protects you from evil spirits. I bet you don't know how to get up it without a ladder. Even your dad doesn't know. There're no branches near the bottom, see? You think I fly up there?"

Iris frowned. "Is there a rope?"

"No. And you can only jump down to the wall, not climb up from it."

She was interested now, standing on tiptoes to peer about. "Have you got a secret trampoline?"

"There's a trick I'm going to show you. But you must promise never to tell anyone, OK? Only me and Kass know. You have to shake on it."

She nodded solemnly and put out her hand. "I promise."

As we crossed the grass there was the sound of yelling behind us from the apartment building. Iris held my hand tighter, so I knew she'd heard. I told her we needed to concentrate on the tree. I told her I'd already checked it wasn't rotten or dead and she should never do what I was about to show her with any other tree in case the branches snapped. I told her to adopt a good mind-set.

"What's a mind-set?"

"It means you accept the challenge. It means you're going to be brave, like when you have a ballet performance."

"They make me feel wobbly."

"Exactly, but you overcome the wobbles and launch yourself onstage anyway, don't you?"

She touched the trunk. It was gnarly and full of crevices. "Hello, tree," she said.

I liked her talking to it. "Remember what it's called?"

"Ash."

"Correct. Now, watch very carefully."

I pulled the length of fabric from my pocket and showed her how I'd made a loop for one wrist. "You can borrow it anytime," I said. "I'll show you where I keep it."

I slipped my left wrist in and tightened the knot. I flung the loose end around the tree and grabbed it with my right hand. I wound it round my fist until the material was tight. I planted one foot on the tree and quickly pushed out and up, using the material to support my weight until both feet were flat on the trunk.

"You have to practice holding this position until you can do it for one whole minute," I said. "Then you can start moving higher."

Kass said once that, in terms of physics, I was overcoming gravity with my force pushing upward while my outward force was met with the opposing force of my hands. I made him say it three times so I learned it. I said it to Iris now. It made me sound smart. "You try it," I said. I jumped down and looked at her. "You might not be able to do it straightaway."

Of course, she couldn't. Her arms were too short and had no muscle. The first time I'd tried without Granddad's help, I'd been nearly eight and had practiced for weeks. I told her to trust the material, that it was made of hemp and wasn't going to rip. I stood behind her and took her weight, letting her press her spine into my stomach, but she said she was scared. I took off her shoes so she could grip the bark with her feet, but she couldn't do that either.

She kept glancing back at the apartment building. "You think we should go in?"

"I think we should sit in the tree. How about I lift you up?"

She weighed nothing. I got her sitting on my shoulders and she put her feet into my hands and I pushed up while she grabbed the lowest branch and then I shoved her bottom until she was sitting on it. "Hold on tight," I said. "I'm coming up."

I threw the material round the tree again and wound it tight in my fist. I jumped and planted my feet. To move higher I pushed up

142

with my feet, slid my hands up, and pulled again. Slowly, slowly I inched up.

When I'd finally settled on the branch next to Iris, I pointed out all the things she needed to know—which windows were ours and how you could count along from the blue curtains in Mom and John's bedroom to get to the kitchen, which was the best room for spying into. I told her that when I lived here with just Mom we only had the middle flat, and that after her dad turned up on the scene, he bought the one above and joined them together. I showed her the lines of new bricks, like a pink scar where he'd changed the windows.

"The sun always hits those bricks last," I said. "In summer, once it goes completely dark on that wall, then you know you're in massive trouble because you're late for supper."

"Then what do I do?"

"Go in and get yelled at or run away and hide. Kass and me used to hide for hours. When you're older, I'll show you how to balance along that branch and drop down to the wall. You can jump straight into the cemetery from there, even when it's closed."

"I wish I was you," she said dreamily. "Doesn't it smell nice up here?"

It smelled wild—a mix of bark and sap and growing things. I pointed out the magpie nest that was way above us in the top branches. I said the magpie had been building it for weeks.

"I think the weather up here makes it smell nicer too," I said. "It's because the clouds are closer."

Far away I could hear John shouting and Mom pleading, which meant they were still at it, but it felt like something on TV that had nothing to do with us. If we climbed up to the branches Kass and I had pushed the boards onto, we could stay until they'd worn themselves to silence.

"There's someone in the kitchen," Iris said.

"It's Mom."

"How do you know?"

"Your dad's head would be higher."

We watched a shadow get closer to the glass and peer out and then we could tell very clearly it was Mom.

"She's looking for us," Iris whispered. "She doesn't know where we are."

"We're not going in yet. She'll be fine."

But Iris started to fidget and said she needed the bathroom, and could we get down now? I tried to distract her, but her focus was back on the apartment. I told her to stay there and let me get down first so she could jump into my arms.

"An important thing to remember," I said, "is that it's harder to get down than to get up."

Maybe I cursed her. Is that how it works? Because she flung herself at me rather than letting herself drop and we both fell backward and, even though I mostly caught her, she made a sound like a cat crying as we thumped to the grass.

I thought she was kidding. I scrabbled out from under her. I told her, "OK, you can stop pretending now."

And then I saw blood dripping into the mud at the side of her head.

There was a stump from another tree. I'd never noticed it before, spiky and sharp in the grass right next to her. Had she hit that?

"Iris?" I said. "Iris?"

But she didn't answer.

It felt like hours passed as I looked down at her and all she did was give a little moan and bleed some more. I didn't know what to do. Should I try and pick her up? I shook her shoulder. "Iris?"

She opened her eyes and then shut them again. She let out a whimper. I hopped around. I looked at the apartment building. All the windows were glazed with sunshine.

"Help me," I whispered. "Somebody help."

I ran to the nearest downstairs apartment and knocked on a window. Nothing happened, so I knocked louder. I knocked on the apartment next door and the one next to that.

"Please," I called. "Please, is anyone there?"

A woman opened a door and peered out. She was young, with her hair in a ponytail. "What's the matter?"

"My sister's hurt."

The woman came out and sprinted across the grass and knelt by Iris, who had her eyes open again and was groaning and trying to sit up. There was blood all down her T-shirt and the woman asked her to turn her head. There was a ragged hole above Iris's ear that was full of grit and darkness. Blood oozed out and matted in her hair.

The woman turned to me. "Are your mom or dad in?"

I nodded.

"Run and get them. Tell them to bring a phone."

As I ran up the stairs I was thinking, he's going to yell. He's going to hate me. I kept wishing I could turn everything back to the

time only half an hour ago when me and Iris had walked downstairs hand in hand. Or further back to when Mom told John to
please stop talking to her like that or she was going to take her kids
and leave, and John said, "You just try it and see what happens." I
could've left Iris to put up with it and just got myself out.

John was at his desk when I barged in. I was breathless and gasping. "Where's Mom?"

"Flounced off."

"Iris fell. You have to bring your phone."

His face collapsed. He aged a hundred years. That is how much
he loves her, I thought.

He bolted down the stairs and I grabbed his phone and gal-
loped after him. He stalled when he saw the woman—like he'd got
it wrong, like this woman was stealing or hurting Iris instead of
helping.

He's never going to forgive me, I thought. It might be delayed
now because the woman was here, but it would happen.

"I don't think it's deep," the woman said, "but it probably needs
stitches. She's a bit groggy too. I guess she might have a concussion?"

John didn't answer as he scooped Iris into his arms. "Let's get
you inside, we need to wash that dirt off you, baby."

The woman stood up. "I think she needs an ambulance
actually."

I held John's phone out to him, but he walked past me and away
across the grass.

The woman looked at me. "Is he going to take her to the
hospital?"

I shrugged. I never knew what John would do.

The woman dashed after him. "Excuse me, but I think it's probably best to let a doctor look at her. I can give you a lift somewhere if you want."

He kept walking. He started up the stairs. He said nothing. He never usually missed an opportunity to charm strangers, so I thought maybe he'd gone mad. I thought love for Iris had done that.

The woman turned to me. "Where's your mom?"

"I don't know. She went out."

"Do you have her number?"

I scrabbled with John's phone and gave the woman his emergency number, which I knew was Mom.

When I got back upstairs John was in the bathroom with Iris on his lap. She was very quiet and pale. He was mopping the side of her head with a sponge and whispering to her. He was telling her she was going to be fine. I wanted to remind him about the ambulance, but he was the adult and, if Iris died now, it would be his fault.

His phone rang, and it was Mom, so I answered. "What's happened?" She sounded wild with fear.

She's going to hate me too, I thought.

I told her Iris fell and hit her head and John was washing the blood off. She told me to put the phone on speaker.

"John?" she said. "What's going on? How bad is it?"

Her voice came out high and ghostly and echoed around the bathroom.

"John, if she's hurt her head, you have to take her to the hospital. Are you listening to me? Is she conscious? I can't hear her crying. Is it bleeding a lot? Why aren't you answering? Can you please answer me, John?"

It was like she finally woke him from a trance. "It looks worse than it is," he said.

"Head injuries need a doctor, John. You don't always know best."

"OK, OK."

"If I get a cab and meet you there, will you take her to the emergency room?"

He gathered Iris up in a towel and walked out the door with her in his arms. I grabbed the car keys and followed. He never said I couldn't. He buckled Iris into the passenger seat and I sat in the back. I wasn't totally sure he knew I was there, although I'd handed him the car keys. He still wasn't saying anything, apart from whispering soft words to Iris that I couldn't hear.

Mom met us in the parking lot at the hospital and took over. She was brilliant—not tearful and anxious like she'd been that morning, but calm and focused. It was like seeing someone I used to know. She pulled back the towel to look at the wound and didn't seem freaked out by the blood. Iris whimpered, and Mom told her she was brave.

Every bit of me was cold. "Is she going to be all right?" I asked.

"Of course," Mom said. She told John to sort the car out and meet her inside. She picked Iris up and cradled her. "Don't go to sleep," she said. "Come on, we're going to find a doctor."

I don't know why I stayed with John while he parked the car. It was stupid. There were no spaces in the hospital parking lot and all the surrounding streets were for residents only.

"Why are there no fucking meters?" he said.

I wanted to be with Mom and Iris. I wanted to be in the hospital with doctors and nurses. I wanted to explain to sensible people that I'd tried to catch her, that I was sorry, that the last person I ever wanted to hurt was Iris.

We got stuck behind a delivery truck and John slapped his hand on the horn and it blared on and on until the driver came out from a house and asked what John's fucking problem was. I sank lower in my seat. John opened the window and said his fucking problem was that he had a child in the hospital and the man's fucking truck was blocking the road.

The man said, "Two minutes, mate."

John said, "I need it moved now!"

I am not here, I thought. I am invisible. I tried to breathe small and light. I tried not to swallow. Soon this would be over—the truck would move, we would park, we would be in the hospital, and there would be people and bustle and noise. But even though I was trying to be invisible, John looked at me in the driver's mirror and I looked back at him and he said, "Why do bad things always happen when you're around, Alexandra?"

I shook my head. "They don't."

"Your grandfather might disagree."

I stared at him. Tears blocked my throat.

"Nothing to say, no? Not your fault he lay on the floor all night in agony?" He regarded me in the mirror. "On and on it goes, doesn't it? First your dad abandons you, then your granddad dies, and now your sister plummets from a tree. What's the common denominator?"

I was crying properly now. Salt tears washed into my mouth.

He slapped the steering wheel again. He leaned out of the window and blared the horn. "Will you please just move your fucking truck?" he yelled.

The driver came out of the house, waving. "I'm moving it now."

"About damn time," John said.

We did a big circle and ended up back in the hospital parking lot. There was a space now and John put money in the machine and a ticket on the dashboard. Neither of us spoke. I walked behind him to the main entrance and he marched ahead.

You don't have to follow him, I thought. You could just walk away.

But I followed as he went to reception and asked where Iris was, and still I followed as he jogged along the yellow lines on the floor to the emergency room.

Iris was in a cubicle with Mom and a doctor. She was fine. It was a scrape, the doctor said, and only needed cleaning and some special glue.

John threw his hands in the air. "Didn't I say?"

Mom apologized for making a fuss and the doctor said head injuries often looked worse than they were. John said that's what he'd told Mom on the phone, but Mom was a worrier and what could he do? The doctor gave him a smile as if she understood how exhausting that might be. The doctor told Mom not to let Iris go to sleep until bedtime and to bring her straight back if she seemed altered in any way. There was some paperwork to fill in, but then we could go. The doctor looked at me. "You the tree climber?"

I nodded, my eyes filling again.

"Hey," she said. "I'm not telling you off." She looked at John and smiled. "These things happen, right? In fact, I encourage children to climb trees. I'm fed up with treating kids who've tripped over the TV cable. At least this is a good old-fashioned injury."

"Absolutely," John said. "Couldn't agree with you more."

They shared another smile.

It was in the car on the way home that John turned the charm off. He twisted around in the passenger seat and looked at me. "A tree," he said. "You took your four-year-old sister up a tree! Are you insane?"

"Don't," Mom said. "Leave it for now. Let's just get home."

"Iris could've been killed," John said.

"But she wasn't."

"No thanks to your daughter." He glanced at his watch. "How long have we been in that hospital? Two hours? What a total waste of time. I knew Iris wouldn't need stitches. Why does no one listen to me? Why does no one ever take notice of anything I say?"

We were all silent.

John turned to Mom again. "And you love dishing out the advice, don't you? You call me up, and without even seeing Iris you insist on dragging her to the hospital. What did you tell me? 'You don't always know best, John.' Turns out I do, though, doesn't it?"

Please, I thought. Please leave her alone.

John said, "Why did that doctor want all that information from us at the end, eh? I tell you why—because she thought we were irresponsible parents. She thought we were low-life scum. Well, you might be low-life, but I'm sure as hell not. How do you think that made me feel?" He leaned back in his seat to get a better look at her. "I've a good mind to call that doctor when I get home and tell her I was innocently sitting at my desk trying to earn this family some money when you swanned off and left the kids up a fucking tree."

"I didn't know they were there. I had no idea."

"Christ, woman—you only had to look out the window."

"I did. I couldn't see them."

"Oh, so you had zero clue where they were, and you left anyway?"

"It wasn't like that. I knew they were in the yard. I thought they'd come upstairs when they got bored." Her voice was wobbling. "I didn't leave them by themselves. You were there. You were in the apartment."

"Oh, so this is my fault?"

"That's not what I'm saying."

"Take some responsibility." He jabbed a finger at her. "Our daughter could have died. Do you understand how serious this is?"

I stared at him. At his jutting chin and furious eyes. I stared at Mom. At the tremble of her lips and the way her hands had turned white clutching the steering wheel.

And I grabbed the book of maps that was tucked into the back pocket of the driver's seat, unrolled the window, and let the book fall. It broke as it hit the road and lay there flapping like an injured bird. The car behind us honked. A cyclist slapped the roof of our car as she passed.

John whipped round to me. "What did you just do?"

I snatched a handful of trash from the floor—an empty bag of chips and several toffee wrappers and let them flutter away into the wind.

"Stop it. Why are you doing this?"

I blinked at him. I wasn't sure.

He looked back at Mom. "Have you no control over her?"

She glanced at me in the mirror. "Lexi," she warned. "Whatever you're doing—stop."

I wrenched the plastic ice scraper from the side pocket and threw it out after the wrappers.

"Christ," John said. "She's a fucking monster."

"What's she up to? I can't see in the mirror."

"Chucking stuff." He turned to glare at me. "Are you nuts?"

I shook my head at him.

"Should I pull over?" she asked him.

"No, because she's going to stop." He sat there glaring at me to make sure I did. I put the part of me that wanted his golden smile into a box and shoved it away.

When he turned back to Mom, he said, "She was a nightmare earlier as well."

"What did she do earlier?" Mom said.

"Apart from take her sister up a tree, you mean?"

"Apart from that."

"She got the neighbor involved, for one thing," John said. "I had that interfering cow going on and on, chasing me across the yard insisting it was an emergency." He twisted back to me. "You should have come straight upstairs and got me. I don't know what the hell you were thinking knocking on other people's doors."

"Oh dear," Mom said.

"You told her to call Mom as well, didn't you?" John said. "You gave her Mom's number?"

"I didn't. She had it already."

"Don't lie to me."

"John," Mom said. "Let me deal with her when we get back."

"Hear that?" he said to me. "You're in trouble with your mom when you get home."

I nodded. "OK."

He shook his head at Mom. She shook hers at him. He reached out and patted her knee. She gave him a small smile.

"We have a monster in our midst," he said.

"She's upset, that's all."

"We're all upset. You need to keep a tighter rein."

She nodded. "Any chance of candy?"

He pulled open the glove compartment and got the tin. He took one and popped it in her mouth. He took another for himself and put the tin back in the cubby.

A Monster in Our Midst

I WAS OFTEN BAD after that. It was like something came over me.

If it were a movie, I'd grow extra muscles and my T-shirt would rip, but it was just my life, so all that happened was I'd knock a plate to the floor or drop a cup or accidentally swear and John's attention would turn on me. It reminded me of the way Granddad had used to hunt for snails at night with a headlamp. They'd get caught in a beam of light and he'd pick them up and dunk them in a bucket of salt water. John would switch his beam on me and shout and wave his arms around and tell Mom I was out of control.

Once, I took John's favorite ashtray (the one he'd had since being a student) and smashed it on the kitchen floor. Mom had been washing it in the sink and knocked it against the tap.

"Oh shit," she said. "Oh hell."

I snatched the two halves from her and flung them.

"Lex!" she said. "No!"

She probably thought she could have fixed it with glue and John would never have noticed the crack. But he would have.

He came bounding in. "My ashtray!" He dropped to his knees to get a better look at the damage.

"It was annoying me," I said.

"Go to your room," he whispered.

I went to my bedroom and sat by the window. It was ages before I was allowed out.

The first time he grounded me, I ran away. I sat on the low wall at the front of Ben and Meryam's house and watched them eat together. I couldn't hear a word they were saying, but I liked watching them. When I got home, I wouldn't say sorry and John wouldn't let me eat supper. It was fish pie and I said I didn't care. I said it looked like vomit.

It was different when Kass came to stay. He'd dare me to put chili powder in John's pajamas or fake soap in his bathroom or salt in his tea, and if we got caught it would just be funny. If John ever got mad when Kass was there, we'd hide in the laundry room or climb the tree and drop down to the cemetery and lose ourselves for hours.

One time, after Kass had gone home and I knew I wouldn't see him for ages, I got a bus by myself and stood in the dark at the bottom of his block of apartments and longed for him to come back. I thought about asking his mom if I could live with her instead. I stood there for so long building up courage that by the time I got the bus home, Mom was hysterical, thinking I'd been abducted.

I wrote her a note saying, *I wish we were a pair of whiptail lizards.*

She looked it up and discovered they're an all-female species.

"Why would you wish such a thing?" she asked.

I said I didn't know.

John was trying to be a good father to me, she said. But I wasn't making it easy. I needed to make more of an effort. The world was a difficult place and we all had our crosses to bear.

Seventeen

KASS, MY KASS, WAS coming for supper. While I waited, I sat in the living room with my hoodie up and my eyes cast down and tried to be as invisible as possible. But it seemed like everyone kept saying Kass's name, and whenever they did I could feel my face burn and John would give me these looks, like he was thinking, *You better leave my precious son alone, Alexandra!*

He asked why I was moody. He asked if I was protesting about something. He told me it was all very well to have a study plan, but how about I got my act together and did some actual studying before supper? Mom made me herbal tea to help me focus. Iris sat next to me on the sofa and asked me to tell her about sleeping over at Kass's place last night.

"Did you play games?" she said. "Did you watch movies?"

I shook my head and pulled my hood lower.

"Did you order pizza and get it delivered?"

I yawned massively. "Stop bugging me, Iris."

"Dad said you were drunk—did Kass's mom tell you off?" She poked me with her sharp little elbow. "If you don't tell me, I'll ask Kass when he gets here."

"Well, he won't tell you either. So, don't be an idiot." I sounded high-pitched and furious. They all turned to look at me.

"Apologize to your sister," John said. "You're supposed to be treating family members with respect."

I had to deliberately breathe slow and long. "Sorry, Iris."

I decided it was easier not to talk at all. I answered questions with a bored yes or no, and whenever anyone mentioned Kass's name, I pretended to be deaf. John got pissed off—*Seriously, Alexandra—you want me to add* sulking *to the contract?* Iris kept being annoying and Mom kept offering me jobs, as if peeling carrots and potatoes was going to cheer me up. It was a relief when I had the fantastic idea of watching a French movie with subtitles to improve my vocabulary and John reluctantly agreed. I curled up with my iPad and headphones and watched the whole of *De rouille et d'os*, where Marion Cotillard has her legs chewed off by a killer whale and then gets to be in charge of her boyfriend's martial arts fights.

It was strange when Kass walked in. He looked scruffy and tired. He hailed us with the flat of his palm from the doorway and then slumped on the only free seat.

"So," he said, rubbing his hair with both hands as if he was trying to wake up his brain. "How's it hanging here?"

John stared at him. "What's wrong with you?"

"Nothing." Kass smiled innocently. "I'm fine."

"Why are you so late?" John tapped his watch. "We said six and it's nearly seven. We're all starving."

Mom came to the doorway in her apron. "You're here, good. Should I start serving?"

"Sorry I'm late," Kass said. "My mom had a freak-out."

Mom froze in the doorway. "What about?"

"Is this because of last night?" John said, glaring at me. "Is it because this one turned up on her doorstep?"

"No," Kass said, shooting me a quick look. "It was nothing to do with that."

"Well, what, then?"

Kass shrugged. "It doesn't matter."

"If she's upset about you coming over here for supper," John said, "then she's out of order."

"Funny," Kass said. "That's what she said about you."

We all looked at him and there was an awkward silence.

John said, "What the fuck is that supposed to mean?"

Kass looked startled. "Nothing."

"I hope you're not taking your mother's side? I hope you're not going to tell me I should know where this one is at every moment of the day?" He flipped a thumb at me.

"That's not what I meant."

"Kass," Mom said, stepping between them, "could you give me a hand in the kitchen, please?"

"I don't want him wriggling out of this."

"Of course not," Mom said. "But I need help carrying things in."

John shook his head. "I expected more from you, son. I'm disappointed."

Mom and Kass went out to the kitchen to serve up and Iris was dragged with them to get cutlery. John glared at me. "This is your fault."

I didn't care. Kass hardly ever went against John. The power of a kiss, I thought.

The meal went OK. There was wine, but I wasn't allowed any. Kass and John made up and I wondered when John was going to start talking about my dreadful behavior and Kass was going to defend me and insist I didn't need a doctor. But apart from thanking Kass for "taking care of things" last night, John didn't mention me at all and Kass didn't bring any of it up either. Iris chatted nonsense and Mom made wedding plan suggestions and John talked about work and architecture and it turned out to be one of those times when John was happy, and it drew everyone in and changed the mood. They all relaxed, except for me. I wasn't part of the golden picture. I sat there saying nothing at all.

John opened a second bottle of wine. As I watched Kass drink, I thought of us kissing. The memory felt like a dream, like it was something that hadn't really happened to me. I wanted Kass to wink at me or pass a secret note under the table so I'd know it was true and that he was thinking about it as well, but he never did.

For dessert, Mom brought out a cheese platter and slices of melon and various yogurts. I spooned hazelnut yogurt into my mouth while watching John slice cheese. The knife curved upward and had spikes on the top like a weapon. John made the slices so thin they were almost see-through, like dried-up pieces of paper. He picked them up gently and laid them flat upon a cracker. He lifted it carefully. His mouth opened like a cave, his tongue reached out, glistening.

Kass watched me watching John and reached for more wine.

"Don't drink it so quick," John said through the cracker. "It's good wine, that."

"Too good for me?"

John laughed. "Too good for someone who prefers cheap beer. Come on, don't leave me with sediment."

Kass laughed back at him. "Good wine doesn't have sediment."

"You're wrong there, son. The high quality stuff isn't filtered." John took the bottle away and poured a glass for himself, right to the brim. He wiped his mouth with a napkin. "So, given your dad knows a thing or two—it's back to school tomorrow, yes? And then you're going to knuckle down for exams? And we've agreed—no more sudden visits home?"

Kass nodded and my whole body clamped. That sounded like they'd talked about me already. That sounded like Kass hadn't fought for me at all and had simply agreed to stay away.

"It's not that I don't want to see you," John said. "But your job is to study, not to come hurtling down whenever Alexandra gets into trouble. I'll pop more money in your account to tide you over, so don't worry about finances."

Kass pressed my foot under the table as John sliced more cheese. Maybe he wanted me to know he was sorry, that he'd tried to talk to John about the doctor, but there was nothing to be done.

I moved my foot away. He was leaving and wouldn't be home again for weeks.

"I need air," I said.

I sounded like an idiot from a movie, and I bet John rolled his eyes.

*

I sat on the fire escape steps. The yard was quiet and smelled of rain. It was the kind of evening the dead might come walking. If I still had the necklace I'd summon Granddad and tell him to bring his friends and they'd materialize through the fence together and walk across the grass. They'd smell of good things like wood smoke and wet leaves and that gas smell garages have. "We're here for you," Granddad would say, and all his dead friends would nod and smile.

"You OK?" Kass said when he finally came out and sat next to me. He'd topped off his wine again and some sloshed on the step.

I nodded. But I wasn't OK. Everything in me was hurting.

He said, "I got it in the neck from my mom. That's why I was late. She went off on me for letting you get drunk and for abandoning Cerys."

"She had a go at John too. She grassed me up, telling him I spent the night at your place."

"We told her my dad knew, that's why. She only called to check he was treating you right."

I hadn't thought of it that way. I felt warm toward Sophie again. "Did you tell her we kissed?"

Kass flicked a quick look of alarm up the stairs. "Keep your voice down."

"Is that why she went off on you about abandoning Cerys?"

"Of course I didn't tell her."

"I don't mind if you did. I like your mom."

"I'm not going to tell her, OK? I got the third degree from her this afternoon. She reckons I'm turning into my dad."

"You're nothing like him."

"I freakin' hope not."

I loved the way he shivered. "Imagine living without them," I said. "Imagine having an apartment and yard like this."

He shook his head. "I don't want what they've got."

"No, but a place of our own. Wouldn't that be cool?"

"What about Iris?"

"She can come."

He laughed as if it was a game.

I took a breath. "I've got a plan, Kass. One that means I don't have to see a doctor."

He stopped laughing. "Oh yeah?"

"I'm going to come and live with you in Manchester. I'm sixteen in thirteen days. I'm going to come then."

He turned to look at me. Whole seconds ticked by. "Is that even legal?"

"Strictly speaking, I need parental consent, but the website said I was unlikely to be made to come back unless I was in danger."

"Then the website doesn't know my dad. He would *not* let that happen. You can't just leave your life."

I could, actually. I'd looked it up. I'd also looked up what would happen when John refused to top off Kass's living costs in revenge and discovered that once Kass had proved estrangement, he could apply for student loans. If that wasn't enough to keep us, I'd get a job.

"Everything will be legal in two weeks, Kass."

"That makes no difference. I live in student accommodation. It's for a single person."

"I'll live there secretly until we find something else."

"You'd get discovered in five minutes. There's always people milling around."

"I'll hide in the wardrobe if anyone comes."

"Lex," he said slowly, "this is a terrible plan."

"Think about it at least?"

We were quiet then and I stared at the jagged rooftops and the tree cutting the sky and I ran my fingers along the cool metal of the stairs.

"I guess Cerys might not like it," I said.

I don't know why I brought her up. Maybe because she'd asked me to talk about her and I had to have something to report. Or maybe I was checking if he still had feelings for her.

"Cerys is going to Bristol to study law and will forget all about me."

"If she gets in."

"She will."

"And you're going back to Manchester to forget all about me."

165

"I'm not."

But it felt like he had flint in his soul. "Did you talk to your dad about the doctor? Can you stop that happening at least? I mean, that is why you came back for the weekend, isn't it?"

"I told him to stop coming down so hard on you."

"And what did he say?"

"That he would."

"Oh, all sorted, then, thanks."

"I did my best. I'm not denying he's a control freak."

"What if he tells the doctor I'm insane? What if they lock me in a madhouse?"

"This isn't Victorian England, Lex."

"I had to sign a contract. And every night before I go to bed, he wants my phone in the safe. He says it's to make sure I get enough sleep."

"Maybe it is."

"Every morning when I wake up he wants to know my plans—down to the last detail."

"He wants you to work, to get some exams under your belt."

"Why are you on his side?" I grabbed his wine and downed it in two great gulps. "I went round Meryam's today and she didn't want to help either."

"You shouldn't've done that."

"Why not? Is it a secret your dad hates me? When Iris fell out of the tree, he called me a monster, did you know that? He thinks I killed my granddad."

"You're angry at him, but it's not just you that gets the shit. Your mom gets a lot of it."

"Oh, so that makes it all right?"

He sighed, and I knew I was irritating him. I bet Cerys never went off on him, never raised her voice, never disagreed or asked for difficult things.

"Is it because of my temper that you don't want to let me live with you?"

He smiled. "No, Lex."

"Is it because you think I'm an ogre?"

"Not that either."

There was a plant on the steps, some feathery thing in a pot, and I reached out and plucked off a tawny leaf. "Close your eyes," I said. I took his hand and pulled his arm out straight toward me and stroked the leaf at his wrist. "No peeking."

It was a game we'd played a hundred times as kids—with feathers, leaves, fingers, tongues. You had to say "stop" when the tickling reached the exact crease of your elbow.

In the past, Kass would grab me when I got there and spin me over and sit on me. He'd hold both my wrists above my head and turn his free hand into a tickling spider until I begged for mercy.

But tonight, he let me inch achingly slowly up the length of his arm to his shoulder. I thought maybe he'd fallen asleep, but when I got to his throat he opened his eyes.

"How many times have we played this game?" he said.

I know, I thought. I know, I know.

He said, "I'm not sure we should be playing it right now."

It's not a game anymore, I thought.

"Mostly," he said, "because I've drunk three-quarters of a bottle of wine. But also because one thing leads to another and my dad's upstairs."

"One thing leads to another?" I said, smiling.

I didn't move. We were so very close. I could hear the dull thud of our hearts.

"It's not happening again, Lex," he said.

"Why not?"

I moved closer. My eyes locked with his. I could feel the warmth of his breath mingling with mine. If we kissed again, he'd let me live in Manchester.

"Give me this," he said, and he took the leaf from my fingers and let it drop over the edge of the stairs. I watched it flutter away like something burning. "Now give me this." He took my hand and threaded his fingers with mine. "You're like a sister to me."

"Bullshit."

What are big brothers for? To go to school with. To look out for you in the corridor. To tease you when you have a crush on their friends. To share the complicated fact of your parents with. A girl in my year went hiking with her big brother. They cook together. They have mutual friends. When she turns eighteen he's promised to take her on a pub crawl.

Big brothers are for eating ice cream with. They help you with homework. If you say you're scared, they promise to save you. They do *not* press the length of their leg against the heat of your thigh and say, "I'm not denying I enjoyed that kiss, Lex, because I did."

I yanked my hand from his and stood up. "What are you doing?" I raged. "Why do you keep doing this to me?"

"Calm down," Kass said. "I'm not doing anything."

"You are. You're doing *this*." I waved at myself, at him, the yard, the apartment building. "All of this is what you're doing."

"Lex," he said. "Shall we go in?"

"Why? You think I'm being weird?"

He smiled. "Maybe just a bit."

"Of course I'm fucking weird. I've got a condition, haven't I?"

"Don't," he said. "Don't say that. Come on, Lex, what's wrong?" He tugged at the lace on my sneaker. "What do you want? Tell me. You want to climb our tree?"

Our tree? He hadn't been up it for years.

"Oh, just go back to Manchester, Kass. Get on with your life and leave me to mine. That's what I want."

✳

For the rest of the evening I ignored him and talked only to Iris. I read with her, drew with her, held her on my lap, and taught her how to thread melon seeds on a string.

Mom cleaned the fridge out. She wore yellow rubber gloves and hummed show tunes like a fifties housewife. Kass and John sat together on the sofa and watched soccer streams on John's laptop and clinked their glasses after each refill and talked about Kass's classes.

John loved it that his son studied architecture. He sunbathed under it, like Kass would turn into a copy of him in some new world. He glugged the wine and asked Kass questions about essays and coursework and his plans for the summer. What about an internship in Europe? he asked. Would Kass like him to pull a few strings?

I zoned out from John's words, away from his smug face, and looked at Kass instead. I looked at his bare arms and the hairs turning gold in the light from the lamp. I watched Kass's lips move and thought, I kissed those lips.

"I love you," I'd said. "I always have."

"I love you too," he'd whispered.

I thought of standing up and spilling it out loud. I wanted to blast something apart. John was suggesting that when Kass went into sophomore year, he move out of student accommodation and rent a house so that he could stay in Manchester during the holidays and concentrate on his academic work.

Kass was being pried away in front of me. First an internship, now never coming home at all. I wanted to pick up John's wine glass and sling it across the room. What had Sophie said? *You're allowed to be angry.* Except, I'd be sent straight to a doctor if I was.

I concentrated on John's weak things instead.

I saw that he'd cut himself shaving. Plus, he was puffy under his eyes and had a small stain on his shirt. Three weak things. I breathed easier. But when Mom came in and pointed out that John's phone kept buzzing and asked why he wasn't picking up, he told her to stay out of his business and that made him strong again.

At about half past ten, Kass said he had to go. Iris ran to get her shoes so she could walk downstairs with him. John said it was too late and she should stay inside.

"I'll stop her," I said.

"This is not an excuse for a send-off party," John said.

I knew that was a threat, but I ignored him. I wanted to say goodbye to Kass alone. Because even though I was furious with him, I wanted to give him one last chance to pull me close and tell me yes, I could come to Manchester. We'd build a barricade, make plans, be together forever . . .

But Iris escaped and raced out of the apartment with no shoes. I ran down the stairs after her and grabbed her sweater. "Go back up," I hissed.

"No way! I'm coming to the bus stop."

"Leave her," Kass said, coming down behind us. "It's fine."

So, now we'd have to talk in code, which was stupid. Had he let her come on purpose?

"I won't see you for ages," I said as we walked across the parking lot to the gate.

"It'll fly by." He wouldn't look at me. "And you'll be distracted by exams."

"So will you," Iris said. Kass had her on his back so she didn't hurt her feet. Which meant I'd have to carry her home, which meant I'd have to *go* home and couldn't wander off into the dark and disappear.

"Will you see Cerys before you go?" I said.

"Your girlfriend," Iris said. She drawled out the word, giving the *r* a roll, making it rude somehow.

Kass shook his head. "We said goodbye already."

We were at the bus stop and a bus must've just come because there was no one waiting. I was glad. I wondered if he meant he'd split up with Cerys. And if he had, was it because of me? I didn't know how to ask that in code.

"Iris," I said. "The bus could be ages. You should go in."

"I'm not even listening," she said.

I envied her his arms around her legs, her body pressing close to his back, her arms looped loose about his neck, her breath hot in his ear.

"Call me," she told Kass. "Twice a week."

"You don't have a phone, Iris."

"Skype me, then." She kissed him passionately on his cheek. "I miss you."

"I haven't gone yet."

"I miss you anyway."

Me too, I thought. I know exactly how you feel.

The world was so sad and close. Maybe we should be a band of three? Tell Iris the truth? We could get on the bus and just leave together. This was our chance.

"Hey," I said. "How about we all go to Manchester?"

"Yes!" Iris whooped. "Let's run away."

"Don't," Kass said. He gave me a look—one of the deep ones that usually made my heart scud, but now just made me want to weep. "I'll be back," he said. He kissed me on top of my hair. "It's going to be OK."

172

"Is it?" I said. "Are you sure?"

He shook his head, irritated with me again. He gazed down the road, wanting the bus to come. He'd always hated goodbyes, said they made him feel awkward, as if there was something profound he should be saying.

"It'll come soon," I said. "Don't worry."

"It'll never come," Iris said. "I called the bus people and they canceled it."

Kass laughed. "You and your phone calls."

And his laughter brought the bus. I felt a pang of anxiety. He would get on it, he'd hand Iris over, he'd leave. In Manchester, there were girls—hundreds of older and smarter and more glamorous girls. There was freedom. There was no John.

Kass could spin himself a whole new story.

It felt like boxes slamming shut as he made Iris hop down, ruffled her hair, bent over to me, and gave me a rough hug. Our lips went nowhere near one another. We looked like brother and sister. But he wasn't my brother. Windows crashed shut inside me as he walked to the bus, got up the step, and scanned his card on the reader. He went upstairs. I knew he would. He waved down at us. He looked more cheerful than he had all evening. I was so cold standing there with Iris hopping barefoot beside me.

"Watch out for glass," I told her. My voice came out gravelly and old.

"Watch out yourself," she said.

The bus took off. Kass, *my Kass*, in it, surrounded by strangers who had no idea how precious he was.

I had weeks to get through without him. Exams. John. Contracts and threats of doctors. Day after endless day. How would I ever bear it?

We heard the shouting as we walked back up the stairs. "Shush," Iris said.

I propped myself against the wall of the stairwell. I wanted it to suck me in.

"Get them to stop," Iris said. "Do your furious thing."

"My what?"

She shrugged.

I sat down on the carpeted stairs and made her look at me. "What fucking furious thing?"

"Don't swear."

"What are you talking about?"

She stuck her bottom lip out and pretended to be younger so I'd forgive whatever she was about to say. "Do your monster."

Eighteen

JOHN'S FRIEND DEREK LEAMAN had an office at the top of a building on Harley Street, where all the expensive doctors had their practices. I sat on one side of the desk, sandwiched between Mom and John, and Derek sat on the other side with a blank sheet of paper in front of him and a sympathetic smile on his face.

He said, "Could you tell me a little more about what happened on Saturday night, Alexandra?"

Behind him, through the window, was a stretch of blue sky and a single London plane tree. It wasn't fully in leaf yet and its branches looked like scribbled ink. If I was down there on the street with my granddad, he'd point out the camouflage-patterned bark that breaks away in large flakes so the tree can cleanse itself of pollutants. He'd tell me that when the leaves matured, they'd look like five-pointed stars.

But I wasn't outside in the fresh air; I was in an office with central heating and a deep pile carpet. It was Wednesday morning. Iris was at school. Kass was at school. Granddad was in his grave.

"Alexandra?" the doctor said.

"You want me to go over the detail?" John said. "Would that be useful?"

Mom stroked my arm. "If you agreed to come, Lex, maybe you should agree to talk?"

I agreed to come because John said he'd go through the school if I didn't. He said he'd call the principal and get her to ask all my subject teachers to fill in a report. He said the more input, the more likely I'd be to receive a decisive diagnosis.

"I'm happy to kick things off," John said. "Maybe Alexandra can interject if she wants to?"

I was sitting on a gray chair. The carpet was beige. Mom was to my left and John to my right. He'd given us the silent treatment the last few days, but now he couldn't stop talking. Ever since we'd walked into the office and John and Derek shook hands and asked how each other's kids were, words had been gushing everywhere. John had asked if there was a definitive test for ADHD (there wasn't) and if it was genetic (it could be). Mom had asked if it might be something else (it might), but John had interrupted to ask if today would be the only meeting (probably not) and was there a complete list of symptoms he could look at? The doctor made a lame joke about reading out a list and every person in the world putting their hand up and saying they had a disorder.

"Everyone experiences these symptoms at one time or another," he said. "What we're looking for is consistent demonstration in multiple settings."

No brain imaging, blood test, or computer analysis was going to give John an immediate verdict. Instead, we had to sit through a diagnostic interview to see how I functioned in everyday life. Starting with Saturday night.

Do your monster.

"My son, Kass, came round for supper," John said, "and after he left, Alexandra got distressed."

Mom was still stroking my arm. "She's missed him since he's been at college. They're very close."

"Anyway," John said, "it was about half past ten when she and Iris went down to wave him off at the bus stop. They'd been gone maybe twenty minutes, when Alexandra came storming upstairs and proceeded to rant and rave at me and her mother. She said it was our fault Kass had gone, that we were trying to control everyone, and why had we suggested he didn't come home again for so long? When we asked her to stop shouting, it made her worse. I told her to go to her room if she couldn't behave and she ramped things up another notch. She threatened to throw the television out the window, but when it proved too heavy for her to lift, she opened the sash and hurled my laptop out instead."

"It was frightening," Mom said. "Really scary. I've never seen her so angry before."

"It landed in the parking lot," John said. "Smashed to pieces, with all my work on it. I know she was distressed, but someone could have been killed. The neighbors called the police, who came marching up the stairs thinking it was a domestic disturbance."

Outside the office window, a magpie landed in the tree. From this far away, all you could see were oily wings and a creamy chest, but up close, magpies had purplish-blue wing feathers and there was a green gloss to their tail.

"The police would've been within their rights to press charges," John said. "They told her she'd potentially endangered anyone who might have been walking below and that she'd behaved in a culpable and reckless manner. I suppose they were trying to scare her, but she didn't bat an eyelid." He turned to look at me. "Would you say this is an accurate presentation of events, Alexandra?"

✳

It was bullshit that I tried to throw the TV out the window. Our TV was attached to a bracket on the wall with three bolts and any idiot would know you needed a screwdriver and another person to come anywhere close to chucking it anywhere. It was true I'd *threatened* to throw it out, that I'd rattled it about on its bracket, then opened the sash window and rattled that. It was also true that I grabbed John's laptop from the table where he'd been watching soccer streams with Kass and, yes, I lobbed it in a beautiful arc down to the parking lot. But I'm sure I looked first. I'm not a maniac.

When the cops asked me why I'd done it, I gave a secret sideways glance at John and said, "I was pissed off."

The youngest cop said, "What about?"

I looked at Mom, but she had that "please don't break my heart" look in her eyes. So I shrugged, and the cop sighed and then he looked at John as if he might be able to read his mind.

"Don't look at me," John said.

"You don't want to add anything?"

John shook his head and looked mystified. "I gave my son money to stay at college until after exams. That's all I can think."

The cop looked at Mom, who asked if he'd like some tea, and he looked at Iris, who smiled angelically, and he looked at his colleague, who said, "I think a warning will suffice."

And the young cop nodded and said, "Well, it's your lucky night, Lexi."

*

Dr. Leaman had clearly given up getting me to talk. He concentrated on Mom and John, telling them that ADHD symptoms can present differently in girls. "Many of the usual questions don't pertain because girls often experience things more internally and so the questions oriented toward them are different."

He ran his finger down the questionnaire in front of him. He'd given me a copy to fill in when I got home. He'd given Mom and John a copy to look at. Each question should be answered with a mark from one to five depending on if I strongly agreed or disagreed with the statements.

Do I often feel as if I want to cry? Do I get a lot of stomachaches and headaches? Do I worry a lot? Feel sad a lot? Do I not know why I feel sad? At school do I dread being asked a question? Do I forget what the teacher asked the class to do? Even when I have something to say, do I not put my hand up? Do I ever volunteer in class?

I turned the paper over on my lap, hoping for blank whiteness, but there were questions on the other side as well.

Am I unable to control my temper? Do I think other girls don't like me? Do I have arguments with my friends? When I want to join a group, do I feel unsure how to approach or what to say? Do I often feel left out?

"What we're looking for are patterns," Dr. Leaman said. "If Alexandra has any of these feelings both at home and at school, then that would be of interest. Or if her feelings interfere with schoolwork or friendships, or if she's felt a certain way for a long time, say longer than six months."

I gripped my fingernails into the side of the chair and concentrated on the tree outside. Plane trees require little root space and can survive in most soils. They grow up to 100 feet tall and can cause problems for buses and overhanging wires. After rain, their leaves are rinsed to a lush green shine—all the grime washed away.

"The questions are a marker of emotional reactivity more than anything." The doctor pulled his attention from the paper and looked at me. "What all this means, Alexandra, is that if your feelings change a lot—if you find yourself getting upset, hurt, and angry more than your classmates do—these are signs. These are the things I want you to tell me about."

He smiled at Mom and John. "It's important to remember that

Alexandra can meet all the diagnostic criteria without having ADHD. To deliver a more accurate diagnosis, I need to see clear evidence that her symptoms reduce the quality of social and academic functioning."

"She's doing badly at school," John said.

"She's smart," Mom said. "But it's like she's choosing not to be."

"She doesn't have any friends," John said.

"Again," Mom said, "it's like she's choosing not to. She was popular in elementary school."

The doctor turned his smile on me. "I'd love to hear your side of things, Alexandra. The more I get to know you, the more I can help."

I met his gaze. I wasn't afraid of him. What could he do if I didn't speak or fill in his questionnaire? How would he diagnose me then?

John and Mom were given parental forms to fill in. They sat with pens and clipboards ticking boxes and circling numbers.

This is what John's questionnaire should ask him:

Do you ever shout at your partner? Do you ever (on a Saturday night, as your children sneak up the stairs) yell, "Fuck off with your ridiculous accusations"?

And does that make you: (a) a guy doing his best to deal with a paranoid woman? or (b) a man under pressure, who temporarily lost his cool? or (c) a complete and utter bastard?

When your partner asks who was calling your cell all evening and tells you she couldn't cope if you left again, do you suggest she goes instead? And then, do you walk menacingly toward her and say, "Go on, what are you waiting for?"

And when your six-year-old daughter comes creeping through the door and takes her mother's hand, do you say, "And don't think for one minute you're taking Iris with you."

And when your partner starts to cry and the older daughter (who isn't yours and who you wish someone *would* take away) comes hurtling in the room, do you: (a) glare at her? or (b) say, "What the fuck are you looking at?" or (c) say, "Christ, have I got to put up with you as well now?" or (d) all the above?

We were in Dr. Leaman's office for one hour and thirty minutes precisely. A social history was taken (Have we moved a lot? Are we financially challenged? Is a family member ill? Has anyone in the family ever had mental health problems?). John said no to everything until the doctor moved on to a symptom history when John swapped to yes—I was inattentive, impulsive, and unproductive and, yes, I had been for years.

At one point, the doctor asked for a few minutes alone with me. "Standard procedure," he said, and Mom and John reluctantly left the room. The doctor smiled when they'd gone and said, "Anything you tell me is confidential, Alexandra. That means that although John and I know one another, I'm not allowed to tell him anything we talk about."

A small part of me wondered if this was a chance. I could confess, "I think it might be John, not me." I could ask, "Do you think he might have a condition that makes other people feel wrong? Is there such a thing?"

But that sounded paranoid and I didn't want to be locked up, so even though we sat there for a while and he asked me several leading questions, I kept my mouth shut until he brought Mom and John back in again.

It was suggested I see the family GP to test my hearing and an optician to test my sight, so that physical causes could be ruled out. John asked about medication and the doctor handed over some leaflets and said we could discuss treatment options next time.

Then the doctor looked at his watch and said what a pleasure it was to meet us. He shook Mom's and John's hands. He told me he looked forward to seeing me again soon.

John paid the bill at reception. It was nearly five hundred pounds. I felt sorry for him as he handed over his credit card and tapped in his PIN. But in the car on the way home, I stopped feeling sorry when he said, "I'm glad Derek wants to discuss medical options. Did you hear him say that, Georgia?"

"We haven't got a diagnosis yet," Mom said.

"Of course, it's every parent's nightmare to have to consider medicating their child, but it's a relief to have professional input at last. Don't you feel relieved, Georgia?"

"Yes," she said. "I guess so."

John looked at me in the mirror. I made myself look back at him. He said, "You didn't do yourself any favors with the silent treatment."

I breathed slowly and deeply and just kept looking.

He said, "Did you think you were being clever?"

I blinked once for *yes*.

"Keeping silent is pathetic behavior, you know that?"

I blinked five times for *I learned it from you.*

He shook his head at me. "You're not going to win this, Alexandra."

Nineteen

THAT NIGHT WHEN I was in bed, Mom came into my room and shut the door behind her. She came right inside and knelt on the carpet next to me. I knew John had gone out and I hoped she was going to tell me he'd gone for good, packed his things and left. I hoped my silence had driven him away, or that he couldn't afford the doctor's fees and he'd finally given up and gone to find himself a new family.

"How do you feel?" she asked. She spoke in a soft voice as if we might be overheard and this was only between us.

I propped myself up on my elbow to look at her. "What, now I'm officially crazy?"

She shook her head. "Nobody used that word, Lex."

"You all think it."

"What I think is that you're finding life tough."

"Are you going to let them drug me, Mom?"

"Believe me, it's the last thing I want."

"They put kids with ADHD on Ritalin. I looked it up."

"Let's see what the doctor says when we see him again, shall we?"

"He'll just agree with John."

"I'm sure he'll do whatever's best for you."

"John always gets his own way. Have you noticed? Even though I obeyed all his new rules, he still sent me to a shrink."

"You threw his laptop out of the window, Lex."

"Something came over me."

She studied me for a long time. Then she put an arm round me and I put both mine around her. "I wish I could make everything better."

She started to hum. She hadn't done that for ages. It was the sunshine song. When I was small, before John, she used to read me a story and then sing me a song every night before bed.

"Do it properly, Mom."

She was embarrassed. I could tell by her laugh.

"Please, Mom, go on."

She sat back on her knees and I sat up against the pillows. Her voice wavered because she was trying to keep quiet, but it was her voice. Just for me.

I was her sunshine. I made her happy. Even when it was raining outside, she felt cheerful because of me. She loved me so much that if I ever went away or stopped loving her back, it would be like the sun died.

I felt loved and valued. I felt as if we could talk about anything.

I said, "What were you arguing about? When me and Iris were coming up the stairs on Saturday night?"

"Nothing."

"Something."

"Nothing for you to worry about."

"John didn't speak to you for three days afterward."

"Couples argue." She stroked her hand along the duvet, ironing it flat with her palm. She tucked the edges under me, like she used to.

"You could talk to me about it. I'm a good listener."

"I just came in to see how you were, Lex."

"I could offer you advice."

"Come on, it's late. Let's say good night."

"Or I could ask useful questions. Where's John now, for instance? Do you know?"

"Let's not do this, Lex. I don't have the energy."

"One night we should go out. You, me, and Iris. We should leave a note saying we've gone to the movies, but really we've gone to stay in a hotel, and when we don't come home he'll be pacing around the apartment wondering where *we* are for a change."

I don't even know where the words came from. They fell out of my mouth without going via my brain. She looked right at me and I could see the wonderful velvet possibility of revenge right there in her eyes.

"What *would* he do?" she said, and her voice was light like a girl's. Her hands kept smoothing the duvet flat.

"He'd be very surprised," I said.

She laughed. "He would, wouldn't he?"

I loved her laughing. I loved that I could make her laugh by coming up with such a splendid idea.

"He wouldn't manage without you," I said. "He'd forget to go to work. He wouldn't eat. He'd probably starve to death."

I might've gone too far because she stood up and brushed herself down, sweeping imaginary dirt from her jeans. "Enough now."

"Mom, don't go. This is fun."

She shook her head. "Not for me it isn't."

"Don't get upset."

"I don't think you realize, Lex, but every time you have a go at John, I have to defend him." She gazed sadly down at me. "I'm so tired of defending him to you."

"I'm sorry. I won't say anything else. It's only because I want you to be happy."

"Oh, happiness!" She waved a hand dismissively, as if I'd said I wanted her to be ten years younger and such things were impossible.

"You used to be," I said. "Didn't you used to be happier than now?"

"Time for sleeping," she said.

Twenty

IT WAS LIGHT, BUT too early for my alarm to have gone off, when John stuck his head round my bedroom door the next morning.

"Where's Mom and Iris?" he said.

I pulled the duvet up to my neck. "I don't know."

"What do you mean you don't know? You were here with them last night, weren't you?"

"Aren't they in bed?"

"No, they're not. You think I didn't look? There's no note—nothing."

"You mean they're not in the apartment?"

He glared at me like I was an idiot. "Check your phone, will you?"

"You put it in the safe."

He huffed off, and while he was gone I put my robe on and tried to work out what day of the week it was. Thursday, a school day. Maybe they'd gone to get milk? But the shop was only around the corner—why would Mom take Iris? And why so early?

John came back with my phone and stood in the doorway while I turned it on. No new messages. No missed calls.

He took a step into the room. "When was the last time you saw them?"

He smelled of smoke and booze. Had he only just got in? A terrible thought crossed my mind that he'd done something to them and was going to blame it on me, but he didn't look like a killer as he sat on the end of my bed. He looked afraid.

"Alexandra?" he said. "When did you last see them?"

"Last night. Iris went to bed and then I did. A bit later, Mom came in my room and we spoke. That was about eleven thirty."

"Spoke about what?"

I hated how urgent his voice was. And the way he was holding his chest as if it pained him. It made everything seem deadly serious. I told him me and Mom had talked about the doctor. I didn't tell him about the singing or my suggestion we disappear.

"That's it? Nothing else?"

"Nothing."

He looked at me suspiciously as if I knew more than I was saying. "Try ringing her. See if she picks up for you."

It felt wrong to call her when John was in the room. What if she'd run off and was going to send for me and he heard the plan? But her phone went straight to voice mail.

John sort of collapsed into himself. "Where on earth are they?"

I shook my head. "Maybe there was an early assembly?"

"At seven o'clock in the morning?" He collapsed a bit more. Then he had a sudden thought and stood up. He left the room and came back only a few seconds later with Mom's and Iris's passports and waved them at me. "Well, at least they left these behind."

"You think Mom would take Iris abroad without telling us?" I whispered.

He called her cell again, but she didn't answer. He left her a message saying she had no right to withhold information about his daughter. Would Iris be going to school today? Did she know it was against the law to pull a child from education? He told her to call him immediately. He checked her Facebook and WhatsApp, but she hadn't been online since yesterday.

I was beginning to feel sick.

He went through the coatrack and announced that both their coats were missing and both pairs of shoes. Iris's school bag was on the peg, so she hadn't gone in early. Mom's handbag wasn't there, but her suitcase was on the top of the wardrobe as usual. I went into Iris's room to see if she'd left me a clue. Her stuffed elephant and her pajamas were missing. Had Mom picked her up while she was asleep and carried her away?

"What about Mom's car?" I said.

"Gone. It was the first thing I checked." John stood by the living room window looking down at the parking lot, and then he turned to me and said, "Are you sure Mom didn't mention an appointment? Maybe Iris had the orthodontist?"

He went to fetch Mom's planner from their bedroom and I pulled my robe tighter and sat on the sofa looking for signs.

He strode back down the hallway and handed the planner to me. "Nothing. But there are phone numbers at the back. Call Meryam and see if she's heard from them."

"Why me?"

"She won't tell me anything, will she? Call from the landline so she recognizes the number."

I pushed the planner back at him, but he shook his head. "Just call her."

I felt like a grass as I dialed. What if Mom was with Meryam? Or what if Meryam knew where she was and told me and then John went there and did his "you're a useless parent" speech and snatched Iris for himself?

Meryam didn't pick up, which was a relief, but John made me call her again and she picked up the second time. I wondered if she was avoiding me. "It's Lex," I said. "Sorry, did I wake you? John asked me to call."

He shook his head at me, but I was glad to have snuck him in like that. Now Meryam would know not to give any secrets away. I told her the whole story and when I'd finished she said, "Has your mom ever gone off like this before?"

"For a couple of hours sometimes. But never with Iris."

"Yes," Meryam said quietly. "I see that's worrying. Let me just check my phone. Hold on." I could hear her breathing and I wondered if she was in the kitchen with the cat and the view of the yard or if she was upstairs in her bedroom. Was Ben still asleep? Would my call have woken him too?

"No," Meryam said, "nothing here. Why don't I call her and see if she picks up? I'll call you right back."

She didn't wait for a reply but cut me off. Her ending our conversation like that made my heart flare. I turned to John, sitting on the sofa behind me. I said, "What if Iris got sick in the night and Mom took her to the hospital?"

He blinked at me and I felt my words fall into him. It was like the tree accident all over again. I wondered if he was thinking that too. "She'd have woken you up, wouldn't she?" he said. "Or left a note?"

Not if it was an emergency, I thought. Not if Iris broke her neck climbing out of her bunk bed, not if she had meningitis. I said, "Should we call the hospital and check?"

He didn't answer. I watched him breathing—his belly going in and out. He hadn't shaved, and he had dark circles under his eyes. He looked old and tired. He looked like he couldn't decide anything. I clamped my fists shut and dug my nails in because I didn't want to feel sorry for him. This was the same man who took me to a doctor.

When the phone rang, we both jumped.

"Quick," he said.

I reached for it. "Meryam?"

"Yes, yes, it's me. OK, I got hold of your mom and everything's fine. She was driving, so couldn't speak much, but she's on her way to Brighton with Iris. A day trip, apparently. She did send John a text, but only a few minutes ago, which is probably why he hasn't seen it yet."

I put my hand over the receiver and told John and he scrambled for his cell.

"There's nothing else?" I whispered. "No message for me?"

"I'm sorry, Lex. It was hard for her to talk while she was driving, and she sounded stressed. Why not give her a call in an hour or so?"

"I called her just now and she didn't pick up."

There was a long pause and Meryam said, "Are the two of you in a fight?"

Why did she think this was something to do with me? Why couldn't she say, "Poor baby, being deserted like this. I imagine your heart is breaking into pieces."

But then I remembered that last time I'd seen Meryam I'd slammed out of her house without even saying goodbye and she'd stood on the doorstep calling after me.

"Come over after school if you want," Meryam said. "Come and have tea with us."

I mumbled something about an after-school club and having homework. I wanted to be at home when Mom got back.

"Anything happening with that text?" Meryam said. "Has he got it?"

I turned to look at John. He was huddled over his cell. Every bit of him was angled, like he suddenly had corners. Even his knees and elbows looked sharp.

"What does it say?" I asked.

"Has he read it?" Meryam said. "Can I speak to him?"

194

I didn't know how to tell her that he wouldn't want to speak to her, so I just passed the phone to him, and when he shrank from it, I said, "She asked for you!" in a loud voice so he had no choice.

I couldn't tell what the conversation was, because John was mostly monosyllabic. But I guess she asked if he knew why Mom had gone because he said, "I have zero idea what goes through that woman's mind." Then Meryam must've asked if there was anything she could do to help, because he said, "I'm perfectly capable of managing, thanks." He got impatient after that and said, "This isn't helping. *You're* not helping. Just let me know if you hear anything else, OK?" And he put the phone down.

"Shit," he said. Then he closed his eyes and slumped back on the sofa.

"What did the text say?" I asked him.

He opened his eyes and looked at me. "Shouldn't you be getting ready for school?"

"Was it about me?"

"Go on, or you'll miss homeroom. And leave me your phone, in case she gets in contact."

Twenty-One

EVERYONE TURNED TO LOOK as I walked into media studies over half an hour late. I glowered at the lot of them. "What are you staring at?" I snarled.

"Lexi," the teacher warned.

Ben waved at me across the tables. "You OK?"

I shook my head.

He scrambled to his feet and I motioned him to sit back down. His mom had clearly told him mine had abandoned me. I was the sad case, that was obvious.

"We're going over coursework," the teacher said. "So, get your project book out, please, Lexi. You've a great deal of catching up to do."

I wanted to smash something. Saturday, Kass left. Followed by John doing his silent treatment for days. Wednesday, the doctor. Today, Mom and Iris were gone. And now I was stuck at school with no phone and a massive backlog of work. I took the doctor's questionnaire out of my backpack along with my project book and began to circle my answers. Yes, I wanted to cry. Yes, I had a stomachache and, yes, a headache too. Did I get angry a lot? Definitely. Feel sad a lot? Every day. Did I dread being called on in class because I hadn't been listening? Absolutely. Did I feel left out and argumentative? All the time. I hated everyone, and everything was wrong. I was a misfit surrounded by misfits. I circled so hard I made holes in the paper.

I felt a bit better after that and passed some time staring out the window while the teacher droned on about deadlines. The sky was blue and tightly stretched and I watched a plane skim its surface and thought of all the people in their seats above us. Kass told me once that there were a million people airborne at any one time, like a city in the sky. I wished I was up there right now. None of them would know me, so I could be anyone.

Ben wrote me a note. It said, *Talk after?* I put it in my pocket and didn't look at him.

I felt him watching me across the room. I didn't want him to do that. I didn't want people thinking we were together—the gawky redheaded boy and the weirdo girl.

He wrote another note and got it passed along: *Lex—u want 2b a movie star?*

I put that note in my pocket too. Wasn't it him who'd said to concentrate on exams? I scrawled a reply and passed it back along the line. *Fuck off. I'm trying to work.*

He smiled as if he was impressed and put that note in his pocket. I made a show of listening to the teacher get all enthusiastic about exam technique and the importance of timing ourselves with practice papers. I was never going to do that. Panic rose in my throat again. What if Mom never came back? What if I failed all my exams and had to live with John by myself forever? I had to find a way of getting hold of Mom, finding out where she was and going to her. What was I doing sitting in a classroom doing nothing about anything?

When the bell rang, Ben dodged other kids to walk next to me in the corridor. "So," he said, "can I ask you something?"

I thought he was going to ask me on a date and my face turned to fire. "I don't have time."

"I'll be quick," Ben said. "It's just that we both need to submit a media project and we both know you haven't done yours yet. So, I was thinking—why don't you be an actor in mine? It's a win-win situation because you're brilliant, so I'll get a great mark, and you have no other options, so you can't refuse."

Not a date. Of course, not a date. Meryam had put him up to it. *"Poor girl—even her mom can't stand her. Be nice to her, Ben."*

I stopped in the corridor and folded my arms at him. "Why are you asking me?"

"Because you're an amazing actor."

I thought of the note in my pocket. He'd written my name in the same sentence as the words *movie star.* "You're making a documentary," I said. "It doesn't need an actor."

"A presenter, then. Or I could change the format."

"You'd change the format of your film so I could be in it?"

He glanced along the corridor. I'd raised my voice and people were looking. "Why not?"

I took the note out of my pocket and handed it back to him. "I can't believe you're asking me about this when my mom's missing."

Ben looked down at the note squashed in his hand. "I thought she'd just gone off for the day?"

"Yeah, leaving me with a psycho."

He flicked me a look. "What's he done?"

But words never quite cut it and I didn't have time for searching for ones that didn't make me sound ridiculous. "I have to go, Ben, sorry."

I walked quickly out of the door, across the playground to the main entrance. I didn't look back. At the reception desk, I asked one of the women if they had my mom's cell number on file. She checked, but only had the landline or John's cell, would either of those do instead? I asked if she had Kass's number. She told me the school didn't keep ex-students' details, but surely, if I rang John, he'd have my mom's and brother's details, wouldn't he?

"Kass isn't my brother," I said.

She nodded sympathetically. I asked her to double-check for Mom's number and she patiently searched again and still didn't have it. One of her colleagues came over and asked if everything was OK? They both looked at me. Was I feeling nauseous? they wondered. I looked a bit sickly. Did I want to sit down?

I said, "If I tell you the name of my sister's elementary school, could you give me that number? They might have details for my mom."

One of them looked it up and the other one warned me that the elementary school was unlikely to give information unless I physically went there and proved who I was. A slip of paper with the school's number was passed over. They blinked at me over the counter. Was that everything?

"Can you lend me a cell?" I said. "One of the confiscated ones, I mean? Just until tomorrow?"

They couldn't do that, they said, their eyes moving from sympathy to suspicion. School policy didn't allow students using phones, and lending me a confiscated one would be an invasion of some other child's privacy, wouldn't it? And no, of course they couldn't give me money for a train fare if I promised to pay it back and anyway, whose class was I in? Because they were thinking they should call my tutor to come and have a word with me. Wasn't I the girl who broke the window? But then the bell rang for third period and two boys turned up covered in blood from clashing heads on the Astroturf field and the women's eyes turned sympathetic again and they lost interest in me.

The ache in my stomach got heavier as I turned away. I took a deep breath, had to stop, had to sit on the low wall by the gate and put my head down. I didn't know what else to do, where else to go. I watched my own hands gripping my bag, my own feet in my shoes. This is you, I thought. This body is yours. It's the one you were born with and the one you'll take to your grave. This is your life. And your mom has left you.

Ben came bounding over. "I'm sorry about just now. Of course you're worried about your mom. I'm an idiot. Have you heard from her? Do you know why she went?"

Help me, I wanted to say. *I don't know what to do.* But I just shook my head and breathed some more.

Ben said, "Are you ill? Is that why you were at reception? Did they say you should go home?"

I did feel sick. But it was probably sadness. Did that count as an illness? Whatever was wrong with me, I wasn't going home. If I couldn't have Mom or Kass, what I wanted was for some giant to pick me up and carry me somewhere cool and safe. A forest maybe, a Canadian forest with pine trees and a brisk wind.

"Have you got a cell on you, Ben? Do you have my mom or Kass's numbers?"

He shook his head. "Cerys will have Kass's, won't she? You want me to see if I can find her?"

My life was a mess. Everything was falling like a card house. It was useless to think I could come to school and be normal. Nothing about me was normal. Even asking Cerys for Kass's number was weird because the last person to kiss her boyfriend was me, not her. But she was the closest thing to Kass I had. And my only chance at speaking to him.

I stayed sitting on the wall as Ben scampered off. He reminded me of a puppy I'd made friends with on a farm once. I heard the second bell ring and watched the gate swing open and shut as kids hurried in from break, eager not to be late. I sat there for ages before Ben and Cerys came walking across the playground. She looked brisk and efficient.

"Hey, Lex," she said. "What's going on?"

I wondered if I should tell her I'd suggested me, Mom, and Iris run off together and that Mom had taken my advice, but only taken Iris. I wasn't sure Cerys would understand how it felt to be left behind.

"Well," I said eventually. "My mom seems to have gone to Brighton."

"Do you know why?"

"She says it's a day trip. But she took Iris out of bed and left without saying anything."

Cerys narrowed her lovely eyes at me. "Do you have a theory?"

I could tell by her face she had one of her own and was waiting to see if mine tallied. I toyed with giving her unhelpful and stupid theories, such as alien abduction or brainwashing and cult membership. But I just stared at the ground instead. "Maybe John did something terrible and she's run off with Iris to punish him?"

"Surely, if he did something terrible she'd kick him out?"

"She's not that brave."

"Why not? John doesn't have a gun, does he?"

"He doesn't need one. He's scary all by himself."

"If he's so scary, why did your mom leave you behind?"

I looked at Ben for help and he said maybe we needed to turn the question round and ask why John was frightening? But I wasn't going to answer that either. There was no point. Instead I said, "Can I borrow your phone, Cerys?"

"Of course, yeah. We have to go off campus to do it, come on." She used her sixth-form pass to open the gate and me and Ben followed her through. It made her special somehow—older and more mature than us fifteen-year-olds, who had no such thing.

"I'll text him first," Cerys said, "so he can get out of class if he's in one. I'll say it's urgent."

I nodded and sat on the curb and stared at the community center across the street. I used to go swimming there when I was at elementary school. Mom took Iris for lessons now. I wiped my sleeve across my eyes. What was wrong with me? This was so exposing. Ben kept shooting me worried looks. Why did that make me feel sadder? Why did his concern feel so moving and unusual?

"He's not answering," Cerys said, handing me her phone. "He probably thinks it's me. Tell him it's you and see if he answers then."

She stepped away into sunlight, leaving me in the shade of the wall. I texted:

IT'S LEX, NOT CERYS. IMPORTANT.

It took him twenty-two seconds to call. We were bound, that was why. Girlfriends came and went.

"Lex?" he said. "What's happened? Why are you calling from Cerys's phone?"

I loved the urgency in his voice. "Can we FaceTime? I need to see you."

"I'll call you back from my laptop."

Behind me, Cerys and Ben weren't talking. Cerys had her arms folded and was gazing at the school buildings. Ben was sitting on the wall by the gate, hunched up, still watching me. I moved along the pavement out of earshot.

"So," Kass said, "what's up?"

He was in his student room and his face on Cerys's phone looked elongated and in shadow and there was a tiny lag with FaceTime. It made him seem as if he might be in a different time zone.

I told him the whole story—from the moment he'd got on the bus, through the argument and the laptop incident to the doctor and how I'd suggested me, Mom, and Iris take off.

He laughed. "Might've known it was your idea!"

"But why didn't she take me?"

"You've got exams coming up."

"You think I'm his punishment? You think she took his favorite child and left me behind to piss him off?"

"Hey," Kass said. "You're a beautiful human being, OK?"

The look between us was profound. It held all the mystery of our kiss in it.

I nodded. "OK."

"Just lie low. Keep out of his way. This is them going round in their ridiculous circles. He'll buy her flowers and she'll come back and it'll all be fine. You never know, this might give you and my dad a chance to get along."

I sighed and looked away across the road. The community center doors swung open and a line of little kids came out with wet hair clutching their swimming bags. Watching them made my throat swell again.

"Please, Kass," I whispered. "Can't you come back? It's an emergency."

"Your mom had a tantrum and left. How is that an emergency?"

"A tantrum?"

He raised an eyebrow. "They've had a fight, then. A tiff."

"You think I'm exaggerating?"

"I think you need some perspective."

A text came through on Kass's cell and he looked away from his laptop to click it open. "Sorry, I need to get this."

I watched him read it. I watched him tap out a reply. I sat on the curb doing nothing while he scanned through other messages. Behind me, Ben and Cerys were quietly talking now. I felt a strange stab of envy.

I had to look away, back at Kass—remind myself of his hand gripping mine, his lips feverish on mine, his arms pulling me close. "Kass, can you put your phone away?"

He made a big deal of turning it facedown on the table and then leaning back and folding his arms at me. "Right, I'm back."

"I know I've already asked you this once, but can I come to Manchester? I wouldn't get in the way."

"That can't happen, Lex. You know it can't."

"Why not?"

"Because you're too distracting?"

I didn't want that to thrill me, but it did. Especially when he smiled his beautiful crooked smile. "Go to school," he said, "feed yourself, and stay out of trouble until tonight when your mom gets back. That's all you have to do."

"That's a definite no, then, is it?"

Silence. Because it was. Because he was busy and had a new life. Because I had to get some perspective.

"I'll go, then," I said.

"Call me again if you need me."

"Sure."

"I mean it. Anything at all."

I clicked the phone off. I was on my own. I had to stop being needy, stop asking for stuff, stop being weak. As Cerys said, John didn't have a gun, did he? Kass said it was a chance for me and his dad to get along, that it wasn't an emergency. Even Ben had said, "Isn't it just a day trip?"

All I had to do was get through school, go home, and manage an evening with John.

How bad could it be?

Twenty-Two

THE NIGHT AFTER MY granddad's funeral, I wet the bed. I crept along the hallway to let Mom know, scared she'd be mad. But she helped me off with my nightie and wiped me down with a towel and gave me one of her T-shirts to wear and let me sleep next to her. She tucked me warm beside her, kissed me, and told me not to worry about a thing. I'd been scared for no reason at all.

Maybe I'd made a mistake about John too. He was always lovely to Iris, wasn't he? He adored Kass. Mom was the love of his life. It was only me he seemed to have constant trouble with.

Maybe he wasn't a bad person at all?

Looking at him now as I walked in from school, slouched at his desk with his head in his hands—he seemed so harmless. He's just a man, I thought. He's just a guy trying to get by in a difficult world.

"Hey," I said. "How's it going?"

He looked up and smiled. "There you are. I was getting worried."

"Sorry I'm late. I walked the long way home, through the park."

He turned to the window as if checking things like parks existed. He said, "I haven't been out all day. I was going to go to the office but couldn't face it."

I stood in the doorway, not sure what to do next. "Fancy a cup of tea?" I said when the silence got mildly awkward.

He looked round and smiled again. "Sure. Thanks."

I made it properly in the pot and I used his favorite cup, even though I had to wash it out and I could just have got a different one from the hooks. I didn't stew the tea too long or fill the cup too high, because he hated that, and I put precisely half a teaspoon of sugar in and stirred it thoroughly. I was pleased I knew what to do—exactly what—but also surprised, because I didn't think I'd been taking that much notice of Mom's routines. I put two shortbreads and two chocolate cookies on a plate and put that and both teacups on a tray and went up to John's study. I stood in the doorway until he noticed me because I didn't want to assume I should put the tray on his desk.

He moved some papers and gestured to me to put the tray down. "Wow," he said, "great service." He swung his legs onto the leather sofa and picked up a shortbread.

I took my tea and sat carefully on the sofa. His feet bounced a tiny bit, but he didn't say a word.

I knew shortbreads were his favorite so, in case he wanted both, I took a cookie to give him a choice. I sat there and sipped my tea and I wanted to ask stuff, like: *Where were you last night?* Or *Do you have any idea why Mom took Iris and not me?* But I knew questions stressed him out and that kind might make him yell at me, so I just kept quiet.

Eventually he said, "So, how was school?"

He said it so warmly, like he genuinely wanted to know. "It was OK. I had media and then drama, so that was good."

He nodded, as if he understood.

"But then I had double math, which wasn't much fun."

"What did you have for lunch?"

I couldn't remember, and my guts literally clamped. Then I remembered I'd had chips and a chocolate bar because the line had been too long at the cafeteria, so I told him I'd had a tuna salad sandwich and a bottle of water and he raised an eyebrow at me and we both laughed.

I really liked him knowing I was bullshitting.

He took the other shortbread and I knew I'd been right not to have taken it. I watched him eat it and watched the crumbs fall on his shirt and I wondered if I should lean over and brush them from him. But Mom wouldn't do that. She'd come back later when he was out of his study and discreetly sweep the carpet with a dustpan and brush. I'd do the same. He always watched the news in the living room after supper—I'd do it then.

He took another sip of tea and said, "I've had an idea. Want to hear it?"

I nodded. I had no clue what he was about to say. I stopped chewing, so I'd hear every word.

"Your mom's finding it hard that you and I aren't getting along."

"That's what she said in the text this morning?"

"The laptop-out-the-window thing freaked her out."

"She actually wrote that?"

"So how about we try and get on brilliantly? We can send her regular updates and make living with us sound like a blast."

"But won't they be back tonight?"

He rubbed a hand across his stubble. "Yeah, well, apparently they've checked into a hotel."

"How do you know?"

"Your mom texted again."

"Why didn't you tell me?"

A flash of irritation crossed his face. "I'm telling you now."

"Why didn't you tell me when I came in? Why are you telling me so casually, like it hardly matters?"

"Jesus, Alexandra, give me a break."

His anger rippled in me. I felt it in my chest, like a wave. Don't get angry, I thought. Be nice to him. He's hurting too.

"Sorry," I said. "It's just that I've been worried."

"And you think I haven't?"

He rubbed at his stubble a bit more and then picked up his cup and drained it. I watched the lump in his neck go swallow, swallow.

I said, "So, she left because of us?"

"It makes sense, doesn't it? You hurl things out of windows and then give us the silent treatment at the doctor's. I go out for the evening and leave your mom to cope alone." He put his cup back on the tray. "I didn't take you to the doctor to piss you off, you know. I'm genuinely worried about your future. Are you going to study, for instance? Are you actually going to bother at all?"

"I hope so."

"You're an idiot if you don't. You're smarter than you know."

"You think I'm smart?"

"I wouldn't be trying to help you if I didn't."

I stared at him. Trying to help? Was he?

He said, "Oh, you can look at me as if I'm talking nonsense, but I see your brightness every day. Kass and Iris might be more obviously academic, but you've got something school can't teach."

"What have I got?"

He studied me with his head to one side, as if I mattered and was interesting to him and he wanted to tell me something true. "You're a survivor. If the world was ending, you'd pull up your sleeves and get on with it. Your mom would be hysterical, Iris would hide, Kass would run. But you? You'd look it in the eye and stick it out."

It was the nicest thing he'd ever said to me. I said, "You'd survive too."

"Oh, I'd try and buy my way out, but I'm not sure credit cards work in an apocalypse." He chuckled. "I genuinely admire you, Lex. You'll outlive all of us."

I had to stop myself from cheering. I wanted to hug him. I wanted to say, *See! I knew I was worth something.*

"Hey," I said, "shall I make us supper later?"

"If you want."

"I could do pasta?"

"Sounds good."

We smiled at one another as the late sun glimmered through the blinds.

Twenty-Three

I FELT AS WHOLESOME as Snow White skipping around the apartment tidying up. I wouldn't have been surprised if a flock of birds had flown through a window to help. I emptied the dishwasher and restacked it with the dirty cups and plates. I wiped the tea tray and put it back in the cupboard. I even took a cloth and lemon spray to the kitchen counter and sink. I checked the fridge for anything decent for supper, but since Thursday was Mom's supermarket day, it was bare. I googled "simplest pasta recipe ever" and discovered we had enough ingredients for a carbonara. Even I could fry some onions and fling some cheese, eggs, and bacon together.

I tried to study for a while so that John would think his talk had inspired me. I got out my biology book and read about energy and plants. I gazed out the window trying to see if I could remember what I'd read without checking. I took out my chemistry book and wrote "Molecules" at the top of a blank piece of paper.

But I was too excited to concentrate. I wanted the evening to be perfect, so I began a list of tasks. I'd start to cook supper at six. I'd offer John a whiskey with a single cube of ice at half past and give him a fifteen-minute warning before the food was ready so he could wind down his work and wash his hands. It might be awkward, the two of us together at the dining table, so I'd serve supper in front of the TV. I'd clear the coffee table and give it a wipe, make sure there was a coaster for his drink and the TV remotes were in place. I'd let him choose the channel, and if he chose the news or a political program, I wouldn't talk or interrupt, but listen carefully in case he asked me questions afterward.

I took off my outdoor shoes and put on Mom's slippers. I went around the apartment taking note of how things were so I could keep it exactly as John liked it—the alignment of the soap to the tap in his en suite, the way the towel hung in the exact middle of the rail, the toilet paper facing outward with one sheet hanging down. I knew these things were important because I'd seen Mom fussing over them. The living room had to be free of any clutter—no toys or used cups, all the cushions neatly plumped. I noted that yes, the curtains were tied correctly, and that a clean ashtray was sitting next to a lighter. The carpet was supposed to be vacuumed daily, but Mom would've done that yesterday, so I might get away with it. She usually did that when he was out because the noise bugged him. I guess if he went out later, I could do it then.

Next, I checked that none of the soap dispensers or toothpaste tubes was empty and wiped a cloth around the bath Iris and I shared, because even though John never went in there—what if he did tonight? I didn't want him revolted by stains. I opened doors quietly and shut them carefully as I checked things, but I occasionally made a regular noise, such as a small cough or a quiet humming, just to let John know I was about and that I wasn't creeping around spying on him or anything bizarre. He'd once told Mom off for being *too fucking quiet*. I didn't want to surprise him or make him jump or feel stupid because he forgot I was there. I didn't want to humiliate him by catching him picking his nose or farting.

When it was time to start cooking, I tied my hair back and put Mom's apron on. I pretended I was a famous chef and made small and accurate movements as I got all the ingredients together. I wasn't going to drop or break anything. I was going to make a perfect meal.

I was frying onion and bacon in oil with plenty of black pepper, when John came in and said, "That smells great." It was so easy to please him, to make him happy. Why had I never known this?

He said, "I've had a new idea. Want to hear it?"

"Sure." I wiped my hands on a tea towel and flapped it over one shoulder like Mom did when she cooked. I tipped the chopped garlic from the board into the olive oil and mixed it all together with a wooden spoon. *To ensure the onion caramelizes, cover with oil and occasionally stir.* I didn't mind John watching. I was certain and solid and in control. Nothing was burning. I wasn't making a fool of myself. I'd never felt so relaxed with him in the same room.

"I was thinking," he said, "if we can find out which hotel they're at, we could drive to Brighton and surprise them."

"After supper?"

"Or now. We can get food there."

I turned with the wooden spoon in my hand to tell him he could piss off with that idea because I'd spent ages preparing, but the

214

spoon dripped oil onto the kitchen floor and he gave a quick glance down and then back up again and he opened his mouth to let me have it, but decided not to and closed it again, so I took a breath and swallowed my anger too. We're both trying hard here, I thought.

He said, "Your mom needs some love and attention from us. We've been taking her for granted." He sat down in the rocking chair and pressed his toes to the floor and slowly rocked. "It'd be fun, wouldn't it?"

I imagined turning up at the hotel—the surprise of it. Would it be fun? Would Mom be pleased?

He said, "If you call her and get the name of the hotel, we can be there in a couple of hours. We'll have drinks in the bar, dinner in the restaurant, and stay the night. You girls can have the day off school tomorrow. It'll be like a vacation."

A vacation? Maybe he was right. Maybe after dinner, we could go for a walk along the seafront in the dark. Maybe there'd be a pier with slot machines or a carnival? We'd be like a proper family. Mom might say how pleased she was to hear that me and John got along without her. "It's such a relief," she'd say. "I'm so very happy. This makes all the difference to me. I feel so much better."

"Hey," John said, "if it helps you to decide—I think I know why your mom didn't answer when you called her this morning."

I turned to look at him. "You do?"

"I'd locked your phone in the safe, hadn't I? So, she thought you didn't have it. She thought it was me using your phone."

Of course! Just like Kass thinking it was Cerys calling him earlier and refusing to pick up. It wasn't *me* people were avoiding.

"So," John said, "why not leave her a voice mail, let her know you've got your phone back and ask her to chat?" He pulled my cell from his pocket. "Here you go. Don't tell her we're going to surprise her, though, eh?"

I did as John said and left a voice mail.

"Attagirl," he said.

I put my phone on the counter and went back to stirring the sauce. Behind my back, I knew John was watching the phone and willing it to ring. And when it did, I was so happy that Mom hadn't hesitated to call back when she knew it was me.

I flung the tea towel over my shoulder again and picked up. "Mom?"

"Lex. Oh, baby, is that you?" She sounded urgent and upset. She sounded like she was missing me. "I've been so worried. I had no way of getting in touch with you."

The relief of hearing her voice released something in me. "You could've left a note."

"I didn't know I was going anywhere. Iris woke up at some ridiculous hour and I just wanted to get out of the apartment. I was planning on a little drive. I didn't mean to come all this way."

"You didn't mean to?" I was suddenly hot and furious. "No one accidentally drives to Brighton!"

She spun me some story about a sunny morning and quiet roads and a car full of gas. "Iris had a tummy ache, so wouldn't have gone into school anyway. The seaside seemed like a good idea at the time and then I remembered you didn't have your phone."

The fury built. I hadn't realized I was mad at her. It was like I'd been holding a bunch of stones in my fist all day and now I could throw them. "You could've called school. You could've emailed. You could've given Meryam a message to pass on. Hey, you could even have turned round and come back to get me."

"Oh, Lexi, I'm sorry."

"What kind of mom takes just one of her kids away?"

"Baby, I promise you're not missing much. Right now, I'm sitting in a grotty B&B next to a boarded-up nightclub. The TV doesn't work and there's no room service."

"I don't care. I'm glad it's horrid. You shouldn't've left me. Even though you're pissed off with me, you shouldn't have done that."

"I'm not pissed off with you, Lex."

"Then why did you leave me behind?" My eyes pricked with tears and my throat tightened. "I thought you were dead. If we hadn't rung Meryam, we wouldn't have known anything. I thought Iris was sick. I wanted John to phone the hospital."

I had to stop speaking because my voice was breaking up and anyway, she could piss off with her stupidity. I passed the phone to John and he gave me the kindest look, as if he really understood how it felt to be abandoned.

"Hey," he said, "so your daughter's pretty upset here."

He stood by the window, looking down at the yard. I sat in the rocking chair and wiped my eyes on my sleeve. Last night she'd sung to me and I'd said *let's go away and not tell him where we are*, and she'd done it without me.

"Listen," he said, "you have to come back. We miss you. Yes, both of us—of course both of us. Christ, Georgia—if you don't know how much I love you by now . . . No, babe, listen. It doesn't matter about the hotel, never mind the money. No, listen to me."

But she didn't want to. She wanted to talk. I could hear her voice, shrill and insistent in the background, and it did something to him. I saw it happen. His face flickered with fury and then a hardness slammed down.

He said, "Tell me where you are. I want the name of the hotel."

She said stuff I couldn't hear, but whatever it was, it made the anger build in him like a river being dammed—like all his systems got clogged with it.

He said, "You know I could get an emergency court order to find out where you are? You want me to do that?"

He said, "What's wrong with you, woman? What on earth's wrong with you?

"Normal people don't do this," he said. "Sane people don't behave this way. The kind of people who drag a kid away from school and run off without a word are hysterical people, who shouldn't be left in charge of children. I'm telling you, there will be major consequences unless you get in that car right now and come home."

I heard her shout, "You don't get to tell me what to do. You do *not* get to tell me."

"Let me speak to Iris."

She shouted some more, and he held up a hand to stop her, even though she couldn't see it. "No, you can't speak to Alexandra again. I want to talk to Iris. Put my daughter on the phone immediately."

But she wouldn't. I knew she wouldn't because he called her an emotional idiot and then maybe she hung up, because he growled furiously and threw my phone at the kitchen door, where it bounced and crashed to the floor in pieces. That was my phone, not his, and I wanted to yell at him, but he was standing in the middle of the kitchen clutching his head like a madman, so I walked slowly across the room and picked everything up. The case was broken, and the screen was cracked, and a strange milky light flickered where the icons used to be. I sat back in the rocking chair and cradled the pieces.

"It's only a fucking phone," he said. "Nobody died."

Again, I swallowed the anger. I tried to make a joke. I said, "Well, maybe you'll get me an upgrade now?"

"Jesus, do you only care about yourself?" He looked at me as if I was subnormal and then stormed out of the kitchen and up the stairs to his study.

I sat with my broken phone on my lap and the pan sizzling beside me on the stove. I sat very still. On the counter was my list of tasks and the whiskey glass and bottle all prepared. Five minutes ago, John was smiling and telling me the food smelled amazing. Five minutes ago, we were planning to drive to Brighton together.

I shouldn't have turned around with the spoon and dripped oil on the floor. I shouldn't have got mad. Or cried. I'd failed to find out the name of the hotel. I shouldn't have picked up my broken phone as if it was the most precious thing on the planet. I shouldn't have made a joke about an upgrade.

Is this how Mom feels? I thought. Is this what he does to her?

I sat there in her slippers and apron and wondered what was going to happen next. Maybe John would come downstairs and tell me he didn't mean it, not to take things to heart, not to be so emotional. *Was I still making supper?* he'd ask. He'd make out it was all a joke. Or he'd come downstairs and make a great show of putting on his coat and shoes and telling me he was going out to eat. *You can fuck off with your supper*, he'd say. He didn't need to sit around with a tortured martyr who saw him as the bad guy. What about his pain?

And if I were Mom, I'd either make supper and accept he'd been joking, or I'd beg him not to go. Because if he left, there were two ways he could come back: silent or mean. And if it was mean, there were a hundred ways that could play out.

Is this why Mom never seemed to have any energy? Was she exhausted from trying to work out what may or may not happen next? Is this how he weakened her?

Here he came now. I could hear his feet on the stairs. My stomach gripped. My pulse raced. Living with him was like following the rules of a complicated and terrible game.

He stood in the doorway, one hand on the frame, and smiled. "I'm sorry, Lex."

That wasn't what I was expecting. *Don't fall for it*, a small voice warned.

"I'm such an idiot," he said. "I broke your phone."

I felt myself softening. That sunny mirror smile was so warm. "It's all right. You didn't mean to."

"I'll get you a new one."

I nodded. "OK."

He raked a hand through his hair. "They will come back, won't they?"

"Of course."

"But what if they don't?"

I could hardly bear it. His eyes were the same color as Kass's and he looked so upset. He looked like a dog I'd seen hit by a car once, standing lost and bewildered in the road.

"I'll make the food, shall I? We can think of a plan while we eat."

"Did your mom say anything about the hotel at all? Any defining detail?"

"She said it was a B&B and not very nice. Oh, and it's next to a boarded-up nightclub."

He nodded. "Thank you."

"You're welcome."

"And food would be lovely. Thank you for that too."

He left. I quietly returned to stirring the pan. It was such a relief when John was warm. I felt soft as marshmallows. As clouds. I felt like the hair that drifts across old ladies' heads. Harmless as fluff.

Ten minutes later, he came bounding back. "White Horse Inn. I called them, and a Georgia Robinson just booked in with her daughter." He stabbed a celebratory fist at the ceiling. "Oh yes."

"You found them? Does this mean you want to drive there?"

"It means I'm sending flowers."

"So, we're not going there anymore?"

"New plan. Give your mom time to calm down." He grinned at me. "Maybe some champagne too. She loves a glass of fizz, right?"

"Why are you sending her presents?"

"A man has the right to spoil his fiancée, doesn't he?"

"But you only buy flowers when you're apologizing."

He looked guilty. I saw it flash across his face. "Now," he said, clapping his hands together, "how's that pasta coming along?"

"What did you do?"

"Come on, Alexandra, are you making supper or not?"

"You told me Mom left because I threw the laptop out the window, but she said on the phone she wasn't upset with me at all."

"Don't start."

"Which means it's your fault."

The slammed look came back in his eyes. "I'm not listening to this."

"Which means you did something so bad she'd rather be in a crap hotel than come home."

"I said that's enough."

Whatever he'd done, he'd get away with it. He just needed to shine his sunny mirrors on her. And when he did that, she'd do anything. Just like I'd been doing all evening.

I was such an idiot.

I wanted to break apart in front of him. I wanted my head to come off and roll across the floor. "What was it?" I said.

"I'm warning you."

"What horrible thing did you do to make her leave?"

He took a step toward me. "You don't know what you're talking about."

"I know Mom's gone. I know she's taken Iris. I know you've pissed her off."

He took another step. *Hit me*, I thought. I wanted a black eye— some evidence to show the world. I'd go to the police and they'd arrest him and lock him away. No one believed words, but they'd believe a bruise.

"Mom'll chuck your flowers in the trash," I said. "She'll swap hotels and tell me where she is, and I'll join her."

"What nonsense you talk, Alexandra. What absolute crap you come out with."

"We'll get Kass to come and we'll change our names and move somewhere new and you'll be all by yourself forever."

"Pathetic." He shook his head very slowly at me. "Absolutely pathetic. I spoke to your mom when I called the hotel. I asked them to put me through to her room and she begged me to let her come back. She was sorry for not letting me speak to Iris, she knew it was wrong. Should she still drive back tonight? she wanted to know. Would I forgive her?"

I grabbed the handle of the frying pan and upended it. Onion, bacon, and oil spattered onto the floor.

"What the hell are you doing?" he bellowed.

I snatched an egg from the counter and hurled it at the window.

"Stop it. Stop it right now."

I swept my arm across the countertop and brought the chopping board, knives, salt, pepper, and all the other eggs crashing down. I pulled a cup from the hooks and lobbed it hard at the wall, where it smashed into pieces.

He grasped me by the arm, eyes blazing. "Stop."

I grabbed another cup and he pushed me down on the rocking chair. I tried to scramble up, but he rammed me down again. "Sit. Stay there."

"I'm not a dog."

"No, you're a spoiled brat."

I threw the cup right at him. He ducked, and I was almost out the kitchen door when he grabbed me again. I pretended he was a crazed stranger who'd broken in, because that was less scary than a man who could make people weak, who could steal their real selves away, who could change brave people into cowards.

I shoved and pushed and kicked. "Get off, get off me."

He gripped both my arms and backed me against the wall in the hallway. "You've done it now."

I was breathing all wrong and my throat ached with tears. I didn't want him to hurt me. He was holding me so hard, squeezing my arms.

"I'm sick of you," he hissed. "So sick of you stomping about demanding attention as if you're the center of the universe."

I didn't want bruises anymore. I didn't want evidence, didn't want him to be holding me there.

"Sick of you breaking stuff. Sick of your temper. Sick of everyone thinking I live with a lunatic."

I wanted to get away from his smoky breath and his eyes all narrow and that look on his face that said, *I will destroy you.*

"You think you can trash the apartment and get away with it? You think it's OK to hurl stuff at my head? Well, it isn't. It's fucking demented."

I closed my eyes to block him out.

On and on he went. I was out of control and everyone thought so. Mom hadn't a clue how to handle me. He knew exactly, and he was going to break me. He was going to prove I had no power in the world and never would. "*I'm* in charge," he spat. "You get it? Now go to your room and fucking calm down."

I asked the dead to help. *Granddad*, I said. *Tell your friends I'll give them anything. I'll give up Kass, give up all hope of love, just help me!*

I thought it. I didn't say it out loud. And the answer came roaring silently back.

Do your monster.

Twenty-Four

AN APOCALYPSE STARTS WITH a change in the smell of the air—a wet dust smell, like rain after weeks of dryness. The light changes too—starting off bright like an overdeveloped photo, then darkening at the edges. A pressure comes next, a kind of tugging like a fish caught on a line, like being pulled toward destiny. People huddle in terrified groups. They whisper, "Is this the end of the world?"

"Yes," I said as I held out my arms for balance, as I tiptoed forward. "But not for you. This is John's apocalypse."

At the almost-end-of-the-branch, just before it would no longer take my weight, I looked out through the leaves at the rows of windows twinkling. Behind each window was a room. I counted two up and three across from the fire escape and found Mom's bedroom, where the blue velvet curtains were still open. It looked very still and dark. Had John noticed I was missing yet?

I leaped from the tree and landed neatly on the wall. Kass and I had done it hundreds of times. But not for years. I jumped down the other side and started walking. The cemetery footpath was worn from dog walkers and cyclists, but I knew the turning where people rarely went. Down there, the trees sounded loud because everything else was quiet. It sounded as if all engines had stopped, all power had gone down. No phones, no radios, no TVs or computers made noise in here. There were scuffling sounds that might be foxes, but could also be rats or even the cold, bright fingers of the dead.

But I wasn't afraid.

If Mom were here, seeing me walk along the path that led away from the main drag, to the very center of the cemetery, she'd say, "Don't do this, Lexi."

I'd take her hand. I'd say, "I know you're not strong, but I'm going to sort this for you."

"Will it hurt?" she'd say.

"I guess you'll miss him at first, but after a while you'll be glad. So, no—it won't hurt much at all."

"I meant him. Will it hurt *him*?"

Wild arum berries contain needle-shaped crystals that irritate the throat and result in difficulty breathing. Stinkweed causes hyperthermia and memory loss before it sends you into a coma. Just touching aconite (the queen of poisons) can result in multiple organ failure.

Granddad warned me never to go near certain plants. But I'd asked his dead friends for help and they were drawing me close.

"Just think, Mom," I'd say, "how uncomplicated John will be when he's dead."

"Yes," she'd say, "I see that. It will be such a relief. Thank you, Lexi, for being braver than anyone else."

"You're welcome," I'd say. "Now go back to the gate and wait for me there."

The gravestones glimmered in the dark. The statues winked at me. Above me, in the trees, magpies cried, their wings like rainbows caught in oil.

Don't be afraid, they called.

"I'm not," I said. "I'm a monster."

When I was a kid I used to wonder about my future. I never imagined it would be like this. I'd turned out to be the scary one. I was the noise. I was the cold.

Out in the world, Cerys was probably working her way down her study plan. Out there, teachers were marking coursework, examiners were setting the papers and sealing them in brown envelopes. Iris would be getting ready for bed. Mom would be raiding the minibar. Soon, there would be a phone call from reception. "Can you come down? There are dozens of flowers here with your name on them."

Names are powerful. Babe, sweetheart, darling.

Pathetic. Bitch. Idiot.

Once, I called the police. I said a woman was in danger and they came. Me and Iris watched the blue light flashing down in the parking lot. We watched a policeman walk slowly up the steps. We listened to the buzzer. When no one answered, the policeman stepped back into the parking lot and looked up at the windows. Me and Iris ducked. I don't know why. A policewoman got out of the car and the pair of them looked up at the windows together. Then they got back in the car and drove away.

A dead rat lay on the cemetery path, its belly torn apart and strings of intestine exposed, the blood dried to black paste in the dust. Farther along, there was a dead pigeon—a mess of matted feathers and a single wing like the dark sail of a child's boat.

The world was a difficult place, Mom said, and we all had our crosses to bear. She didn't buy a newspaper anymore. She switched off the TV when bad things came on. She put a good newsfeed on her phone and read out stories of rescued puppies and people finding Christ's face on a slice of toast.

But you can't avoid bad things by pretending they're not there. You must look the end of the world in the eye.

Names are powerful. *Snakeroot. Nightshade. Hemlock.*

But action is more powerful.

When Kass and me were kids, we played in the cemetery. We knew that even though it was sheltered, it was colder than the streets, the cold came up from the ground and down from the sky. There were no buildings to churn out heat. Only thirty acres of the dead.

"How many dead people are here, do you reckon?" I asked Kass once.

"Thousands," he said.

We tried to imagine it—all those rattling bones, all those grinning skulls.

Once, we made a shelter out of pallets to hide from the wind. Once, we plucked flowers from graves that had loads to share with those who had none. Often, we sat on a bench, simply breathing— feeling special, because we were alive when no one else was. Once, when we finally trailed in too late for supper and John refused to let us eat, so we'd understand what a *fucking boundary* was, Kass said, "Lex put a spell on me."

Bad things happen when you're around, Lex.

That wasn't true, though. The opposite was the truth. Bad things happen when *John's* around.

In stories, if you want a favor from the dead, you have to offer them something special. I'd offered to give up love. Now I had to tell them what I wanted in return.

"Poison," I said. "The strongest you have."

And under the ground, the dead shuffled and sighed. "Are you sure?" they said. "Giving up love is a considerable price to pay."

As I walked, I told them why it mattered. "I wanted him to like me. But that's the wrong thing to want."

I said, "When Mom gets back, she'll do the same, hoping for scraps of warmth. Even though he did something terrible to make her leave in the first place."

The dead shuffled some more and whispered among themselves.

I said, "He'll say she's the love of his life. He'll say they were made for each other and how could she even think of leaving him?"

I said, "She'll smile and soften and tell herself he means it. And when she's safely hooked in, he'll treat her badly all over again. He's like a magician casting spells to mess with people's minds."

"We recommend the common ink cap," the dead whispered. "Consumed with alcohol, they're deadly. It's an easy mistake to make."

I dropped to my knees and combed the grass. I was wearing Kass's coat. I breathed it in. It smelled of leather, which in my memory smelled of him. I could never walk past a market stall selling bags and purses without stopping to breathe.

Kass.

If I hadn't met John, I'd never have met Kass.

Never mind, never mind.

I found twigs and small stones and leaves. But eventually I found a mushroom with an orange umbrella. It looked ancient and rusty. It had grooves running from the center and was covered with a deadly-looking white dust. After one, they were easier to find. They stood around in groups calling me.

Take them, the dead whispered, *and you'll have the power.*

A Third Tale of Love and Death
(But Mostly Death)

ONCE, THERE WAS A girl who plotted to kill the man her mother loved. This was because the girl knew him to be a powerful magician who'd cleverly disguised himself as a handsome prince. Everyone had fallen for his charm and no one except the girl seemed to notice the appalling things he did.

So, one night, when her mother was away, the girl stole out to the local cemetery and asked the dead for help. In return for assistance, she promised to give up love. The dead advised her to gather poisonous mushrooms. She followed their instructions and crept back home to make a deathly brew.

Climbing the stairs to the apartment, the girl was like a wild creature coming in from the night. She smelled different—of earth and cold and the ghostly air of the cemetery. The mushrooms whispered in her pocket and she felt strong.

Soon, she thought, I will live happily ever after.

But when she opened the door, the magician was standing in the hallway as if he'd been there forever, waiting for just this moment.

And he looked calm and powerful, like he knew everything. And fear washed through the girl's bones.

"Where the hell have you been?" he said.

The girl pretended to be sorry. She offered to make him a special breakfast as way of an apology. A mushroom omelet perhaps?

But he clearly didn't trust her an inch. He ordered her to remove her muddy shoes and go to her room and change out of her wet clothes. He handed her a dustpan and broom, a mop, a bucket, and a packet of trash bags and told her to clean up the mess she'd made in the kitchen.

He said, "Wait until your mother hears you went swanning off all night."

"You've heard from her?"

He glanced at his phone. "ETA is ninety-seven minutes, so I suggest you get a move on with that tidying."

"You've got Mom on location tracker?"

He leaned against the wall and folded his arms. He told her that her mother was driving back right *now*, and the clock was ticking. He was going to the bakery to get croissants and they were going to have a family breakfast and the girl would behave properly and sit quietly, and if she didn't do those things, he'd be straight on the phone to the doctor.

"I'll get him to prescribe a sedative," he said. "After your behavior last night, I'm sure he'll agree you need calming down."

"There's nothing wrong with me."

He held out his hand for silence. "I'm going out. Now get tidying."

She didn't bother. She knew it wouldn't matter if the kitchen was a mess once the magician was dead. She'd meet her mother in the parking lot and explain there was a corpse in the apartment and they'd get back in the car and go somewhere lovely. They'd get specialist cleaners to fumigate the place before they moved in again.

The girl waded through broken crockery and smashed eggs to wash the mushrooms under the kitchen tap. She put them in a saucepan with some water, then placed them on the stove and stirred them with a wooden spoon until the water was bubbling. She made a double espresso and poured it in, then whizzed the mixture together with the milk frother. She strained out the lumps before adding two spoonfuls of brown sugar and a glug of whiskey because the ink caps were only toxic when consumed with alcohol.

She went to the living room and looked down at the parking lot. Her head hurt, and the light outside seemed too bright for an April morning. She thought of her mother and sister driving closer and she thought of how much her sister loved the magician (who was her father by blood). Every time he wanted to smoke he sent this youngest child from the room, and each time the little girl patted him on the head like a dog and told him smoking was bad for him. "Give up," she'd say. "There's a good boy."

The girl shook these thoughts from her head and went back to the kitchen and looked at the coffee again. The kitchen was her favorite room in the apartment because it was the place she'd spent most time with her mother before the magician turned up. It was here that the girl used to make up stories and act them out. She was a wonderful actress, and in another, different life, she could have become famous and gone to Hollywood. But her role was to kill the magician, and for that she'd probably go to jail.

She checked the living room window again—nothing. She checked the time.

"Come on," she whispered. "Hurry up. I can't kill you in front of them."

She got the cream out of the fridge. The spoon was supposed to be cold to make the cream pour, so she put two ice cubes in a cup and watched them thaw.

She went back to the living room. No car. No magician. She would've texted him, but he'd broken her phone. She jumbled the cushions and untied the curtains. She stood on the chairs one after the other. She hid his ashtray behind a book and pocketed his lighter. These were small things, but they passed the time.

Finally, his car came through the gate and she ran to pour the coffee. She drizzled cream across the back of the icy spoon, so it pooled like white velvet. Her hands were shaking as she came out of the kitchen and shut the door behind her.

When the magician walked in, she was sitting in the living room with the cup on a silver coaster. She looked innocent, like a fairy-tale daughter. She was a wonderful actress after all.

"Hello," she murmured, "I've made you a lovely warming drink."

His cheeks were red, and he had the cold of outdoors upon him. He was carrying a bouquet of white roses and a large paper bag with ribbons for handles. "Not bad for early morning shopping, eh?"

He sat opposite her and emptied the things from the bag onto the table—chocolates, a selection of pastries, a bottle of champagne, and a card that had a picture of a key on the front with the words *the key to my heart*. He grinned at the girl. "What do you reckon?"

She thought of the key in that Bluebeard story that opened a door where he kept his dead wives. Bluebeard discovered his new wife had peeked, because the key bled.

She thought of her mother coming back to these gifts, smiling at the magician's effort. Her smile would be reluctant at first, but soon he'd cast his spell on her and she'd be back to keen and shiny, wanting to see the best in him.

"Here," the girl said. "Drink this delicious coffee."

He leaned back on his chair. "You trying to win me over, so I don't grass you up about going AWOL all night?"

"I'm trying to show my appreciation for all that you do for us."

He shook his head as if she was a simpleton. She knew what he thought—that he'd frightened her enough to keep her under his control forever. Well, let him think that if it made him drink the poison. She slid the coaster across the table like the most tender of waitresses. "I'm sorry about being such a difficult person to live with."

He looked suspiciously at the cup. "What is this?"

"Irish coffee. It's got whiskey and cream in it."

He hunched forward and sniffed. "You sure that's all it's got in it?"

"What else could there be?"

"It smells very strange."

In "Snow White," the witch eats half the apple when the girl gets suspicious. "Give it here," the girl said, sliding the coaster back.

"Be my guest."

She picked it up and breathed it in. It smelled of sugar and fallen leaves. She took the smallest sip of cream. Cream wouldn't kill her. The magician watched her with eyes the same color as his son's.

Ah, yes—the magician's son . . .

He was the girl's downfall. She'd accepted the magician in her life for years because he'd brought his beautiful son with him. The girl could put up with any number of terrible things to be close to such a boy. But now the son had gone away and all she had left was horror.

Now the magician said, "When your mom gets back, things are going to change."

The girl took another small sip. "What things?"

"You'll see."

She slid the cup back. "It's not so bad."

The magician picked it up with both hands. "You think she'll like her gifts?"

"She'll love them. You're very clever. She's lucky to have you."

He nodded in agreement as his hands lifted the cup.

The hands that ruffled the hair of the boy she loved.

The hands that cradled her sister.

The hands that caressed the mother and made her swoon.

The girl's grandfather had warned her never to touch wild mushrooms. He'd known someone who died from eating the wrong ones. The guy had got cramps and started throwing up. Then his throat constricted, his head got hot, his mouth got salty, and then he'd started spewing blood. After that, his liver shut down and he fell in a coma and died. "No antidote," Granddad had said. "Even if you go to the hospital, there's nothing they can do."

The girl watched the cup make the journey to the magician's mouth. The mouth that told the son how proud he was of him, that kissed the mother, that blew raspberries against the sister's neck while she squealed with laughter.

How long would it take him to die?

The girl checked the time. Her mother and sister would be where? Did they come back through the Blackwall Tunnel? She imagined her sister doing what she always did and trying to hold her breath for the length of it. She and Mom seemed so frail under all that water. The girl imagined it inky and cold above their heads.

"Don't drink it," she said.

The magician looked at her. "What?"

"I can't give up love."

"What are you talking about?"

"I love too many people. I can't just stop. I'm not cruel like you."

"Don't be so rude," the magician said.

The girl picked up the poisoned drink, opened the window, and threw it out.

She was afraid, shivering. She'd come so close to being just like him—to having a heart that couldn't love. To having eyes that saw nothing but their own reflection and a mind that never once inquired how it might feel to be anyone else.

She ran from the room. The magician called after her, but she crashed out of the door and down the stairs and away.

Twenty-Five

BEN LAUGHED WHEN I told him I'd tried to kill John. "Yeah, right."

"Serious, I poisoned his coffee."

My scalp prickled as he stared at me in horror. I stared back at him for what seemed like hours. Don't be afraid of me, I thought.

"He didn't drink it, though?" Ben said.

"I kept thinking how upset Iris would be."

"I'll take that as a no." He moved to one side. "You want to come in?"

He led me through to the kitchen. The clock ticked merrily away and the light through the window was butter yellow. "Why is your house so holy?" I said.

"Holy?"

"Peaceful and good, like a Christmas story."

"Are you high right now?" Ben said.

I turned round and smiled for him. It was hard to summon one up, but I didn't want him to throw me out. Where else would I go?

He peered at me. "Honestly, you look kind of wild."

I smiled at his pretty red hair that shone like chestnuts and I smiled at his freckles that seemed dabbed on with a pencil and I told him I'd spent the night in the cemetery communing with the dead and they'd advised me how to kill John and I'd picked poisonous mushrooms and put them in his coffee, but basically, I was fine.

"Shit, Lex—are you serious?"

I liked him being so concerned. I wanted to shiver under all his lovely attention. "I'm not entirely sure I picked the right ones. A lot of ink caps are edible. Do you think that'll be a point in my favor when I get arrested?"

"No one's going to arrest you. John didn't drink it, you said. Does he even suspect anything?"

"I threw his coffee out of the window. That's pretty suspicious."

"It doesn't make you a killer." He looked at me curiously. "All night in the cemetery? Didn't anyone wonder where you were?"

"My mom's in Brighton, remember?"

He made a noise like an angry sigh. "And John just let you go?"

"Let me? I didn't tell him. In fact, I ran out. If you asked him if he knew where I was, he'd say no and that he was very worried about me. But he'd be lying." I sat on the sofa and sank back into the cushions. There were strange shadows on his ceiling—one looked like a face and the other was a dancing bird. I had to close my eyes when the face grew horns and the bird began to shrivel.

Ben came and sat next to me. "Have you got your phone back? Do you want me to get my mom to call yours?"

"Why? You want me to go home?"

"I thought you might like to know where your mom is."

"Well, where's *your* mom? Maybe she's run off too." I waved a hand at the room. "If someone isn't in front of you, they could be anywhere, right?"

"I guess. Though I'm pretty sure my mom's around the corner buying milk."

I was so envious I had to stamp my feet on the carpet and try not to imagine Meryam carrying a basket around the local shop choosing delicious things for Ben's breakfast.

"Well, that's nice," I said. "Aren't you lucky?"

He smiled uncertainly, like he agreed, but didn't want to say so because it would be rude to compare our lives. Minutes slipped by as the kitchen clock kept ticking.

"Lex," Ben said eventually, and his Bambi legs almost touched mine as he turned to face me on the sofa. "Why were you trying to poison John?"

I knew what he wanted, but there was no point giving it to him. Every time I'd tried to explain what John did, people found excuses. Even Meryam couldn't cope.

"Do you remember," I said, "when we went to Portugal?"

Ben shook his head.

"My mom called your mom and said we were having a shit vacation because John flew home in a rage and left us in the hotel by ourselves. So, you and your mom got on a plane and came to join us. There was a pool with a slide, you remember that? And a table tennis table. And a lizard lived on the balcony and your mom chased it with a broom and it bit her."

He smiled. "It's coming back to me now."

"Your mom came all that way to be with us. That's a sign of friendship, isn't it? That's a sign of something good." I swallowed. My mouth tasted sour. "Last week, I told your mom we needed her, but she wouldn't help. You know why? Because she's afraid of what goes on with John at the apartment."

"Lex," he said gently, "what *does* go on with John? I don't actually know what you mean."

I pulled my feet up onto the sofa and hugged my knees. I wished more than anything for a power where I could touch Ben and he'd know everything without me speaking at all.

"Tell me to shut up if you want," Ben said, "but does John hit your mom?"

I shook my head.

"Does he throw things or break stuff?"

"He broke my phone. But he's never done anything like that before. It's usually me who throws stuff."

"Is it a money thing?" Ben said. "Does he try and control you by being the only one with cash?"

Words took shape in me. But they were slippery, like fish in a bucket. They kept writhing and sliding over one another. Would Ben believe that John blocks out all that's good in me, like a cloud over the sun? That he makes me afraid. Makes me clumsy. I drop things when he's watching. I lose words around him, feel stupid saying things in front of him, forget everything I'm supposed to remember. I don't do these things on purpose or with anyone else.

"He never stops," I said. "He just never stops."

"Never stops what?" Ben said. "Shit, Lex, are you talking about . . . ?" His voice had a tone I'd never heard before. I looked at him to see what it meant. He looked furious and terrified all at once and I knew he meant sex. "If he's laid a finger on you . . ."

"He hasn't. He hates me. He'd rather chop his hands off."

"Then what?"

How could I speak when there were so many words? I could have vomited words all over Meryam's carpet. John did things that hurt Mom and made me furious, so I looked like a monster and everyone said I overreacted and why couldn't I just calm down? And when I looked back at the thing he did to make me angry in the first place, it didn't seem so bad and I believed everyone was right about me.

"Lex?" Ben said. "What does he do?"

The room stepped sideways, and my blood thickened. "Get your camera."

"What?"

I turned to him and grabbed his hand. "I want you to film me."

"Why?"

"You wanted to do a media project together, didn't you?"

"Is it a good idea to do it now?"

"It's a great idea." I could hear my own breathing like the tide gathering. "I want never to forget."

"Forget what?"

"What he does. Who he really is. For years I've caught glimpses, but last night I saw it completely. He has these smiles that he uses like drugs or rewards so everyone wants one. And he does this hot-cold thing, so you never know what's going to happen next.

One minute you're an idiot and the next you're amazing. He doesn't let Mom have friends or a job or a bank account, and if she complains he calls her names and threatens to take Iris away. He made me sign a behavior contract and he's stuck it on the fridge. He's forcing us to sell the apartment and he's in charge of the TV and Wi-Fi and phones, and he has a safe where he locks stuff when we annoy him. Please, Ben, film me. Why aren't you filming me?"

"Because this is making me really uncomfortable."

"Your mom didn't like it either. But I have to say it before it dis-appears. That's his best trick—making you forget what he does, so you trust him again." I grabbed his hand. "He sent me to a doctor and now he's going to sedate me."

"That's ridiculous."

"That's what I'm trying to tell you. If he drugs me, there'll be no one to protect Mom and Iris."

"He can't sedate you. That's fucking nuts."

"Don't feel sorry for me."

"I don't," he said simply. "I feel angry."

"He's never hit me, never laid a finger on my mom. It's a quiet thing he does, a smoke-and-mirrors thing. He takes away every-thing good inside you and replaces it with fear. You wanted to make a film about fear, didn't you? Well, make it about the private things John does. Because nobody sees them, and nobody believes them, and nobody wants to hear about them."

"I do," Ben said.

"Then get your camera."

I didn't notice Meryam walk in and drop her bags on the carpet. "What's going on?"

"Shit," Ben said. "Terrible timing, Mom."

"Why?" she said. "What's the matter? Lex, why are you here so early?"

"I poisoned John."

Ben flicked her a look. "She didn't."

Meryam said, "Is she drunk?"

"Please," Ben said, "don't worry."

"Is she stoned?"

He turned and frowned at her. "She's wired, that's all. She spent the night in the cemetery."

Meryam softened. She came rushing over and put her arm around me. "Why didn't you come here?" she said.

Meryam stroked my hair and I liked it so much that I crumpled into her. I felt like a pet. I wanted to be her cat so it would always be like this.

"You can come round here anytime," she said. "Did John know you were out all night?"

"I didn't tell him. I trashed the kitchen and ran off."

Meryam cringed away from me. "You trashed it?"

"It's all right," I said. "It was self-defense."

"I should call your mom. She's on her way home, you know that?"

"Yeah, John bribed her."

"I think she was worried about how upset you were on the phone last night."

I shook my head. "I think she was flattered he spent a fortune on flowers."

"I'm still going to call her."

"Fine. She'll need a friend when I tell her John's an evil magician."

"What?"

"Nothing," Ben said. "She's wired, I told you. Mom, can you stay out of this?"

"No, Ben, I can't. I've spoken to Lex's mom a few times over the last twenty-four hours, so I think I know a bit about what's going on. Shouldn't you be making Lex a hot drink if she's been out in the cold?"

Ben was a good and obedient boy and he did what his mother wished, but I felt his thoughtful gaze on me and I knew our story wasn't finished. We could make a video and send it to the television stations or the newspapers. I'd seen movies where that happened.

I walked to the window while Meryam went away to make her call and I breathed on the glass and ran my finger through the condensation and made a snake. Then I made a flower. Ben said, "I'll believe every word if you ever want to tell me, Lex."

It was the best thing anyone had ever said to me. Better than Kass saying I was distracting, because maybe he said that to lots of girls. I turned from the window to tell Ben how much his words mattered, when Meryam came back looking stern.

"Your mom's stuck in traffic," she said. "I've told John you're here and I've offered to take you home. He says he'd appreciate some help tidying the kitchen."

She'd spoken to John and she'd changed. Her face was set in a sharp line. She put her palm flat against my cheek and made me look at her. "What did you put in his coffee, Lex?"

Here it comes, I thought. This is where I get arrested. "Well," I said, "it's complicated . . ."

"Laxative," Ben said, coming up behind me and putting a hand on my shoulder. "John was being a prick."

Meryam looked horrified. "You can't do that to people. That's a terrible thing to do."

Not as terrible as poison.

"She didn't go through with it, Mom." Ben squeezed my shoulder conspiratorially. "Even though he deserved it."

Meryam looked at us both uncertainly and then she nodded. "I'll talk to him, explain you were upset. Come on, let's go and help tidy up and then I'll take the two of you to school."

"Don't abandon us, Meryam," I said. "Mom doesn't have any other friends."

Meryam shook her head very slowly. "I have no intention of abandoning you."

Twenty-Six

ME AND IRIS SAT on the pillar by the front steps and swung our legs and stared at things—cars on the road, people walking past, the newsdealers getting a delivery, the traffic lights changing color. It was comforting watching ordinary things.

I said, "Did you have a good time in Brighton?"

"Not really."

"What did you do all day?"

"Sat in a café. Went for a walk. Got wet in the rain."

I know it was wrong to be glad about how boring it sounded, but I was.

"I didn't have proper clothes," Iris said. "I had to wear my pajamas all day. It was embarrassing."

"Still, at least you were together."

We let that hang for a bit, because however dull it had been, Iris was the chosen one.

"When Mom started driving out of London, what did she say?" I asked. "I mean, it must've been weird being told you weren't going to school. How did she explain it?"

"She said it was a day trip."

"So, how did she explain the fact I wasn't coming with you?"

"She said you wouldn't want to."

That made my throat go tight. "That's crap. She never even asked. I woke up in the morning and you were just gone."

Iris shook her head miserably. "I didn't want to go. It wasn't fun. We never did anything nice, and when we got to the stupid hotel, Mom was on her phone all the time."

"Who with?"

"Meryam. Talking secrets."

"What secrets?"

Iris shrugged and banged her heels against the pillar. She bit her lip. She fiddled with the hole in the knee of her jeans.

"What were they talking about, Iris?"

She gave me a look. It was the kind of look that said she knew things she shouldn't know, and she really wanted to tell me but thought she probably shouldn't.

"Tell me quietly," I said. "And then it won't really count."

She banged her heels some more and faked interest in the traffic beyond the gate.

"You'll wreck your sneakers doing that. Come on, stop being a pain and tell me what Mom was saying to Meryam. Was it about me?"

"It was about my dad."

"What about him?" I watched her take a breath and let it out again. "Honestly, Iris, there's nothing your dad could do that would freak me out."

"He's got a girlfriend."

"He's fucking what?"

Iris closed her eyes, leaned forward, and rested her head on her knees. "He's got a girlfriend and Mom found out." She opened one eye and peeked at me. "And now they're getting married."

"Whoa! Your dad's marrying his girlfriend?"

"He's marrying Mom, but sooner than before. Like next month or something."

"Why would they still be getting married when he's got a girlfriend?"

Iris flinched. "It's Dad's last chance," she said to her knees. "He's done it before with other girlfriends. Please don't be mad."

"He's a serial cheat and she's still marrying him! If he's been seeing other women, Mom needs to dump him, not marry him. I'm not going to any fucking wedding now."

"You have to."

"I don't have to do anything."

Iris sat up. "Mom said you'd be like this. She told Meryam if you ever found out, you'd go crazy."

"Well, she was right about that. What girlfriend anyway? What's her name?"

"Monika."

I jumped off the pillar and stalked around the parking lot. I wanted to break something, so I kicked the hubcaps on John's car. He was having an affair with the intern and Mom was upstairs snuggled in his arms? None of it made sense.

I stalked back to the pillar. "Are you making this up?"

Iris shook her head and rammed her thumb in her mouth.

"When Mom was on the phone talking to Meryam, where were you?"

"Watching a broken TV."

"Take your thumb out of your mouth. Did she know you were listening?"

"No, and I wish I'd never told you. You're being scary."

I leaned closer, so she could feel my breath on her cheek. "I can be scarier."

She squeaked and pushed me away, laughing. "You're mean."

"Not to you, though. Never to you." I gave her a quick kiss. "Listen, I need to talk to Mom about this because she's clearly lost her mind, so is it OK if I tell her you heard her on the phone?"

"She's going to announce about the wedding."

"But not the bit about the girlfriends. She's going to hide that from everyone because it'll make her look like an idiot. Can I tell her you told me about that?"

Iris nodded and shoved her thumb back in her mouth. I paced the parking lot again, trying to work things out. Mom found out about Monika and ran off. This wasn't John's first offense, so she probably threatened to leave him forever and he panicked. He needed something more impressive than flowers to win her back, so he moved up the wedding. He'd have made all sorts of promises about commitment and monogamy and Mom fell for it. He'd treated her badly for years in all sorts of ways, but it was an affair that got her to react.

Maybe John having a girlfriend was exactly what I needed to get rid of him?

As I was kicking his hubcaps again, Iris ran over to me and held her hand out, fist closed. "I've got something for you. Want to see?"

She opened her fist finger by finger. It made me think of a flower unfurling. In her palm was the necklace from John's safe—the string of precious rubies that my granddad bought his wife as a true love gift.

Iris tipped it into my hand. It was warm from hers. "I took it when no one was looking."

I said it was the bravest thing she'd ever done. I told her I'd cherish it forever. I told her that if I got caught with it, I'd say I'd stolen it myself. I kissed her all over the top of her lovely head.

"While you were away," I said, "I decided that the only way to survive is not to lose my ability to love. You know, despite the bad guys."

She blinked at me. "What does that mean?"

"It means that I will always love and protect you." I smiled at her. It felt like the truest thing I'd ever said.

Twenty-Seven

"I'VE NEVER BEEN SO certain of anything," Mom said. "It's wonderful to finally have a date for the wedding."

"Your fiancé just betrayed you with the intern. Why doesn't that break your heart? Why aren't you throwing furniture? Why aren't we changing the locks?"

"I'm not saying it doesn't hurt, Lex, because clearly it does. But please calm down. This isn't about you."

She was sorting clothes on the bed and I was leaning against the window watching. I couldn't bear to be any nearer than that. She'd cried when I told her I knew about Monika, bowed her head, said what a fool she'd felt when she found out. I told her I knew he'd done it before with other women and she said, yes, he had, but it wasn't happening again. "Last chance," she said. "We all need one of those."

I said she should kick him out. I said she was beautiful and worth a million Johns. How much more crap was she willing to put up with?

"Adult relationships are complicated," she said, dabbing at her tears with balled-up tissues. "And the only reason I'm talking about it now is because you already know. I would've done anything to keep this away from you and Iris."

I said he was a womanizer and could never be trusted. But she didn't want to hear. She collected up her tissues and threw them in the trash.

Now she picked through clothes to categorize them—charity, chuck, and keep. It was a technique she'd read about to clear bad karma and welcome a positive future. Stuff for the charity shop was folded into a suitcase, things to keep went back in the wardrobe, and the rest got flung in a heap on the floor. She said, "Did you know that John has never felt properly accepted into this family?"

"He lives here, doesn't he? You gave birth to his daughter. How much more accepted does he want to be?"

"Maybe I should've changed my name. Or signed over the deed to the apartment."

"That can't be a rule! You can't force someone to give up everything."

"It's not a rule. I'm just saying. Getting married will be the start of a new commitment. We're going to be a proper family—for richer or poorer."

"Well, I'm not changing my name."

"Oh, Lex." She looked forlorn, holding some tatty cardigan to her chest. "You won't seem included if you don't."

"I don't want to be included."

She threw the cardigan on the chuck pile. She held up a bathrobe, then folded it into the charity suitcase. Next were her blue-checked pajamas. I'd forgotten them. She used to wear them on long-ago movie nights. If I grabbed them and held them close, I bet they'd smell of ancient perfume and maybe a hint of popcorn.

I hated watching her throw the past away and be excited about the future. John and Iris had gone to the park. He was being the perfect father and fiancé now. He wouldn't be able to keep it up, though. Mom had been back from Brighton for four days and that was already pushing his limit.

I said, "People don't change overnight."

"John's made a promise to me, Lex, and I believe him."

"You took Iris away. He'd promise anything to get her back."

"That's a horrible thing to say." She looked at me, her eyes filling with tears again. "He loves me. And I love him. I miss him whenever we're apart. That means something, doesn't it?"

"People miss heroin, Mom. That isn't the point."

"Then what is the point, Lex?"

Name it. Tell her.

But it felt terrifying to say she was weak. What would she do? How could I say she'd let John get too powerful and that she was supposed to protect us? I knew what it was like to fall under his spell. Hadn't I spent an evening in Mom's slippers and apron trying to please him?

"The point is, maybe you shouldn't rush into things. Have you asked Iris what she thinks? Because she seems pretty upset about the whole girlfriend thing."

"I think you'll find your sister's excited about being a bridesmaid."

And even though there was no way I wanted Mom to get married, I felt a small prick of disappointment that no one had mentioned me being a bridesmaid.

"You can't get rid of that," I said, leaping across the room and snatching up the scarf she'd just lobbed on the throwaway pile. "I made you that."

She picked it up and held it out. "You glued two pieces of material together. You were five."

"So?"

"I bet you'd forgotten it even existed until now. You want me to keep it?"

"I want you to *want* to keep it." I took it from her and held it close. "What will become of me if you throw my childhood away?"

"These are just things, Lex. What will happen is that you'll grow older and make new memories and none of this will feel so bad." She smiled. "You'll study. You'll pass your exams, stay on at school, and go to college. One day, you'll get a job. You've got your whole future ahead." She packed the lid down on the charity suitcase and rammed it shut and clicked it.

Seeing her shut that case made something rear up in me.

Weeks ago, I'd asked Cerys for advice and she'd told me to be nicer. I'd begged Meryam for help and she'd refused. Kass had run away to Manchester. And now, even though John cheated on her, Mom was giving him a last chance. Maybe I was cursed? Whenever I spoke about John, people refused to listen. If I went to the police station and made a formal complaint, they'd probably give him an award or make him chief inspector.

I walked back to the window and looked out at the yard, the tree, the wall, the clouds. The wedding was in just over three weeks. And I had to stop it happening. Words didn't cut it. They didn't make the slightest difference.

But Mom giving John one last chance gave me an idea.

Twenty-Eight

I CYCLED TO JOHN'S office on Ben's bike and loitered at the edge of the parking lot. I was wearing sunglasses and had my hair tucked into a hoodie. I didn't want John looking out the window and recognizing me. When I told Ben what I was doing, he said I was the most courageous person he knew and asked to come. I told him if he really wanted to help he should call the office at exactly 4:00 p.m. and ask for Monika.

"Tell her there's a florist's delivery for her out in the parking lot."

"Will she fall for it?" he said.

I didn't know, but there was no way I was going into reception, and since I didn't have a phone, my options were limited. I just hoped Monika thought that a bouquet of flowers might be from John and worth coming down for.

When I saw her exit the swing doors and innocently gaze around the parking lot, I felt fierce like a wasp. This woman hurt my mom. It was her fault Mom scarpered to Brighton, her fault Iris spent the day in her pj's listening to Mom cry and her fault I was here now. But it's easy to blame the women. "John's fault," I muttered. I swallowed my fury, slapped a smile on my face, and cycled across the tarmac toward her.

I could see why John liked her. She was prettier in daylight. Maybe twenty-five, dewy fresh skin, her hair loose and shiny.

"Hi," I said, braking in front of her. "Remember me?"

She blushed to the roots of her lovely hair. "Hey," she said. "If you're after your dad, he just left."

"He's not my dad and it's you I want. Oh, and the flowers were a lie by the way."

She bit her lip and looked at the ground. "Did your mom send you?"

I almost felt sorry for her. I knew what it was like to be the other woman. But I also felt bold because she didn't dare look at me. "I want to ask you something," I said. "I'm not out for revenge or anything—but are you still seeing him?"

She shuffled her feet. She looked unbearably awkward. "You should talk to your dad about this."

"He's not my dad."

She looked up, met my gaze. Her eyes were brown, flecked with gold. "Why do you keep saying that?"

"Listen, I *want* you to still be seeing him. If you are, I can go home and tell my mom and she'll throw him out and you get to keep him. It's a win-win situation."

She looked away again, back toward the building. "I should go."

"My mom's given him one more chance. Just one. This isn't the first time he's cheated. So, if you just say the word, you can genuinely keep him."

"Not the first time?"

I felt the spark of elation that comes with giving someone information that changes their life forever. "You didn't know?"

She folded her arms and shivered. "As I said—you need to talk to your dad. I mean, to John, or whatever you call him . . ."

She turned away and I knew she'd be no help now. In fact, I'd probably made things worse, because if they *were* still seeing each other, she might dump him now she knew she was part of a pattern.

"Monika," I said. It was weird saying her name out loud. "Did he invite you to the wedding?"

She turned on the step. "The whole office was invited, but . . ."

"You should totally come."

She frowned. "Why would you say that?"

I smiled in what I hoped was a mysterious fashion and cycled off.

✱

Cerys was next on my list. She was in her yard wrapped in a blanket like she'd been rescued from a fire. She'd been ill a lot since the party, she said. She kept getting sore throats and upset stomachs. She told me her dad had threatened to box Kass's ears if he ever saw him again.

"I just wish he'd let me know one way or the other," she said. "It's like he doesn't want me, but he doesn't want to let me go either."

"Why are you waiting for Kass to decide? What do *you* want?"

Cerys simply shrugged. "I want him not to break up with me."

I felt guilty then. If I didn't want to be like John, then surely I had to stop trying to steal Cerys's boyfriend? But I pushed the thought away, because Kass and me were true love and John and his affairs were painful and wrong.

"I've got just the thing to cheer you up," I said. "You're going to help me wreck the wedding."

"No way!"

I settled down on the grass next to her and told her John was having an affair, but Mom was marrying him anyway. I told her Mom had given him one last chance and I needed him to use it.

Cerys frowned at me suspiciously. "What's this got to do with me?"

"I want you to invite him out for a drink. Then, when he makes a pass at you, you have to record it on your phone and send me the video."

"That's the worst idea you've ever had."

"OK, how about plan B? You invite him for an evening out and bring your friends. Really pretty ones with long legs and swishy hair and tell them to flirt with him and film his responses. That leaves you in the clear."

Cerys pulled her blanket more tightly around her. "I'm not doing any of this, Lex."

I told her the story of Bluebeard to try and convince her. I explained how a young woman fell for his charm even though she was afraid of him. "She wanted a fancy castle and some pretty clothes, so she stopped listening to the part of herself that told her to run."

"Why is this relevant?"

"She's like my mom. We need to rescue her."

Cerys picked up one of her exam books with a sigh. "Well, tell your mom if she doesn't use the key and go in the forbidden room, she'll be just fine."

"But in the story, going in the room saves the woman. She finds out her husband's a murdering brute who killed all his other wives. Surely, it's better to know?"

"Your mom already knows John's faults."

"She's not listening to her get-the-hell-away-from-him voice. She thinks John's going to change if they get married."

"Maybe he will?"

It was useless. Cerys's broken heart had sapped all her strength. I told her I'd come and see her again soon. I'd bring her some grapes, I said, or an energy drink.

As I was leaving, I turned at the door. I said, "Cerys, if anyone ever tells you to stay out of a room, I hope you know that's exactly why you should look inside."

She gave me a small smile. "I wish I was more like you, Lex. Let me know if you hear from Kass, yeah?"

✳

By the time I got home, Monika had, of course, told John about my parking lot visit. I'd had a vague hope she might be into female solidarity, but clearly not. John grabbed me as I came in. "A word?"

He made me follow him to his study and sat me on the sofa and glared at me with his wicked eyes. "Alexandra, are you trying to wreck the wedding?"

I shook my head, played dumb.

He leaned in, lowered his voice. "You might think it's funny to put laxative in my coffee, you might even think it's funny to go to my office and confront my colleague, but I guarantee you won't think it's funny when I add it all to your rap sheet."

I kept quiet, tried to slow my pulse.

"Dr. Leaman's contacting your teachers, did I tell you? The more input the better. Then he can make his diagnosis."

"A diagnosis of what?" I used my innocent voice.

"Don't push your fucking luck with me, Alexandra."

I sat back in the seat and stared at him unblinking.

"I love your mother," he said. "This Monika woman means nothing to me."

But I didn't believe his lies anymore. It was as if I'd smashed some magical mirror and now, whenever I looked at him, I saw right through the golden smile.

He said, "I'm guessing you think it was insensitive that I invited her to the wedding. But it would look odd if I'd left her out, wouldn't it? It would get everyone at the office talking."

I didn't say anything.

"She won't come. She knows not to. No need to upset your mom with any of this."

*

When I was a child, I used to fall asleep in the same bed as my mother. She'd wrap me in her arms and hold me close, our legs entwined. I couldn't tell where I ended, and she began. I felt safe listening to her beating heart. If I woke in the night, I'd fall straight back to sleep knowing she was close. There was nothing that could hurt me, nothing she couldn't protect me from.

Of course, Mom cried when I told her John had invited his lover to the wedding. But he came running and did his big charm act. He explained how he hadn't wanted the gossip that would accompany leaving Monika out, didn't want rumors tainting the day, was certain she wouldn't come and even if she did, he'd ensure she'd be seated as far away from Mom as possible. It was like watching the cogs of a very expensive watch spin and whir. He held Mom's hand, pledged his love, promised to protect her from pain.

"I'm so disappointed Alexandra felt the need to stir this up," he said. "I hate seeing you hurt."

To me, privately, he said, "You just reached the end of the road."

He dragged me back to his study and made me sit there as he jabbed at the screen on his phone. He told Dr. Leaman the severity of my symptoms was increasing. He was worried I had other psychiatric conditions as well—a personality disorder, perhaps? Or a social phobia? "Listen, mate," he said. "Could you fit her in for an urgent appointment? We're struggling to cope here."

*

The next day, he took Mom clothes shopping to cheer her up. My punishment was to stay in the apartment and look after Iris. I set her up with a movie in her bedroom and settled down in the living room with the landline.

My blood was pounding as I called the town hall inquiry line. I told the woman who answered that I'd like to cancel my wedding booking. She said she was sorry to hear that and was I aware that the ceremony fee was nonrefundable? I said that was fine and she asked for my reference number. When I told her I'd lost it she got all guarded and insisted she needed it for verification purposes. I panicked and told her I'd call back.

I went into Mom's bedroom and plunged my face into one of her scarves to feel close to her and remind myself why I was doing this. I was *not* the worst daughter in the universe. This was for Mom's own good. One day she'd thank me.

I took a few deep breaths and put the scarf away. I went back to the living room and called the Crate & Barrel gift list department and explained I wanted all the presents returned to guests with a note saying the wedding was off. The man who answered the phone said that wasn't possible. He asked for my list number, my name, and the date of the event. He sounded very suspicious.

Maybe lots of people tried to ruin weddings?

Next, I called the restaurant where the reception was being held, but it turned out the manager knew John personally. "Is this Monika?" he said.

I banged the phone down. I was running out of options.

I called Kass to see if he had any ideas and after establishing that, yes, my mom had come back and, yes, his dad was a serial cheat, he said I should let them get on with their own sorry lives and stay out of their wedding plans. "Two years," he said, "that's all you've got to get through before you can leave."

"Actually," I told him, "I can leave at sixteen. And that's in two days."

I could hear him smile. "Happy soon-to-be-birthday, Lexi. What should I get you?"

I liked it when he used his soft voice with me. "How about a train ticket to Manchester?"

"Sure," he said, "when your dastardly plot to destroy the wedding goes wrong, just come on up."

I didn't push it, didn't ask if he really meant it. I just let his words fill me and then said I'd speak to him soon because I had an evil plan to be getting on with.

He laughed. I loved his laugh. "You always did walk your talk, Lex."

I was full of light as I called the florist. I walked my talk. That meant he fancied me and thought I was brave. The florist was sympathetic when I told her I needed to cancel a wedding bouquet because the groom was having an affair with his intern. She offered to speak to her manager and try and get my deposit returned. All she needed was my customer reference number.

Iris sidled in. "What are you doing?"

I slapped the phone down. "Shit, Iris, don't creep up on people like that."

"Why are you canceling Mom's flowers?"

I said I wasn't and she said I was fibbing. I said, all right, then, I was, but it was none of her business and she said she'd tell Mom unless I came clean. I made us hot chocolate with cream and marshmallows while I thought about what to tell her. She sat in the rocking chair and watched me with serious eyes.

When I'd made the drinks, I sat on the floor at her feet. I said, "Your dad doesn't make Mom happy."

"Because of his girlfriends?"

"Yeah, but also because he's mean."

"He's not mean to me."

"No, he loves you."

"He loves Mommy."

"He also puts her down a lot and makes her cry."

Iris plugged her thumb in her mouth and looked away. I wasn't telling her anything she didn't know, but it felt like I was breaking her heart. We sat there for minutes with the sun making stripes on the kitchen floor, neither of us touching our drinks.

"Hey, Iris," I said. "Do you know the difference between good girls and badass ones?"

She unplugged her thumb. "Is it a joke?"

"Not a joke. So, in stories, the good girls obey all the rules, don't they? Like Cinderella does the housework and Snow White looks after the dwarves. But terrible things happen, even though they're nice. Cinderella's bullied and starved. Snow White's nearly murdered and falls into a coma."

Iris frowned. "Red Riding Hood gets chased by a wolf."

"Exactly! Rapunzel gets stuffed in a tower. Jasmine gets locked in a castle. Now, can you think of any badass girls in stories? Ones who break the rules and don't care about being good?"

I loved watching her face brighten. "Like Mulan?"

"Great example. She fights for her honor and saves loads of people's lives. Anyone else?"

"Merida!"

"Yep, another good one. She prefers archery and horses to dresses, and there's Tiana, of course. She opens her own restaurant and saves Prince Naveen. They're hard-core. They don't hang around waiting to be rescued, do they? They rescue others."

I told her the stories of clever girls, like Gerda, who saved her friend from the Snow Queen, and Gretel, who shoved a witch in an oven to free Hansel. "They didn't obey the rules, do you see? If they had, the boys would have died."

I told her that this was why I'd been canceling the flowers. I was badass. I was breaking the rules to rescue Mom.

She went quiet again. "You'll get into trouble," she said eventually.

"I don't mind."

Her eyes filled with tears. "It'll make Daddy mad."

"I don't mind that either." I made my arms into a wrestling pose and gritted my teeth to make her laugh, but it didn't work.

"In some stories," she said, her voice wobbling, "the princess gets married and lives happily ever after, even when it starts off scary."

"Like in 'Beauty and the Beast'?"

She nodded, wiping her eyes. "And the one with the bear."

I used to believe in magical transformations—kissing a frog turns him into a prince, being kind to a wounded bear stops him killing you—but it was too late for John. There was no way that marriage was going to turn him into anything new.

I hated seeing Iris upset. It was tough being a good girl. Girls like Cerys and Iris had their own burdens—wanting everyone to get along, smiling and being polite all over the place, desperate for the fairy-tale ending. They were bound to be disappointed.

"I won't cancel the flowers," I said. "I won't do anything else except talk to Mom, OK? Am I allowed to do that?"

"What will you talk about?"

"I'll tell her how Princess Fiona turned into an ogre to match her prince—how about that? Maybe Mom can paint her face green next time your dad's unkind?"

Iris smiled. It was watery and reluctant, but it was definitely a smile.

Twenty-Nine

"LOVEBIRDS COME IN PAIRS," Mom said. She held out a photo of her parents on their wedding day. They looked like they'd walked off a film set in their old-fashioned clothes. "My mom was fourteen when she met my dad. Imagine meeting your soul mate so young. That's ridiculous luck, isn't it?"

I stared at her as she dried her eyes with the sleeve of her sweater. This hadn't been what I was expecting when I sat on her bed and told her I wanted to talk about John.

"What do you love about him?" I'd asked.

I'd hoped she wouldn't be able to think of anything, but instead she pulled a box from the wardrobe and plucked a photo out. She'd found it days ago when she'd first started sorting her keep, charity, chuck stuff.

She tapped it now. "Your granddad was never the same after my mom died," she said. "I know you never met her, but you can see in the photo how much he loves her."

"What's this got to do with John?"

"He's *my* soul mate. It's really that simple, Lex." She wrapped the photo tenderly back into its tissue paper. "Do you know," she said, "when my mom was dying, Granddad promised he'd find her when his time came, wherever she was? Isn't that romantic?" She wiped her eyes again. "They had me very late in life, so they had years of just the two of them. Every time I walked into a room, they were kissing."

"I doubt it was *every* time."

"I'd sometimes wake up in the night and hear music coming from the living room and I'd creep downstairs to see. They'd lit candles— dozens of them—and they'd turned off the lights, so the whole room was flickering. They'd have the record player on and they'd be dancing together." She looked around the bedroom as if she could see them now. "I used to stand for ages watching them."

"They never saw you?"

"No, they only had eyes for each other."

I imagined Mom as a girl shivering in her nightie. I thought of her going back up the stairs in the dark, while her parents danced on and on.

"That sounds horrible," I said.

She laughed. "What's horrible about it?"

"Parents are supposed to put their children first."

She looked at me properly—with her full attention. I felt myself come into focus for the first time in days. "What's that supposed to mean?"

Mom had the date of the wedding circled on the kitchen calen- dar. I couldn't look at it. Or my study plan. Or phones or clocks or newspapers. I couldn't bear that May 19 was ticking closer with each passing minute.

I said, "Parents shouldn't put their own romance at the top of the list."

"This again? Christ, Lexi—me loving John doesn't stop me loving you. You might think I take his side over yours and you might think he comes down hard on you, but that's because you're a teenager. One day, you'll look back and be grateful for a firm hand."

"Is that what we're calling it? Did you know he's made me an urgent appointment with the doctor?"

"He wants what's best for you, Lex."

"You sure about that?"

She scowled at me. "You know, I was thinking about you the whole time I was away. Call me an idiot, but I was hoping you might get along with John if I left you alone together."

"That's not why you left."

"Maybe it's why I left you behind."

"Maybe you're rewriting history."

"I haven't got the energy to argue about this." She picked up the "keep" box and stood up. She walked to the wardrobe and put it back on its shelf. "Now, I've only got two more drawers to go and then I'm finally done. You want to come to the charity shop with me and off-load stuff?"

"Seriously? That's the end of the discussion?"

"I'm sick of it."

I watched her open a fresh drawer and peer in. I watched her face, all keen and hopeful, longing for more of the past to throw away, and I felt a shadow creeping up from the carpet.

I said, "You know, I could give you a list of all the awful things that happened while you were gone?"

"Yes, you told me. You ran around after John and he did nothing."

"He broke my phone."

"Your phone got broken."

"He threw me out."

"You left."

"Because he's a psycho!"

"And what did you do to him?" She glared at me and adrenaline surged in my blood. "Yes, I'm talking about the coffee incident. A laxative? What were you thinking?"

"He pushed me against a wall!"

"To calm you down."

"Because he's cruel!"

There. I'd said it. The words echoed.

Mom stood perfectly still. "Has he ever hit you?"

"Not that kind of cruel."

"Has he ever touched you inappropriately?"

"No, Mom! Listen to me, that's not what I'm saying."

"Then what are you saying?"

It was as if she was a delicate boat and he was a massive ship dragging her around in his wake to smash her up. "He treats women like they're nothing."

She looked up from the drawer. "So, now he's a misogynist?"

"Do all women cry as much as you? Do all guys blame a teenage girl for stuff as much as John blames me? Why does Iris have to be so perfect all the time? Remember the tree? Remember how John blamed us for Iris's accident?"

"You can't hook that on him, Lex."

"Yes, I can! I only took her outside to distract her from the yelling."

"Blame doesn't work like that, Lex. You could just as easily blame me for stomping off, or whoever left the spike in the grass, or the tree for growing too high, or the neighbor for not looking out the window and stopping it happening."

"Or me for taking Iris up there?"

"Yes. Or you."

"So, whose fault was it John went mental on the way back from the hospital?"

She shook her head. "I don't know. I don't remember."

"I threw stuff out the car and he yelled at me."

"Well, that sounds like your fault."

"Even if I did it to help you?"

"What are you talking about?"

It was like a charge between us. Like our eyes got caught and couldn't break free.

I said, "He stopped yelling at you and yelled at me instead."

"You lose your temper on purpose, is that what you're saying?"

"Maybe."

"You chucking chairs and trashing the kitchen is all part of some great master plan?"

"This is what you do, Mom, can't you see? It's *his* fault—all of it. And you never dare point the finger at him."

She turned on me, her eyes glittering. "Stop this war with him, Lex. He's going to be my husband. He's going to be your father. We are going to be one happy family and you're going to like it."

She was honestly suggesting she could force me to be happy? I got up from the bed and walked to the window and looked out at the tree.

Years ago, I had thrown a book of maps from the car and, like a miracle, John had turned his anger on me. A couple of weeks ago, I threw his laptop. And there'd been loads of times in between. It wasn't a master plan, but it was something . . .

If didn't do those things, John would hassle Mom for days. He'd grind her down with counter-accusations and then with silence. He'd refuse to look her in the eyes or answer any questions. He'd eat and sleep separately. He'd be perfectly normal with Iris so Mom knew who was being punished. He'd be late home every night after work and sometimes not come back at all. And Mom would ask: *Where do you go? Why is this happening again? What did I do? Tell me how to be.* She'd do everything she should—shop, cook, clean, remember her kids exist—but only in a vague way, like someone had rubbed out her brightest colors.

Why had I only just seen this?

Why didn't Mom see it at all?

She was supposed to protect us and all she did was tread eggshells around him. It was only his love affairs that got her angry.

I said, "He's never going to be faithful."

"You don't know anything about it," Mom snapped. "You're too young to understand how it's possible to forgive and move on."

"Forgiving him doesn't make him faithful. It just lets him get away with cheating."

"Stay out of it! That's a vicious thing to say."

I turned from the window. "I bet he's still seeing her."

"I'm warning you, Lex."

"Do you know for sure he isn't?"

"Stop it!" She marched over, and I thought she was going to hit me, but she stood right in front of me and I knew she was going to say something terrible instead. "Relationships are complex. You of all people should know that. You have no right to go about dripping poison when you spend most days swooning over a boy who has no interest in you whatsoever."

"What are you talking about?"

"You and Kass and this ridiculous secret relationship you imagine you have with him." She swept a hand through her hair. "Maybe I should have said something sooner, I don't know. I thought you'd grow out of throwing yourself at him."

I was silent. Every bit of me prickled with sudden cold.

"Say something," she said. "Say you know what I'm talking about. I just feel your raging disapproval all the time."

"That's because you're talking bullshit! You don't know the first thing about me and Kass."

"Oh, Lex," Mom said as she reached out for me. "Oh, baby, don't cry."

I pushed her away. I didn't want to be near her. She was weak and ridiculous. How could she possibly know anything about love?

Thirty

I TAPPED KASS ON the shoulder. I said, "Hey."

He turned around and smiled up at me, then immediately realized I wasn't supposed to be in a bar in Manchester on a rainy Thursday evening and his smile crashed. "Lex. Oh my God. What's happened? What are you doing here?"

There were two girls and a boy sitting at the table with him and I felt their interest fall on me. They stopped talking. They knew I was important.

I said, "I came to see you."

"By yourself?" Kass looked beyond me for the briefest instant, as if John, Mom, and Iris were about to appear.

"Sorry I didn't call first, but I've got no phone." I dumped my bag on the floor. "And you can't send me home because the last train back to London already left. And tomorrow's my birthday and I want to spend it with you."

The two girls were checking me out. I could feel the weight of their gaze, trying to make sense of who I was. The boy was looking too, but in a different way. He was doing that up-and-down thing with his eyes. Maybe he thought I was Cerys.

I said, "How about a hug, Kass?"

He stood up and clasped me quickly. We weren't alone, so it had to be brief. He stepped back. "Does anyone know you're here?"

"I left a note."

"Saying what?"

I grinned. "Not much."

"They'll be freaking out."

They all kept looking. But the boy stabbed a sudden finger in my direction. "I know who you are. You're the outrageous sister. It *is* you, isn't it? You throw stuff through windows. What did you throw? A chair? A TV?"

"I'm Lex," I said, smiling mysteriously.

"Stepsister," Kass said.

I wanted to say that we weren't related by blood, but until I got to know these people maybe it was easier to keep things simple. I stood with one hand on my hip, raindrops clinging to my hair and dress, waiting for Kass to remember he loved me.

Remember the layers of us, Kass? The years of us?

"I'm calling my dad," he said.

I shrugged. "I wouldn't bother. I took his wallet, so he's only going to yell at you."

The boy at the table laughed. "I'm in love with your sister, Kass."

Kass scowled at him. "Yeah, well, hands off."

It was thrilling, Kass wanting me for himself like that. It reminded me of the party, when he'd pushed the table over because I kissed a boy.

Kass turned his attention back to me. "Anything else I should know before I ring him?"

I didn't want to tell him my plan in front of his friends—how I wanted him to come back to London and get his mom to team up with mine. I figured we could even involve Monika. Mom made no sense anymore and was too flimsy to rescue herself. I loved the idea of three of John's exes kicking him out of the apartment together and then changing the locks.

I'd get to all that when me and Kass were alone. So I said there was nothing else and that if he insisted on phoning John it was up to him, but in the meantime, I was going to the bar. I smiled at his friends again. "Can I get anyone a drink?"

Kass shook his head. "You won't get served."

"Bet I will."

He watched me reach down and pick up my bag. I put some shimmy in it. I knew I looked good in my red dress. I'd changed into it on the train—the dress that hugged my curves, that John said was "too much" all those weeks ago. I'd done my makeup and hair in a scrap of mirror. *Clackety-clack* went the train as I turned into my new shiny self. I put my London clothes in a bag and sealed it shut. I was a slick Manchester girl now.

"So," I said, flashing John's credit card at everyone. "What can I get people?"

The girls laughed. The boy snapped his fingers. And that's when Kass gave in, like he knew the usual rules didn't apply.

He took the card from me. "I'll do the honors."

He didn't even blink when I asked for a rum and coke. He introduced his friends—Jaydon, Mia, Poppy—and left me with them while he went to the bar. I squeezed myself onto the end of the sofa next to the girls. I liked the dimness of the place, the scarlet walls, the film posters, the fairy lights strung above our heads.

"So, you're pretty hard-core," Jaydon said.

I shook my windswept hair for him. "That's me."

"And it's your birthday tomorrow? How old are you going to be?"

I smiled. "Depends which ID I use."

He snapped his fingers again. "I'm seriously in love with you."

Mia, the girl closest to me, threw a beer mat at him. "Back off, Jaydon. She's way out of your league."

Poppy leaned across and rubbed my arm. "Just deck him when you've had enough."

Jaydon held his hands up in mock surrender, but we three girls shared a knowing look. I loved it that they knew I could take care of myself, that they included me like that. And even though he didn't stand a chance, it was exciting that Jaydon liked me.

They asked me questions about my journey and how I'd managed to find Kass with no phone, and I told them about getting a cab from the station to the halls of residence and sneaking past security, then getting his roommate to draw me a map.

The girls laughed and said I was intrepid. Jaydon called me heroic. They asked me what I'd written in my runaway note (*sod your wedding*) and Jaydon asked what kind of trouble I'd be in for

stealing John's wallet (*What can he do if I don't let him do it?*).
Everything I said was the right thing, and by the time Kass came
back with the drinks, I felt as if all my edges were sparkling.

Kass settled opposite me, his legs under the table, his knees
touching mine, his feet close enough to bump with my boots.

Hello, hello, my feet said to his. He pushed gently back. *I see
you,* his feet said to mine.

"So, I rang my dad," he said.

A thrill of fear skimmed my chest. "And?"

"I persuaded him not to send an armed response unit." He
grinned at me. "It looks like you've got a night of freedom."

Only one night? We'd see about that.

I swallowed the fear and raised my glass at my new friends. "To
freedom."

It was the best evening of my life. I was like a queen holding
court. I wasn't stupid or ugly or wrong or bad or difficult. I was
intrepid and heroic. It made me happier than I could imagine, like a
weight I didn't even know I was carrying had been lifted.

Kass couldn't stop looking. He kept shaking his head and saying
things like "I can't believe you dared to run away. I can't believe you
stole my dad's wallet. I can't believe you're here."

Every time he said something like that, I said, "You better believe
it," and bumped his foot again. *Hello, hello.*

At one point he bent close and said, "What's the plan?"

"What makes you think I have a plan?"

"Because nothing's ever simple with you."

So, I told him about getting his mom to talk to mine and making a team to defeat his dad and he grinned and kissed me on the cheek. "Awesome," he said.

Mom was wrong. I wasn't imagining a relationship with Kass. He'd loved me since the day we met. And he loved me still. She'd see it when we turned up hand in hand to save her.

I told stories about me and Kass growing up and I made us sound like kids from a book—living in trees, playing tricks on the grown-ups, running free.

"She'd do anything I suggested," Kass said. "Utterly fearless."

The girls told him off for leading me on and he laughed and said I should be thanking him for curbing my excesses.

"I am very difficult to curb," I said.

They all chuckled. Jaydon even slapped the table in merriment. I heard my own laughter echoing back at me and it sounded wonderful.

We didn't criticize John. We never had in public. It was a secret scar we carried, like a family tattoo or a branding, and it was difficult to expose it to air. We'd seen John make people we love cry. We'd seen him weaken them. We'd witnessed the accident of their lives— how nothing turned out how they thought it would. Tomorrow we'd go back to London together and destroy him. But tonight was for love.

Kass told them I was brilliant at acting. He showed them pictures on his phone that I didn't even know he had of me in last year's drama project. I said I'd like to go to drama school and they all got excited and said I should apply to Manchester to study theater in college.

I realized I'd misunderstood happiness. I'd always thought that if I could be someone else—someone like Iris or Cerys—that I'd be happy. But I was happy being me. I wouldn't have swapped with anyone.

Kass's eyes turned tender as the night ticked by. I kept catching him looking at me and I wondered if he was doing the same calculations in his head that I was doing in mine.

The last train had gone.

He had a room with a bed.

There were no adults to tell us what we couldn't do.

I turned sixteen at midnight.

I imagined it like a honeymoon—his eyes bright with love, his hands knowing just what to do, his body leading mine, him whispering, *I love you, Lexi*. Us together for hours in some kind of heaven.

It was almost eleven o'clock when our eyes caught and held, and he mouthed, *"Want to go?"* And I nodded.

We said goodbye to the others. They wished me luck for when I got home, and I told them I wouldn't need luck because I had a plan and they laughed and said they hoped it was a good one.

Outside, it was still raining. The streetlights reflected on the wet pavement, stretching yellow and amber ahead of us.

I linked arms with Kass and he grinned at me.

"Ready?"

Thirty-One

I'D SEEN KASS'S ROOM on Skype, but here it was—crimson curtains, brown carpet, shelves full of books. He studied at that desk, read in that chair, slept in that bed night after night. I knew I was walking into womanhood as I stepped in and he shut the door behind us.

"So," he said, "this is it."

"I love it."

He laughed. "It's a cell."

"At least you've got a double bed."

He gave me a long look. "At least there's that."

My heart was beating wildly as he gathered clothes from the floor and flung them in the corner. He moved books from the chair to the desk, switched on a lamp, and turned off the main light. The room sank into a rosy glow.

"Come and see the view," he said.

I put my bag on the bed and followed him over to the window. The rain glistened silver as it fell past the lamps outside. There were trees and a courtyard and a road beyond. On the other side of

the road was the park we'd walked past on the way back from
the bar.

"No buildings," he said, "just greenery. Good, huh?"

"Aren't architects supposed to like buildings?"

"Ah," he said. "You caught me there."

He sounded sad. I turned to him. "You should change majors."

"Should I?"

"You don't have to do what your dad says anymore. I've got a
plan, remember?"

He didn't look at me, pretended fascination with the world outside. "Let's not get into that now, eh, Lex?"

My eyes had adjusted to the dark and I could see all the detail of
his face—the shadow where he hadn't shaved, the beautiful curve of
his bottom lip, each eyelash.

Once, Kass said if everyone in the world had to pick a partner, he'd pick me. Another time he said he could never get married because everyone else was counterfeit. When I asked what
that meant, he said I was his one true thing.

I took a step closer and nudged him with my elbow. "It's me,
Kass."

"Yes," he said. "I know."

Still he wouldn't look. I nudged him again. "I came all this way
to see you. I changed into this dress on the train. I did my makeup
and hair in the little wobbly toilet."

"Stop," he said.

"Stop what?"

"You know what."

But I was a slick Manchester girl. I walked into that bar and found him, and he looked at me like a moth attracted to a light.

"Remember," I said, "the very first time we met? You told me the yard was dangerous and if there was a fire we'd all die because there was no way out. You remember that?"

"Not really."

"I showed you my special way of climbing the tree and how to jump into the cemetery and you said it was clear I could look after myself."

"Why are you telling me this?"

"Because I *can* look after myself, Kass. And so can you. And together, we can rescue everyone else. We're fucking amazing."

He laughed. "Well, you're pretty amazing, for sure—getting all the way here with no phone or money."

"I had money. It just wasn't mine."

He opened his arms. "Come here."

I didn't hesitate. I went to him and we stood together by the window in our coats with the smell of outdoors upon us.

This is me, Kass. This is me, here in your arms.

I pressed myself gently into him and I loved the way his breathing changed. It got deeper and slower and I liked the way he held me tighter the longer we stood there. It was as if we were equalizing pressure between us. Like when people come out of a deep-sea dive and up into air.

"Look at me," he whispered eventually.

I tipped my face up and he looked as if he was really seeing me, as if he knew something about me that even I didn't know. I was so happy to be there with him looking at me like that.

"Thanks for coming to see me," he said.

As he bent toward me, I felt a rush of warmth. As he came closer, I felt his breath on my skin. He kissed me once, very gently on my mouth, then leaned back and smiled.

"That was nice," I said.

"Yeah."

"Shall we do it again?"

"Not a good idea, Lex."

"We're not blood-related, remember?"

He shook his head slowly, as if that was a terrible lie.

Girls are supposed to wait to be taken, however much they want to give themselves. But this was Kass and I was in his room and I'd been waiting for this night my whole life. I wasn't going to let it end before it had even begun. I stood on tiptoes and with my hand behind his head guided his lips back to mine.

Our kisses were soft, barely kisses at all—like we could take them away if we wanted, tell ourselves they meant nothing, stop at any moment. But as we kept kissing, our lips pressed harder and our mouths opened wider and our tongues joined in and it was like we'd been starving for years.

"Fuck," Kass said. Just that word in my ear as he spun me round to the window, pushed me there, and leaned hard against me. We kissed some more, and it was like we couldn't get close enough.

This is it, I thought. This is what love feels like. At fucking last.

But eventually, he pulled away. "This can't happen," he whispered.

I pulled him closer. I'd die if we stopped. I wanted this more than I'd ever wanted anything in my life. I'd dreamed of it for years.

He eased himself gently away. "No, Lex."

"I'm sixteen in about ten minutes."

"That's not the point." He ran a hand through his hair. He seemed suddenly furious.

"Why are you angry?"

"You keep throwing yourself at me."

Mom's words. But from him, they felt like a slap. "You kiss me back. Every time you kiss me back."

He looked at me with cold eyes. "I'm a guy, Lex. That's what we do. You throw yourselves at us and we respond."

"That's so unfair."

"Life's unfair. Listen, I can't be doing this. I've got classes tomorrow and I need to get to sleep."

"Are you kidding me?"

"Not kidding, no. The bathroom's through there if you want to wash your face or anything."

He pointed to a door by the wardrobe that I hadn't even noticed. I didn't know what to do, how to be, what to say, so I did as he told me and went into the bathroom. I went to the bathroom and washed my hands. I splashed water on my face. When I wiped myself on his towel, it smeared with mascara and I was fiercely glad. I wanted to stain his stuff.

When I went back into the bedroom, he was fiddling with his phone. He looked up and smiled as if nothing was wrong. "Did you brush your teeth?"

I didn't bother answering. I got into bed fully clothed and slid over to the wall. I had no idea if he'd get in beside me. Maybe he'd go and sleep somewhere else completely?

"Are you sulking?" he said.

When I didn't say anything, he chuckled. "Back in a minute."

I listened to him pee. I listened to the rush of water from the flush. I heard the tap at the sink and the soft sound of him brushing his teeth, then the swish and spit of mouthwash. If I closed my eyes I could see him do these things as if I was peeking through a spyhole.

When he came out, he turned off the lamp and stood by the bed. "Are you fully dressed under there?"

"Uh-huh."

"You can't sleep in your clothes, that's ridiculous."

"You want me to take them off?"

"I'm just saying you'll be uncomfortable."

I flung the cover from me and sat up. I lifted my dress from the hem and pulled it over my head. I knew he was watching. I tossed it at him and lay back down. "Happy?"

"Come on, Lex, don't sulk."

"I'm not."

"You are and it's boring."

He undid the zip on his jeans and pulled them down right there in front of me, didn't try and hide at all. He took off his socks and

T-shirt, then lifted the duvet, and slipped in beside me wearing only his boxers. He lay on his back, one arm slung above his head— breathing next to me, millimeters away. If I moved the little finger of my left hand, I could touch the skin of his right thigh.

"Want to talk?" he said.

"No, thank you."

"How about we talk about a nice safe subject?" He gently pushed my leg with his. "You want me to ask you math questions?"

I didn't even bother smiling at his joke.

"Suit yourself." He made a great show of turning over away from me. He pulled up the duvet, moved his leg from mine. "By the way—the first cheap train is at half past nine, but guests need to be out of the building by eight, so you'll have to go to a café or some- thing until the train leaves."

"You're coming with me, remember? We've got a plan."

"*You've* got a plan, Lex. Don't drag me into it."

"You agreed."

"I don't think so."

What exactly was happening here? I had no clue anymore. Why did he tell me to take off my dress? Why was he lying next to me in only his boxers? Why wasn't he sleeping on one of the sofas in the communal lounge? Was he coming back to London with me in the morning, or not?

Hardly any time passed before he said, "I can feel the heat of you from here. It's like you're pulsating."

He said, "It's nice sharing a bed with you."

He rolled onto his back again, flung an arm above his head again, and said, "I prefer us being friendly, don't you?"

I scrambled up to sitting. "You keep doing this."

"Doing what?"

"Muddling everything."

"What are you talking about?"

"It's like you give out signals and then deny it."

He sighed. "Here we go."

"When I asked you for a train ticket to Manchester for my birthday, you said, 'Sure.' But when I turn up, you act all surprised. When I told you the plan to get our moms together, you said it was awesome, but now you're like, *That's a crap idea.* You're flirty in the bar and you kiss me at the window and then, when I kiss you back, you stop me. Then you're like, *Hey, let's talk.* And when I won't, you're all, *Actually you have to leave in the morning 'cause you're a pain in the ass.*"

He laughed. "I never said you were a pain in the ass."

"You were thinking it, though."

"So, you're a mind reader?"

"This isn't funny, Kass. This is my life and you're taking the piss."

"Wow," he said, "you were a lot more fun earlier."

"There you go again. It's like you give me stuff and say, *Here, hold this,* and then pretend you never gave it to me."

"I haven't got a clue what you're on about."

"So, you don't know you're doing it?"

"Maybe it's time to go to sleep, Lex?"

But he wasn't going to get rid of me that easily. "Remember that time you spread jam on my tummy so butterflies would land on me, and when none came you licked the jam off?"

"That was a million years ago!"

"No, Kass—I was ten and you were twelve. Remember that time you shoved a boy over on the beach because he wanted to be my friend?"

"He was a jerk."

"What about all the mornings you came into the bathroom when I was brushing my teeth and you told me not to look while you peed?"

"Yes," he said quietly, "I remember that."

I gave him a list. Years and years of things. I was amazed how many I had. All the times we collapsed laughing together onto sofas, and scrambled up trees and hid under beds, and the hours we spent in the small dark place at the back of the laundry room. The notes he left me after each weekend visit. The Valentine's chocolate he slid shyly onto my lap. The time I got tonsillitis and he lay in bed beside me and I had no idea that threaded fingers could be so intimate. The time we practiced love bites on each other's arms. The time I cut my finger and he put it in his mouth and sucked the blood away. The time, only weeks ago, he nearly punched a boy at a party because I kissed him.

"You like me," I told him as he lay looking up at me, his eyes bright in the dark. "You've liked me for years."

"I've never denied I like you."

"In *that* way, I mean." I flung the duvet right off. "You want me to prove it?"

He gave me a slow smile. "How are you going to do that?"

There was only one way and it came to me gleaming and insistent, like something I'd known all my life. I scrambled out of bed and stood on his rough little carpet in my underwear, and I looped a finger through one bra strap and eased it from my shoulder. I watched his face. He watched my hands. I gently pulled the other strap down.

"Stop me anytime," I said.

In the dark, his eyes glittered.

I unclasped my bra at the back. No one had seen this new body of mine. My breasts started growing at eleven, my pubic hair at twelve. I got my first period when I was nearly thirteen. Since then, my breasts had grown, my hips had curved, my thighs had widened.

As I let my bra fall, I felt like a bride taking off her veil. *See me. This is me.*

I tried not to cover myself with my hands, not to shrink into less than I was. *I am strong. I am beautiful.*

I stood there breathing and he lay there looking. "Fucking hell, Lex," he said.

Courage, I thought. Courage to do this. He's always loved you. He loves all your deep and secret places.

"As I said, Kass, stop me anytime."

I hooked a thumb down either side of my underwear. My heart was beating so loud, I was sure he could hear it, and that felt most intimate of all.

Kass once said to me, "Why is it harder to breathe near you?"

And once, John said, "Whenever you say her name, Kass, you have a different voice." Like he knew.

Now, as I inched my underwear down, I imagined myself as a beautiful witch who'd flown through Kass's window and landed on his carpet—and he was a virgin boy in his bed, marveling at all I was showing him.

His eyes shone with tears and it was because I was beautiful. Even though I was a clumsy girl holding on to a desk to step out of her underwear—I was also a witch with thunder in her eyes. He'd always loved my wild side.

I stood naked in front of him and his eyes lapped me up, his gaze traveling from my breasts, down my belly, to my hips and back again.

"You love me," I said.

I took a step toward him and he shuddered as if we'd touched. Taking that step, I could smell my own naked self. I wondered if he could too.

"You love me," I said again. "And you always have." I walked a step closer.

"What are you doing?"

"Proving it."

He shook his head. "Not like this."

"There's no other way. You keep denying it."

He wiped his eyes with the back of his hand. "Put your clothes on, please."

"I don't want to." I was trembling. I hated that he was a crying boy and was about to say he never meant any of it, that I'd misunderstood, got the wrong end of the stick, made a fool of myself. "You don't want me yourself, but you don't want anyone else to have me, is that it?"

"Don't be ridiculous."

"What is it, then? You say stuff and do stuff and then pretend you haven't. Why would you do that?"

He picked up my dress from the floor and threw it at me. "Get dressed."

"No." I threw it back at him. I wobbled like a jelly every time I spoke or moved, but I wasn't going to do what he said. If I cowered, if I covered myself or hid, that would be the end of me. I was a warrior bride, with my head in the sky, my hair whipping a storm. I was fighting for truth.

"Look at me, Kass—stop looking away. You've flirted with me your entire life."

"Bullshit."

"You said you loved me. Didn't you say that? You said it on your bed that time we kissed."

"I didn't mean it that way."

"You just watched me take my clothes off and never said a word."

"I thought you'd stop. I thought you had more self-respect."

"So, it's all in my head?" I felt pure rage. "Oh my God—you're just like him. You're just like your fucking dad."

"Shut up, Lex."

But I was onto him. I could see it now. "It's the same hot-and-cold thing. It's the same powerful magician crap—making us all feel like the mad ones."

"Pathetic," he said. He rolled over and covered his eyes as if that would make a difference.

"You're worse than him, though," I said, "because you're trying to be the perfect son at the same time. All these years you've encouraged me to do stuff you didn't dare do yourself. You obey all his fucking rules and I'm the one who gets in trouble. You secretly lead me on. You flirt with me and kiss me and then throw your hands up in horror. You won't be liable for any of it if your dad finds out, will you? I can't believe I fucking fell for it."

"Lex," he said. "Go away."

"Where would you like me to go?"

He dragged his hand from his eyes. "At least put some clothes on. At least show some dignity."

"Get out," I said.

"What?"

"Go and sleep in the lounge. You should've been there from the start. Go on—fuck off."

He blinked at me in surprise. Was he going to say it was his room and I should go? No, he could barely keep eye contact.

He gathered up his things and I stood there nakedly watching him. I closed all my windows, I shut all my doors, I put up my barricades. I told him I'd get up and leave as soon as it got light. I told him not to contact me. "When you come down for the wedding, bring a girl, but not Cerys, OK—because she deserves better than you. And don't talk to either of us—not once."

"I thought there wasn't going to be a wedding?" he said. "I thought you had a plan."

"Fuck off, Kass."

My hands were shaking. I noticed this like I'd notice an actress in a movie. I felt far away from myself.

He left me the duvet. He turned at the door and said, "I never meant to hurt you, Lex."

"Is that an apology?"

He shrugged. He still couldn't look at me, as if my nudity burned his eyes.

"You know what you should do?" I said. "You should do the exact opposite of what your dad says for the rest of your fucking life."

He nodded. He walked away. I looked at the closed door for far too long.

Thirty-Two

"ARE YOU SICK?" MOM said when I told her I didn't want lunch. She felt my forehead. "You're not hot."

John looked at me with his dark and terrible eyes. "Sick of causing trouble, no doubt."

"You think it's the meds?" Mom said. "You think she's having side effects?"

"Read the packaging if you're worried," he said. "But I think it's more likely she's being a drama queen."

I'd been back from Manchester for a week and he was still livid. My behavior was unforgivable. On top of everything else, I was a liar and a thief. How dare I bother Kass when he had exams? How dare I steal money and run off without a word? I'd apologized over and over, but he'd still taken me to see Dr. Leaman.

Five milligrams of methylphenidate hydrochloride twice daily made me feel far away from everything, like not much mattered anymore—not even a broken heart.

"Best get back to studying if you don't want lunch," John said.

"Maybe she could do with a break?" Mom said.

"She's on study leave. It's called that for a reason."

I was drawing closer to the ground with each passing day. Soon I would be prone and never move again.

Mom opened the sash window an inch and cold air and traffic noise invaded. "Come over here, Lex. Have a bit of fresh air."

"Don't be ridiculous," John said. "It's more carbon monoxide than oxygen. If she's unwell, she should go to bed. If she's not, she should go and do some work. Either way, she needs to pull herself together and stop mooning about the place. We've got a wedding in two weeks. This is supposed to be a happy time."

Mom stood staring at me. "You do look awful."

It was sadness. Even through the haze of medication, I couldn't help thinking of Kass and all that I'd lost. It was also shame. I'd taken all my clothes off and stood naked in front of him and he'd told me to get dressed. Later, he'd sent me an email apologizing for letting things go so far. He'd realized that each time we "got close" he'd been drinking, and would I ever forgive him and had I told anyone? And then he sent other, shorter emails, letting me know he couldn't stop thinking about being like his dad. Was he? Was he really? He was going to talk to his mom about it because it was messing with his head.

And none of his emails said, *I love you, come back to me, I can't breathe without you.*

"You want some chamomile tea?" Mom said. "I could put some honey in it."

It crossed my mind to pretend to have all the worst side effects listed on the packaging. If I had a blocked artery in the brain or abnormal liver function, I could go to bed for weeks, maybe even go to the hospital and lie in a ward with kindly nurses. I'd have to miss the wedding. I'd be given a letter saying I couldn't take exams. I'd go to some country retreat for sea air and sit in a wheelchair and be pushed around the place.

"Is it your period?" Mom said.

"Really?" John said. "You're having this conversation in front of me?"

"Please," I whispered. "Please stop talking about me. No, it isn't my period. Yes, I look awful. I always look awful. I'm going to my room. I'll see you both later."

"Good idea," he called after me. "Do some actual studying while you're there."

Cerys emailed again. Did I know any more about why Kass had dumped her? No, I emailed back, except he's an idiot and you're way too good for him. I knew I wasn't entirely to blame for wrecking their relationship. Kass did most of it by himself, stringing Cerys along while flirting with lovely Manchester girls. But it didn't stop me feeling guilty. She sent me a crying face emoji and asked if I had any fury to spare. I ignored that. All I had was unusual drowsiness and an overwhelming desire to sleep.

Ben emailed—where had I gone? Should he just add my name to his media project? They had to be submitted today. I felt guilty about that too. I'd crept into Ben's room uninvited and taken photos. I'd done precisely zero toward a project and he was offering to share his. I was shamed by his kindness. But still I ignored him.

When Iris got home from school, she came to see me. She'd collected books and toys in a basket and brought them in like a gift.

"Look," she said, "I'm giving you my stuffed elephant."

"What I want, Iris, is a hug—can you give me one of those?"

She climbed under the duvet beside me, wrapped her skinny arms round my neck, and scattered me with kisses. "Don't cry," she said. "Why are you crying?"

"I'm sad."

She wiped my tears with her fingers and laid her hand flat on my forehead as if checking my temperature. "Please," she said, "please be happy again."

"I'll try."

"If I hug you harder, will you be happier?"

I told her yes, because I wanted it to be true, but it wasn't. I felt weak. And weirdly nervous—like something terrible was about to happen.

"I love you," Iris said.

I nodded. I knew. I loved her back. She was the one good thing.

She sang me songs and told me stories about her day. It distracted me to hear her. She told me she had a new plan about the wedding. "I'm going as a boy," she said.

"Why would you do that?"

She shrugged and stuffed her thumb in her mouth. I wondered if she thought boys had the better deal?

John came and stood in the doorway and said Iris should leave me alone if I was sick.

"She isn't sick," Iris said. "She's sad."

"Either way, she might be contagious. Come on, out you get."

Iris planted kisses on my face as if she was going away for weeks. "I don't care about contagious," she cried as John picked her up and carried her off.

Mom came to see what all the fuss was about. "I have something to ask you," she said.

I leaned up on my elbow to look at her. I thought she was going to ask me something about Kass. Maybe she'd heard from him. Maybe he'd told her what I'd done.

She knelt by the side of the bed. "Will you give me away?"

"What are you talking about?"

"My dad would do it if he was here, but of course he isn't. Would you? Would you walk me down the aisle?"

I thought she was joking. I was the one who told her to turf John out. I was the one who told her he was cruel.

"Can't Kass do it?"

"John wants Kass to be best man."

"And does John know you're asking me?"

She shook her head. "Not yet."

"What if I mess it up?"

"You won't."

"I might refuse to hand you over."

She smiled. "You won't."

I told her I'd think about it. She thanked me and blew me a kiss before leaving. I turned to the blank wall and pulled the duvet over my head. I tried not to think about Kass in his best man outfit looking amazing and me in whatever I wore (A tuxedo? An old man's three-piece suit?) as father of the bride, looking broken. I'd told Kass to bring a new girlfriend and not talk to me all night. Why had I said that? I missed him so much it hurt my bones. My only comfort was to remember the way he'd kissed me—the passion in it. And the way his curls turned darker as I ran my fingers through them. And the way he'd got down to just his boxers in front of me. Surely, that meant something? Surely, that was love?

That night, I slept in his jacket. I zipped it over my pajamas and breathed in the scent of him.

Thirty-Three

TWO DAYS LATER, KASS sent me a different kind of email.

I do a lot of the crap my dad does. That hot-and-cold thing, especially. I do it to friends as well as to girls, and now I've seen it, I'm going to do something about it. I'm sorry I hurt you, Lexi. I deserve your fury.

"I'm not furious," I whispered.

I drafted several replies. In one, I said I was sorry too and that I'd overreacted. In another, I said that maybe we should get together before the wedding to talk things through? In every version I said I missed him, that I hated this rift between us, that I loved him.

In one draft I wrote, *Please tell me you love me back.*

And that's when I knew I couldn't send any of them. That's when I made a rule. I made it on Iris's life, so that I could never break it. The rule was *stop begging for love.*

I loved Kass disastrously.

From the beginning.

And he knew. And he played me.

He might not have meant to. He might not have known he was doing it. He was John's son, after all, and things were bound to rub off. But there was no way I was going to let Mom's weakness rub off on me.

My rule didn't stop me hoping Kass would send more emails. It didn't stop me checking my inbox every few minutes or stalking him on Facebook. It didn't stop me getting Iris to call him on Mom's cell, so I could hear his voice. I burned with longing as I listened to him say he couldn't come to the phone right now and to please leave a message. It felt like he was talking directly to me.

"Your heart's gone loud," Iris said.

"Hang up," I told her. "And don't ever let me do that again, however much I beg you."

She looked at me sadly. "Maybe you should stop wearing his jacket?"

I felt deserted, like an empty station or a dried-up cup. I ate meals, but only because I got hassled if I didn't. I sat at the table with everyone and I was polite and nodded in the right places. I took my medication twice a day. But I wasn't there, not really.

Cerys emailed: *Kass got in touch. Loads of bullshit reasons for going silent on me for weeks and then dumping me by text! He needs to "find himself" apparently. I told him to look up his own ass!!*

It seemed she'd found fury without my help. I wrote back and congratulated her, and she replied and said it was entirely down to me. *I've stuck a quote from you above my desk and I keep looking at it.* It was the thing I'd said about looking in a room when you're told not to. She'd taken it metaphorically and found it very inspiring. *I owe you*, she wrote. *You're my role model.*

I told her she could pay me back by helping me write a father-of-the-bride speech because I was clueless. She said as a preliminary idea, how about *All men are bastards*?

Iris lost patience with me. She stopped stroking my head and telling me she loved me and instead, whenever she found me in bed, she ripped the duvet off and told me I should get up and study or do something badass because I was boring.

"I don't mind being boring," I said, clawing the duvet back.

"I mind." She stood there, arms folded, tapping her foot. "I guess it's me who has to be badass now."

"No, Iris. I don't want you getting into trouble."

"We'll see about that." She stomped off, slamming my door as she went. She came back five minutes later wearing denim dungarees with a striped T-shirt underneath. "This is my bridesmaid outfit," she said. "I'm going as a pirate."

"You're going in a frothy pink dress. We both are."

She made a face and went off to show her dungarees to Mom and John. I heard his voice from my bed. It started with laughter and then moved on to, "Don't be silly, Iris. Go away with your ridiculousness."

I couldn't hear exactly what she replied, but I did hear a swear word, followed by her feet pounding down the hallway and John calling, "Come back here, right now."

She was laughing as she leaped into bed with me and crawled under the duvet.

John crashed in. "Get out from under there."

Iris wriggled deeper, clutching on to my legs.

John yanked the duvet from us both. He squatted down on the carpet and held her face between both his palms. "*Do not swear at me.* You get it? It's not funny. What's got into you?"

Her fierce little face was flushed and alive. "I'm badass."

"That's it," he said. "Go to your room." He picked her up under her armpits and pulled. She made herself a dead weight, slumping, difficult to hold.

"Iris," I whispered, "it's not worth it." But if she heard me, she never said. She was too busy laughing and clinging to the doorframe as John dragged her out.

"You, young lady, are in big trouble," he said.

"You, old man, are in bigger trouble."

He took her to her bedroom. I heard some of the lecture—his voice droning on. He wouldn't tolerate being laughed at—it was undermining and disrespectful. She shouldn't go around swearing either. Did she want to end up like me? Did she want a bad reputation?

Eventually I heard her apologizing.

"Sorry, Daddy. I'll be good again, I promise."

✳

A week before the wedding, Kass sent a new email.

Lex, it said, *I'm not going to be best man. In fact, I'm not coming to the wedding at all. I know my dad'll go mental and I know you'll get flak and I'm sorry. I'm sending this from the airport because I'm taking your excellent advice and doing the opposite of everything my dad wants me to do. I'm off traveling (India first). I've cleared it with college staff and my mom and I've emailed my dad to let him know. If it's any consolation—I'll miss you loads. And I promise to keep in touch. Get a phone!! Love always.*

Sometimes, when a terrible thing happens you don't see it at first. I was concentrating so hard on "miss you loads" and "love always" that it didn't click that Kass would be on the other side of the world and I might not see him for months.

It was only when John started hollering from upstairs that I knew he'd got an email too and we were all in for it now. He came bounding down from his study and into my room. He didn't even knock. He looked white-hot, enraged. "Did you know about this? Did you put him up to it?" He slapped a hand on my desk, and my pencils and rulers jumped.

Mom came rushing in from the kitchen. "What's the matter?"

John waved his phone at her. "Kass has taken off for India."

Mom looked horrified. "Does he say why?"

"Oh, I think we all know why, don't we?" He glared at me. "I think we all know whose fault this is."

"How is it my fault?" I said. "I only just found out."

"You run off to Manchester and the next thing we know, my son's left college and gone traveling."

Mom stroked his arm, his shoulder, the back of his neck, told him it wasn't the end of the world and perhaps the architecture course hadn't been right for Kass?

John pulled himself stiffly away from her. "Being an architect is all Kass ever wanted. Did I insist he went to college? Did you see me forcing him to fill out applications?"

"Perhaps he wanted to please you? Perhaps it wasn't quite what he wanted for himself?"

"Jesus, woman!" He wheeled round to face her. "When did you become the world's expert on my son?"

Maybe John would cancel the wedding now, I thought. Maybe he'd go to the airport and catch a plane to India. We could warn Kass and he'd move, and John would follow. Round and round the world they'd go like a game of cat and mouse. How peaceful it would be. How soothing. We could pretend we made them up.

"I paid for his dorm in advance," John said. "Am I getting a refund? Or has he pocketed that? Am I funding this insane expedition?"

He shouted so loud his face went red. He looked as if he might explode. It brought Iris running. She stood in the doorway, both hands on the frame. "What's happening?"

John swung round to her. "Did you know?"

She looked terrified. "Know what?"

"That Kass left school?"

She shot me a look, shot another at Mom. She looked like a young animal caught in the middle of a motorway.

"Christ," he said. "Can't anyone say anything useful?"

He stomped out of the room and away. Mom raced after him. "John," she said. "John, we can sort this."

I closed my eyes as Iris crept into my bed and fumbled around with the duvet, dragging it over both our heads. Far away and muffled, I could hear Mom, her voice high and fretful. "Who are you calling?" she was saying. "Wait a bit. Don't say anything you'll regret. Don't call him when you're angry."

"Listen to music," I told Iris. "Go get your iPod."

She didn't move, and I was worried she'd suffocate, so I pulled back the duvet. She shook her head at me, her eyes wide and dark. "I'm not leaving unless you make them stop."

"I'm not doing that."

"Do your monster."

I turned to her, our faces close on the pillow. "I'm taking special medicine, so I can't."

"Should I do it instead?"

"No, Iris. You're six."

She thought about that. "In some countries, six-year-olds do scary things."

"Like what?"

"Like go down a mine or work in a factory or be a soldier."

"Well, lucky for you, you don't live in those countries. The only thing you have to do is keep out of the way when it gets like this, OK? Just let them get on with it."

She snuggled closer. "I thought it would stop because of the wedding."

"Maybe it will. They're not married yet, are they?"

In the living room, things amped up. John—furious now—was barking at Mom, "Oh, you're loving this, aren't you? You're loving my son being in the wrong. You can be the holy martyr who knows what's best for everyone. Tell you what—how about I call my ex-wife? Am I allowed to do that? Do I have your permission to ask her what the fuck she thinks she's doing consenting to this nonsense?"

"It's getting bad," Iris whispered.

"It'll stop soon."

"But it'll stop *now* if you make it."

"I can't, Iris."

She blinked at me. "I can."

I told her no. I told her to come back. But she launched herself out of bed and ran down the hallway. I felt sick. I'm going to throw up all over the carpet, I thought. I felt fury at Kass and sorrow for Mom and fear for Iris. But mostly, I felt weary. I wanted to fold myself into the duvet and disappear. But instead I got out of bed and jogged to the living room just in time to see Iris throwing her bridesmaid dress through the window.

John and Mom stood agog. And then John turned his terrifying beam of fury on Iris.

Do your monster.

After the shouting was done and Iris had been sent down to the parking lot to rescue the dress and Mom had dusted off the worst of the dirt and Iris had said sorry for being outrageous and I'd apologized for inciting copycat behavior, Mom opened some wine and John calmed down. He suggested he should email Kass and ask him to reconsider. He thought he might contact Roger and ask him to be on standby as best man. Mom thought those were excellent ideas.

She fetched John's iPad and sat at his feet on the carpet while he typed. I took Iris by the hand and led her out of the door and down the stairs and into the yard. We sat on the fire escape steps where Kass and I had sat not that long ago, and I said, "Do you want to have another go at learning to climb the tree?"

Thirty-Four

IT'S BAD LUCK FOR a groom to see his bride on the morning of the wedding, so John spent the night in a hotel and it was just me, Mom, and Iris in the apartment for breakfast. We had fresh orange juice and croissants and then got our dresses on and did twirls in the living room and walked up and down by the windows pretending we were in a fashion show. It was almost possible to pretend we were just messing around and that later we'd fling off our silly costumes, order pizza, and watch Netflix.

It was when I was helping Mom pin up her hair that she took my wrist and said my name and our eyes met in the mirror and she said, "I'm sorry."

"For what?"

"For not being a proper mom."

"What do you mean?"

"For not being strong."

I looked away, ashamed. Of her, of both of us—I didn't know. It was awkward, and I wanted her to go back to being excited and girlish.

"Lex," she said again. "Look at me."

"What, Mom?"

"Keep the necklace. You're sixteen now and Granddad would want you to have it."

I pulled it out from under my dress and ran a hand along the chain, counting each of the rubies with my fingers. "What will John say if he notices it's gone from the safe?"

"It's not stealing if it's yours, is it?"

Our eyes held.

She said, "You will let me marry him, won't you? Promise you won't spoil things."

Did she think I had the energy for destruction? "I promise."

The car arrived to take us to the ceremony and I settled a smile on my face and helped with Mom's flowers and buckled Iris into her seat belt and tried to stop imagining that, by some miracle, Kass would have jumped on a plane and might be waiting for us at the town hall.

Thinking of him brought him. It was always the way. Mom's phone pinged, and I just knew it would be another WhatsApp.

"He's still in Kerala," Mom said, peering at her screen.

Not at the town hall, then.

"He says he's thinking of us and he's sorry not to be here. She flashed her phone at me and Iris. "Want to see the photo?"

He didn't look sorry at all. He was sitting on a bench looking relaxed. A little black dog snuggled against him as if they were best friends. Above them, a palm tree. Above that, an endless stretch of sky.

Mom gently nudged me. "You all right?"

I said, "Yep."

She said, "Missing him?"

I said, "Not really."

She put her phone away. "I don't think I'll show that to John until later."

Good plan. Every time Kass sent any kind of message, John went nuts.

At the town hall, we got out of the car. Mom and her maids. We brushed her down and smoothed her out and walked her up the steps. We were greeted by an assistant to the registrar and shown to a lobby outside the council chamber. We were told our cue was the music and that it would be a couple of minutes. He strode away, leaving us alone.

My mouth was dry, and my tummy hurt. Mom was nervous too. She kept patting her hair and giving little anxious glances through a crack in the door.

"People are still finding seats," she whispered. "There are so many faces I don't know." She eased the door open a centimeter. "Meryam's here. That's a relief."

Iris tapped my arm, then secretively lifted the hem of her brides-maid dress and flashed a denimed leg at me. "Shall I?"

I stared at her, horrified. Was she insane? She had her pirate dun-garees on underneath. "Don't even think about it."

"But I look like a cake."

"You look like a princess." I hurriedly arranged her dress back into place. "And not a badass one."

Mom let the door swing shut as the music began. "It's starting!"

I smoothed my own dress out and gave Iris a warning look. "Be a good girl, OK?"

She nodded. She held her flowers at her waist like she'd been shown. She bowed her head. I linked arms with Mom. Iris fell in behind.

We walked through the door together and the crowd stood up as we slowly made our way down the aisle toward John. People smiled as we walked by. They took photos and videos and nudged one another.

When we got to the front, John looked Mom up and down like he wanted to eat her. "You look stunning," he breathed.

"Ah," said the crowd.

He smiled his public golden smile. "I'm a lucky man."

Roger stood beaming next to him. In his pocket were two gold rings. In the third row, sitting with her colleagues, was Monika.

The registrar welcomed us all. She informed us the room had been duly sanctioned. She told us we were there to celebrate a union and to honor a commitment. She said, "If any person present knows of any legal reason why these two people should not be joined in matrimony, they should declare it now."

Go on, I thought. Do something, Monika.

I'd told her to come, hoping she'd cause a scene. But she sat there doing nothing at all.

The registrar reminded us of the solemn and binding character of the vows. She said marriage was the union of two people voluntarily entered into for life. I thought about Kass then. How warm it had looked under that tree. I wondered if the dog had a name. I wondered if Kass would stay in Kerala for monsoon season and, if he did, how much rain fell and how quickly and was it warm rain. I thought of him laughing under all that water—tilting his face to the sky and drinking it in.

The guests were asked to stand, and Roger was asked to hand over the rings and John and Mom gave each other their token and called upon us to witness it and then it was done. They were pronounced man and wife. They'd promised to be loving, faithful, and loyal in their married life together. And none of us had stopped them.

"You don't need saving," Kass said the first time I met him. "You can save yourself."

But it turned out I couldn't save anyone.

The sunshine outside the town hall seemed startling because it hadn't been there before. There were crowds milling around on the steps and standing in the parking lot in groups. Cerys and Ben were by the gate talking together, and I got that strange envy in my gut again—like a dragging sorrow I didn't understand.

The photographer was perky, like a posh market-stall trader, bossing everyone around. "Bride and groom on the steps, please. Everyone else out of shot for a minute."

I took Iris's hand and moved to one side as John put his arm round his new wife's waist. *Click* went the camera. Mom laughed up into John's eyes. *Click, click.*

"That's it, wonderful stuff."

A tiny airplane flew over as people threw petals and Mom and John posed. They looked like celebrities in their fancy clothes, dazzling the camera with their smiles.

Ben and Cerys came over. Ben said, "Hello, bridesmaids."

Cerys said, "Very pink, the pair of you."

Iris stuck her tongue out and slunk off. But I twirled for them. I don't know why. I felt ridiculous.

Ben went off to take photos and Cerys said, "How are you feeling about the speech?"

I shrugged. "I just want to get it over with."

"I bet public speaking turns out to be your thing," Cerys said. "You're a fantastic actor."

"You've never seen me act."

"No," she said, "but I've heard."

We both knew she meant from Kass. "He didn't make it," I said. "Probably in bed with some girl."

"He sent a message from India."

"That's nice."

"When was the last time you heard from him, Cerys?"

"I haven't. I've deleted his number and unfriended him."

She was stronger than me. I was still stalking him on Facebook.

"Did you know," I said, "that Kerala has two monsoon seasons? They also have a lot of coconut trees. And they produce more rubber than any other Indian state."

"Fascinating," Cerys said, "but it would help me enormously if we didn't talk about your brother all the time."

She used to want to. *He's not my brother*, I'd say. But now I knew I'd have to keep quiet. I didn't want her to suspect me and I wanted to keep being her friend.

"Now," the photographer said, his voice booming across us all, "can we have the bridesmaids back, please?"

Iris had disappeared, so I posed between Mom and John. He even put his arm round me, which I don't think he'd ever done before. When he went off to look for Iris, me and Mom had a picture taken. I took her hand and squeezed it.

Goodbye, Mom. Goodbye. Goodbye.

"Lovely," the photographer said. "Maybe lean your head on Mom's shoulder? That's it. Fabulous."

Clickety-click.

Guests took pictures of the two of us. Cell phone cameras flashed. The groom had gone, and a new order had arrived—me and Mom masquerading in the sunshine.

But John came back, dragging a reluctant Iris, and the four of us were bossed into different positions. Iris shuffled around looking sulky until John said that if we were ever going to get to the wedding breakfast in time, maybe we could get to the group shots? Soon there was a whole crowd of us on the steps and I found myself standing next to Ben.

"I've got something to show you later," he said.

"What kind of something?"

"A video."

"It's too late for all that."

He frowned at me. "What are you talking about?"

I trotted down the steps away from him. I was going to fail media studies along with every other subject and I didn't want to think about it today. I grabbed Iris by the hand and stood by Meryam instead.

She said, "Hello, girls."

I said, "Hello."

"You look adorable, the pair of you."

I said, "Thanks."

"You remember Barbara?"

A woman leaned across and clutched my arm and looked at me tenderly. "It's been too long, Lexi," she said. "We were all saying . . ."

Behind her, a smiling collection of women from my childhood waved at me. I felt like I'd seen them once in a picture book and they'd come to life.

"Who are they?" Iris whispered.

I couldn't remember any of their names, so I hauled her onto my back, so she wouldn't ask again. "Piggyback to the restaurant, Iris?"

"See you this evening," Barbara said. "We're all coming to the reception."

"Reception?" I said.

She laughed. "Girls' night out."

Iris wrapped her arms around me and pressed close. "Don't let me go."

Thirty-Five

WE STOOD ABOUT EATING hors d'oeuvres until the tables were ready. Total strangers told me and Iris we looked lovely and asked about school and exams and wondered if I was looking forward to the summer and was I going away with friends or off to any festivals?

I held Iris's hot little hand and experimented with different personas, because how could I say that I wouldn't pass any exams or that I was permanently grounded and on medication?

"I'm planning on Oxford University," I told one woman. To another I said, "I'm going traveling. India, probably." I told one smiling couple I had a part in a movie.

"You're a big fibber," Iris said.

But at least it made her laugh. She hadn't done that since breakfast. "Now, I've got a dare for you," I said.

Following my instructions, she told the bartender that Mom wanted a champagne cocktail. He prettied it up with an umbrella and tinsel stick and she brought it to me as carefully as an egg on a spoon.

"Are you going to get drunk?" she said.

She looked disappointed when I told her it was liquid courage and I was dreading the speech. What would John's reaction be? Would he get the subtext? I'd spent hours writing and rewriting it with Cerys, but maybe I should change the ending? Would it count as ruining the wedding if John yelled at me *after* the ceremony?

The alcohol helped, but my courage wavered again when John discovered Kass had a place setting at the top table. "What's this extra chair doing here?" he hissed. "I told them Kass wasn't coming. There's even a freaking place card."

"I'm sorry," Mom said. "I'll sort it out."

"You shouldn't have to sort it out."

"No," Mom said, "but I will."

She took the place card over to a waitress. She pointed back at the chair. John stood by Kass's place setting as if it had a neon sign above it saying, *My son let me down.*

Where was Kass right now? Watching astonishing birds flap into palm trees? Kissing girls under the flash of monsoon lightning?

With Kass's place gone, the table was too big for four of us. Roger was sitting with his employees at the far end of the room. Monika had been placed right at the back. It was the one thing Mom had insisted on—she would not have "that woman" anywhere near her.

Between each course people came sidling over to the top table and we sat there in a row, smiling and nodding as they told us how amazing we looked. It was like being in a shopwindow.

Just after dessert, Ben came up and squatted next to my chair. "I need to talk to you."

"Sorry, Ben, I'm busy."

"It's important."

"So are my official duties." I tipped my glass to him. "I'm being nice to people and then I have to do a speech, remember?"

"Shit," he said. "I forgot about that. Can I film you?"

Weeks ago, he'd asked me if I wanted to be a movie star. Who would have thought it would turn out this way?

"Sure," I said, "knock yourself out."

When Roger tapped his champagne flute with a spoon and called for quiet, I stood up smiling. I hoped I looked confident even though my legs were quivering.

I knew Ben was filming me. I could feel his attention on the side of my face. He was leaning on the bar with his camera.

Want people to listen? Wait, breathe, look up from your cue cards, and give your audience eye contact. Be aware of the back of the room, include everyone.

I said, "Some of you will have noticed that I'm not the father of the bride." I waited for the laughter and it came. A gentle rippling and a fading away.

"When my mom asked me to stand in for my granddad today, I said no because I didn't think I'd do a good job. But then I thought about it and realized it was a way of having him here." I tried to calm my breathing. It was too quick and shallow. I cleared my throat. I turned to the next cue card.

"The father of the bride has three main tasks. His first is to thank everyone for coming. His second is to share amusing stories about his daughter growing up, and his third is to pass on wisdom to the groom." I paused to check out the tables at the back. People were smiling. Even Monika. But I still didn't have their full attention. I'd recognize it when it came. It would sound like a hush in the air.

I picked up my glass and raised it. "Thank you all for coming." Around the room, glasses were raised in response. "As for the second task—well, I didn't know my mom when she was a child. So, instead, I'm going to tell you about the man who raised her."

I looked at Mom. She was beaming at me.

"My granddad had a gap in his teeth at the front and he looked like a boy when he smiled. He had gray hair and his favorite outfit was a boilersuit from his days as a mechanic. Whenever I visited, he made a real effort. He had a workshop and we'd make stuff together. Once, we made a wooden car and painted it luminous green. The wheels were coins we hammered flat on an anvil." I waited. I had them now. Even the waitresses, lined up by the window with trays on their hips, were listening.

"We'd go for walks and he'd ask me to pick a plant or a bird and he'd tell me everything he knew about it. He taught me knots and how to climb trees. He came up a lot of trees with me because he said children might be hot-wired to explore, but grown-ups needed to remind themselves."

I looked at Mom again. Her eyes were bright with tears. I was invoking Granddad and I was glad. He had something to say to John.

"He got special food for me and let me watch what I wanted on TV. If I was happy, then he was. And you might think, *Oh, that just sounds like he spoiled her.* But it wasn't about money or treats, it was about time and love." I smiled at Mom. "And he loved you, Mom. I know he did, because your childhood had days like that in it. And I know if he was here, he'd wish you happiness."

She nodded, her hand on her mouth. I took a sip of water and swallowed hard because I could feel my own tears welling. The room was silent. Not a murmur. This was the moment. I put a hand to the necklace and threaded the stones between my fingers.

Help me out now, Granddad.

"The third job of the father of the bride is to give the groom advice. I thought about this a lot and I thought maybe I'd have nothing to say. But then I remembered something my granddad told me, and I figured, why would his advice be any different now?"

I put my cue cards down. I'd rehearsed the next bit in the mirror.

"I never knew my grandmother, but my granddad said she was his soul mate. When I asked what that meant, he said she was the love of his life. I asked if I'd ever have one of those and he said he hoped I would. He hoped Mom would too, because she deserved to be adored and I deserved to have a father. 'How will we know him?' I asked. Granddad said, 'He'll be a good man.' I asked what that meant, and he said, 'He'll make you happy.' Then he told me there are three rules for making another human happy. I'd like to pass these rules on to you today, John."

I turned to him. "The first rule is to be kind." He looked at me, unblinking. "The second rule is to be kind." I wondered if his fists were clenched under the table. "The third rule is to be kind."

There was a strange quiet after I stopped talking. Mom eventually started the clapping, but it was only lukewarm around the room. I thought people would cheer. I thought Granddad's words were powerful enough to make the world a different place.

Mom got up and hugged me. "Attagirl," she said.

I nodded, didn't know what to say. I'd worked on it for hours—trying to put words in an order where they described a good man and gave advice to a bad man.

"What effect do you want?" Cerys had said.

I wanted transformation. I wanted John to hear my grandfather's words and pledge to change.

John didn't say anything about my speech when he got up to do his own. He thanked everyone for coming, although I'd already done it. And he thanked me and Iris for being bridesmaids (even though my official function was father of the bride), and Mom for agreeing to be his wife. He told her she was beautiful, reminded us all how lucky he was, and finally mentioned Kass, who sadly couldn't be with us today.

Then Roger stood up to tell us how reliable an employee John was and how gratifying that he'd finally made an honest woman of Mom. He told a few rubbish jokes, but the people from the office loved it—whooping with laughter at every crap punch line. Maybe they were scared not to be amused in case he sacked them all? Monika wasn't laughing. She had one strappy shoe half off and was gently swinging it backward and forward. I tried to imagine her and John kissing. But then it got disturbing inside my head and I zoned out.

After the speeches, Mom and John went off to cut the cake and the photographer got back into bossy mode and I went to the bathroom and looked in the mirror to see if I was different. I couldn't look myself in the eye for long. I looked like the sort of girl who might tiptoe.

Ben was standing by the toilet door as I came out. "Awesome speech."

"Thank you."

"But now I insist on talking to you."

"You insist?"

"For Iris's sake."

"What do you mean?"

"Come into the yard."

A few people were smoking by the door, but we went to the gate that led to the street and sat at a table. I began to feel afraid. "What's this about, Ben?"

"I've got something to show you. On my camera. Footage of John."

He'd done something terrible. Ben wouldn't want me to watch it otherwise. "I don't want to see, honestly. Don't make me."

He looked at me quizzically. "What's happened to you, Lex?"

"Nothing."

"You seem different."

I shook my head, pretended I didn't know what he meant. I didn't want to tell him I was now on ten milligrams of methylphenidate hydrochloride twice daily.

"I haven't shown this to anyone, Lex, and I'm pretty certain I'm the only one who saw it happen." He looked at me, his eyes serious. "But you have to watch it, so I know what to do."

"Ben, you're freaking me out."

He handed me an earbud and put the other in his own ear. He said, "I detached the audios, so they switch about. Don't be weirded out when you hear yourself."

"I'm in it?"

He nodded. "I whacked a filter on and gave it a title, but we can do more if you want. It's up to you."

He pressed play on the camera. Rose petals spun across a sunlit sky. It was footage from outside the town hall, people milling around after the ceremony, John and Mom laughing, Mom lifting her face up to him. I joined them on the steps and John put his arm around me. The scene died away, and a title appeared: "A Good Man."

"Shit, Ben, what have you done?"

"Just watch."

The title grew faint and the video cut to a long shot of Iris round the side of the town hall in the parking lot, and she was hauling her dress off and underneath were her dungarees. She looked furiously happy as she slung the dress across the hood of a car.

The audio from my speech faded in. ". . . he'll be a good man. I asked what that meant . . ."

The scene evaporated, and the next shot was taken from inside a car, bordered by a window. If I hadn't been terrified of what was about to happen, I'd have complimented Ben on his framing. But John came zigzagging between parked cars toward the camera and his muffled shout took over the audio. "What the hell do you think you're doing?"

The camera cut to Iris, much closer now. She looked scared, but then put her hands on her hips and faced up to him like a small and ferocious warrior.

My voice on the audio said, "There are three rules for making another human happy . . ."

I stared at Ben in horror. "Where were you filming this from?"

"My mom's car. The sound quality improves now because I opened the window. Keep watching."

John marched up to Iris and waved his arms around. She shook her head. He picked up the dress and handed it to her. She threw it back on the hood. The camera zoomed in on her sweet, furious face looking up at him. My voice again. "I'd like to pass these rules on to you today . . . The first rule is to be kind."

The audio cut to John. "Put the dress back on."

Iris shook her head.

"Put the damn thing back on."

She laughed in a half-hysterical way and tried to dodge past him. He grabbed her arm and she reacted as if she'd been attacked by a cobra, madly trying to yank herself free.

"Do I have to make you?"

She tried to shake him off, red-faced and desperate. She was tearful now and he should have let go, but he didn't. He grabbed her other arm.

My audio again. "The second rule is to be kind."

Iris weighed nothing—skinny as a stick and only six. He picked her up by both arms and held her stiffly in front of him. She stared at him. She looked like a toy.

"What's got into you? There are people waiting. Now put your fucking dress on and stop being a little bitch."

"The third rule is to be kind."

He put her back on her feet. She wobbled briefly, then reached for her dress. She looked dignified as she put it back on. I hated watching her be so brave. I hated watching her brush her arm across her face to wipe away tears in between doing up the buttons. But more than anything, I hated knowing that somewhere off camera, me and Mom were laughing on the town hall steps.

"Why did you film this?" I whispered.

"I went to the car to get my mom's coat. It happened right in front of me."

"And you didn't stop it? You didn't get out of the car and do anything?"

"It happened so quick, Lex. The whole thing was over in seconds. I was only filming Iris in the first place because she looked like a superhero getting into her secret costume. I thought it was funny. But then John appeared."

I pressed play, watched it again. Ben took out his earbud and sat quietly next to me.

It was furtive and secret and violent. That's how John got away with it—he bullied in private when no one was watching, and he smiled his golden smile in public and made you doubt yourself.

"He loves Iris," I said. "He never talks to her like that."

"Unless he does?"

"It's because I let down my guard."

"It's not your fault. It really isn't your fucking fault."

I rubbed angrily at my eyes. "What am I going to do?"

"Put it on your Facebook page?"

"I can't let the world see this happen to Iris."

"You could ask her permission?"

"She'd never give it. Why would she? It's humiliating. He's her dad."

"I could blur their faces?"

"And then it's a secret again."

"Except to everyone here today?"

He took the camera, fiddled with it, then passed it back. "Now they're incognito. The blue share button, top right, sends it to Facebook."

"I've only got three friends on Facebook."

"It's a community, Lex. Trust it."

I looked at him. I knew what it might do. I thought of Iris. How lovely she was. How young and upright, like a hopeful flower. I thought of Mom. How she longed for a happy ending, when all John did was whittle her away. I thought of myself and the little white pills he made me take twice a day.

It was a button. It was one click.

"Fuck him," I said. And I pressed share.

Thirty-Six

I BLAZED WITH CERTAINTY as I grabbed Iris and barricaded us behind an empty table. Our lives were about to transform. I held her on my lap and circled my arms around her while Ben went to the bar to get drinks.

"I know what happened in the parking lot," I said. "When your dad swore at you."

She looked at me, wide-eyed. "He said the f-word."

"I know."

"And then he called me the b-word."

"He shouldn't've done that." I kissed the top of her head, in that warm place that always smelled of cookies. "Why didn't you tell me?"

She shrugged.

"Did you think I wouldn't believe you? From now on, we're a sister double act, OK? You promise to tell me everything and I promise always to believe you."

She sighed and nestled close. I loved it that she felt safe in my arms.

Mom came over and said everyone had to vacate the room to let the staff set up for the evening.

I clutched her hand. "Stay here with us."

"I'm expected upstairs. Come on, girls, you'll be in the way here. Come and have a cup of tea with me and your dad."

My dad? Is that what we were calling him now? I shook my head. "We'll be fine."

She didn't want to leave us. But her husband was upstairs, and she'd made her choice.

"Iris?" I said when Mom had gone. "You know my special medicine?"

"That stops you from getting angry?"

"I just flushed it down the toilet."

"Won't you get in trouble?"

"Things are going to change around here, you'll see."

Someone famous was going to see the video and share it with millions of their followers on Twitter. It would go viral and everyone at the wedding would discover what John was really like and rise against him.

I couldn't wait.

Ben brought the drinks and we watched the room jazz itself up. A DJ set up in the far corner, tables were cleaned, the main lights were dimmed, candles were lit. A buffet table was laid out under the windows and a special stand was erected for the remaining tiers of wedding cake.

It was like watching a play. Soon, everyone would come back, and new guests would arrive, and phones would begin to buzz and ping and one by one people would glare at John. Then we'd lock the doors and shut the windows and tie him to a chair and make him watch the video over and over until Granddad's words went into him and Iris's tears penetrated his soul and he begged forgiveness and promised never to be unkind again.

It'd be like an exorcism.

I turned to Ben and whispered, "When everything kicks off, we'll have to get Iris away. I don't want her seeing her dad disgraced."

Ben frowned. "It's not going to be instant, Lex. It doesn't work like that."

"You were the one who told me to trust it."

"Trust what?" Iris said.

"Nothing," I told her. "Never mind. Hey, look who's here."

It was Meryam and the women from earlier—all glammed up and ready to party. I waved at them as they stood twinkling in the doorway and beckoned them over.

"Team handy," I told Ben.

"Told you we'd come," Barbara said, bending down to kiss my cheek and then rubbing at the place with her thumb. "Oops, now I've put lipstick on you."

Meryam introduced the others. "You remember Melis? And this is Gwen, of course. And Stef and Imani." Like spells from a long-ago time, their names, as they each leaned in to kiss me.

They said I looked like Mom when they first knew her. I'd forgotten they all went back years together. They cooed at Iris and told her she looked like her dad. They already knew Ben and covered him in kisses. He didn't seem to mind. They gazed around and wondered where everyone was. "We the first ones here?" I told them to join us, but there were more of them coming, they said, so they took the table next to us and shoved another alongside it. They pilfered chairs from other tables. They dumped coats and bags in a heap on the floor. They marched over to the DJ with early requests and made him write them all down. Barbara took drinks orders and then forgot them and yelled over from the bar and they all shouted back at her.

Iris sucked her thumb and gawked at them.

"They're Mom's friends," I said. "Aren't they brilliant?"

John's guests seemed dull as they wandered back and settled themselves politely at tables around the room. Compared to them, Mom's crowd were like a rowdy soccer team. I knew they'd protect us when John saw the video and things heated up.

"It's going to be OK," I told Ben. "We're a tribe."

He looked up from his phone. "Cerys has seen it."

"Seen what?" Iris said.

It was beginning. I felt a thrill deep in my gut. "Send it to your mom. Tell her to share it with the others."

He nodded, his eyes shining. I wanted to kiss him, just lean over and touch my lips against his. I'd never had that feeling for Ben before and it was shocking.

"What?" he said. "Why are you looking at me like that?"

I blushed, couldn't hold his gaze. Was it gratitude? Was I drunk? I didn't feel drunk. I felt as sharp and clear as a beam of sunlight.

Mom and John appeared at the door, hand in hand. I checked John's face for clues, but he seemed calm. *Not yet, not yet.* There was a smattering of applause and the DJ played Kylie's "Can't Get You Out of My Head," and Mom laughed, her other hand sliding under John's jacket. *I can't breathe without him.*

Mom's friends were like a flock of birds, launching themselves from the table and surrounding her.

"Where have you been?" they twittered. "We started the party without you."

"Upstairs," Mom said, "freshening up."

Barbara winked and mugged, "Freshening up!" and all the women laughed as if Mom had said she'd been having sex.

Meryam wanted a group shot and asked John to take it. Then everyone wanted one and he looked awkward standing there being bossed around, being told how phones worked and which buttons to press.

"Come on," he said to Mom eventually. "We have other guests."

The women clung to Mom. "Stay with us," they cried.

But she smiled and said she had to go. John took her arm and made a neat little bow to the women. "Can we sort this dreadful music out?" I heard him say as he walked away.

"You just wait," I muttered.

Cerys arrived, looking amazing. She swooped on me and pulled me into a hug. She whispered, "It's had fifty likes already." She stood up again and blew a kiss at Iris. "Hey, gorgeous."

I stared at her. "You're kidding?"

"Not kidding. Although 'like' is the incorrect word, obviously. There are comments too."

She passed me her phone and Ben leaned in. There were three comments from people I'd never heard of.

This guy's a shit.

What a loser.

Call the cops on the bastard. That's f***ing child abuse.

My tribe was swelling. For the first time, people were seeing what John was like. "We made this happen," I breathed.

"*You* made it happen," Ben said.

Iris wanted to know what we were looking at, so Ben took her off to the bar to get chips. Cerys slid into his chair. "I'm sorry I gave you such crap advice," she said. "Be nice? What use is that? I should've told you to kick him in the nuts."

I laughed. It came spilling out of me.

She laughed too. "You're literally the bravest person I know."

I wasn't sure that was true, but I wanted it to be. I asked her to help Ben take Iris away when things got dramatic and she agreed at once. I grabbed her hand. "Let's dance."

We were devastating. We were wild. We danced like we meant it, like a new age was dawning and it was one where wicked girls were in charge.

The attention of the room turned toward us. Faces flickered in candlelight. There was Roger with his pale mustache. There was Monika, looking mildly amused. There were groups of people from the architects' office with their intelligent eyes. There was John, his arm loosely slung around Mom. He didn't look happy to see us gloriously dancing, but I didn't care. *Soon, John, soon . . .*

Ben and Iris joined us. I held Iris's hands and spun her. The DJ pumped up the volume. Ben pulled Meryam to her feet and the other women followed. I requested anti-love songs and the DJ stacked them up—"Bad Romance" by Lady Gaga, "Grounds for Divorce" by Elbow, "Tainted Love" by Soft Cell. John put a stop to it after the first one, replacing Elbow with some classic jazz, but still we danced.

Music poured through me. I had an endless supply of energy. I breathed in the perfume of the women, the warmth of our moving bodies. It was Saturday night, and nothing could stop us.

"Kass has seen it," Cerys said at one point, and flashed her phone at me. She may have deleted his number, but he still had hers . . .

My dad's a prick. Tell Lex I'm sorry.

"Sorry" didn't do anything, though, did it, Kass? "Sorry" lets you stay safe under your palm tree. "Tell him to share the video," I yelled.

Mom came over. I knew she'd been sent by John. I could tell from her eggshell walk. "Can you tone it down?" she said. "You're being very rowdy."

I shook my head, pretended the music was too loud to hear her.

She came closer. "You're a bit raucous. Maybe it's time for a break?"

I grabbed her hand, pulled her into the dance. "Maybe it's time to boogie."

Be on our team. Join our tribe.

She was reluctant, embarrassed, probably aware of John glaring at us from the other side of the room. But we surrounded her,

338

encouraged her, and soon she was dancing with the rest of us, lifting her dress and flashing her ankles as she moved. Iris did the same, so we could all see the denim underneath. We danced together—a whole crowd of women and Ben—faster and faster, like fireworks whizzing and spinning.

And under the room, in some electric network, the video was being shared, the private John was being seen, and the world was about to shift.

He grabbed me when I went back to the table for some water. "Sit down," he said.

I did as he asked, just straightaway did it. Like a reflex.

He pulled up a chair and sat opposite me, his back to the room. He bent close. I could smell the alcohol on his breath.

He said, "I've just seen a link to a video that's posted from your Facebook page. A video that's been edited—by your lanky friend, I presume—to present me in a false and malicious light."

I tried to keep looking at him, tried not to look scared.

He said, "You know that video's illegal? You've heard of defamation of character?"

It was happening again—that smoke-and-mirrors thing. The words that made me feel unsure who was right.

He stared at me for a couple of seconds. "You probably don't know much history, since you never listen at school—but I suggest you look up Hitler Youth and see how they betrayed their parents and then ask yourself if you're not a nasty and vindictive little girl."

The words that twisted everything, so I ended up being the bad one.

He said, "How do you think your mom's going to feel about this? Ashamed, do you reckon? Disappointed you tried to ruin her day, despite your promises? And Iris? Do you think she'll ever forgive you for putting her tantrum on the internet?"

"You can't tell it's her."

"Did you think some primitive editing to obscure our faces was going to get you off the hook?" He jabbed a finger at me. "You've unlawfully intruded into my private affairs, you've attempted to damage my reputation, and you've publicized me in an offensive and misleading light. Unless you remove that video immediately and issue a formal apology on the website, I'll get a lawyer to force you to do it."

I should've known it would turn out this way.

"Did you hear me?" he said. "You need to take it down."

"I don't know how."

"Then get your fucking accomplice to do it." He swung back in his chair, his eyes deadly. "Come back when you're done and bring your mother with you."

"What for?"

"Just do it."

I hauled Ben from the dance floor and dragged him out to the yard. It was cold and there was no one outside. The night sky seemed full of pins. Sharp little needles making pricks of white across the dark.

I said, "We have to take it down."

Ben sank down on a plastic chair. "What happened? Did he see it?"

I nodded miserably. "He says it's illegal."

"That's bullshit."

"We still have to take it down."

I was shaking. Maybe Ben could feel it, because he reached for my hand. "We don't have to do anything."

"He's getting a lawyer."

"Then we'll get one too."

"We can't fight him, Ben. He's got all the money and power and rightness."

"He's not right, though, is he? He's wrong."

"Why did he have to see it first?" I peered through the door at Meryam and the other women still dancing under the lights. "Why haven't they seen it?"

"They have."

"Then why haven't they done anything?"

"My mom said she'll talk to yours in the next few days."

"That's it? That's all that's going to happen? You heard your mom promise not to abandon us. What good is talking?"

He frowned. "The video gives you a voice, Lex. It's a permanent record, so you never forget. That's what you wanted, isn't it? It stirs things up, gets a dialogue going. But it's not going to change the world overnight."

Of course it wasn't. Loads of parents lose their tempers. Weddings are stressful—right up there with death and redundancy. It wasn't like John hit Iris. He just swore a bit. He's usually so charming and everyone's allowed a less-than-perfect day.

"Take it down, Ben."

"We don't have to."

A million people could see the video and thousands could comment, but it wouldn't change a thing. Iris, me, and Mom would still have to live with him. And the more comments and likes and shares the video got—the more we'd suffer.

"Please, Ben. It'll make everything worse."

He switched his phone on. "I hate what he does to you, Lex."

Mom was still dancing when I went back inside—magnificent and disheveled in her dress. John was still at the table, his face slammed shut. I knew I was leading Mom to her fate as I drew her away from the dance floor toward him.

She was laughing as she sat down. She poured water from the jug and took several deep gulps. I sat next to her and watched her drink. I watched John watching her.

"Is this how married life is going to be?" he said. "Your friends making me look ridiculous?"

Mom thought he was joking. "What are you talking about?"

"Your friends need to leave."

"What do you mean? What did they do?"

He leaned forward, his face a mask of contempt. "They're drunk, overbearing, loud, and inconsiderate. They're taking advantage of the free bar. They're embarrassing me in front of my guests. You want me to go on?"

She looked suddenly afraid. "I can't ask them to leave."

"Given they weren't invited in the first place—I'd say you can."

"Of course they were invited," Mom whispered. "I invited them."

"Is it just *your* wedding, then? Do I get no say?"

"We discussed it." But already I could hear doubt in her voice. "Please, John, don't make me ask them to go."

"I'm not *making* you do anything." He leaned back slowly, never taking his eyes from her. I knew it was for my benefit. *See what I will do to her? See how I will punish her for what you did?* "It's your choice. Either they leave, or I do."

It was strange and dreadful watching the switch in her. She'd been so happy. And now she sank like a boat with a sudden hole. "What do you mean—you'll leave? We only just got married."

"I mean, I will walk out the door right now and you'll spend your wedding night alone." He shrugged. "Up to you."

"What will I tell them?"

"I don't give a shit what you tell them." He pushed his arms against the table and stood up. "Just make them go away."

Mom looked at me, pale with shock as he walked off. "They'll think I've lost my mind."

It felt like knives. Like glass in my blood. Like the sound windows make as they shatter.

Mom wilted beside me. "What will I say? What excuse should I make?"

Like shards of metal rasping in my head. Like bones being ripped apart and all my insides exposed.

"Oh God," Mom said. "I can't bear it." She pushed her chair back.

My breath was ragged. My fists were tough by my side.

And inside me, the furious thing came roaring.

Thirty-Seven

I WAS THE SHRIEK of a scraping chair. I was the clatter of a table being swept clean with the swing of my arm. *Smash*—the water jug hit the floor and broke into jagged slices. *Crash, tinkle*, went the tumblers.

I was the clamor of my own feet running. I was the explosion of the buffet table slamming to the ground. *Boom!* I was the smash of china plates and the jangle of falling cutlery.

Listen to my racket.

People recoiled. They pushed their chairs back and shrank away from me, clutching themselves.

I was frenzied. Fury spattered out of me like liquid rock.

Bang—over went another drinks table, smashing forward onto wet shards of glass.

"Christ," someone said. "What the hell's wrong with her?"

I was the outcry. The commotion.

"Somebody stop her."

Don't let them near you. Keep moving. You are the storm.

I bumped into tables, lurched into chairs, pitched half-eaten plates of food to the floor, tossed knives and sharp little forks behind me to stop anyone getting close.

The lights snapped on. The music stopped.

"Grab her."

I rushed at the cake, standing proudly on its special plate. I hauled it up, grappled it close, and turned around to face the room, breathing hard.

People stared, their mouths open like gaping fish. The women on the dance floor looked horrified. Ben's face was a mask of shock. Mom stood with Meryam, her hand on her mouth, her eyes luminous with tears.

The room throbbed with silence.

Spikes of broken glass glittered across the floor like ice.

The silence made everything strange. The way people stared made me feel raw. The cake was a dragging weight in my arms.

The fever was leaving me. I was going to be left with horror and mess and I stood there clutching the cake—the icing smooth as a tombstone—and I knew what John would do if I threw it. But he was going to do it anyway.

Whoosh! I lobbed the cake as far as I could. It plummeted more then it flew, spinning once before landing upside down in a soft collapse of cream and sponge at the edge of the dance floor. The plate didn't break, protected by the layers of frosting, but slid slowly to the carpet.

There was absolute silence. Every person in the room was staring at me. It was like the *Tempest* audition all over again and Caliban's words came into my head. *Cursed be I.*

John stepped over spattered cream and broken crockery toward me. He held one hand, palm out, as if approaching a fearsome animal.

"Don't touch me," I hissed.

He stalled. He looked incredulous. "Alexandra, please . . ."

"Stay away."

He came closer, one hand still held out. "Let me help you."

I shook my head, couldn't bear him near me. I had no words, only a hot jumble of feelings in my head as I stood there pathetic and sniveling, wiping my eyes on my sleeve.

John said, "I won't come any closer if you don't want me to. I can see you're agitated."

People exchanged quick glances. They were thinking—she's crazy, she's completely off her rocker. How dreadful for John, to be saddled with a girl like her.

He turned to the room and raised his arms like a conductor. "Ladies and gentlemen—I'm so sorry for this shocking disturbance." He smiled sadly at their troubled faces, at the ruined mess of the room and all the broken things at their feet. "My stepdaughter, Alexandra, is struggling with a psychiatric condition. She's under the care of a doctor and we were assured she'd be able to cope with the pressures of the day." His voice was low and tender. "Clearly that wasn't the case and I can only apologize that we weren't able to manage the situation and support her more effectively."

They believed him. I could feel it happening. People flicked me little secret looks. How true it sounded, how right and sorry he was.

"*I am subject to a tyrant,*" I muttered. But it wasn't loud enough for anyone to hear. Caliban's words were nothing more than whispers from a play written hundreds of years ago.

"We're looking at all possible treatment strategies," John said. "We're determined that Alexandra will get the help she needs to reach her full potential." He rubbed a hand across his eyes as if he was exhausted. "In the meantime, please could I ask you to find it in your hearts to forgive her for what's happened here today?"

I felt a chill in my bones as people murmured softly that, of course, I was forgiven. I was young, troubled, only a girl. Poor John, having to cope with me. Poor me, having to cope with an appalling illness. The cold burned deep in my ribs and chest and spread along the length of my spine.

Caliban wanted to kill Prospero. He got Stephano to help and they crept toward the tyrant as he slept, and Caliban told Stephano to tread softly, to speak softly too, because if Prospero woke up, he'd fill their skin with pinches and make them into "strange stuff."

That's what John did. Made me into strange stuff. I was trembling violently. I felt like something peeled, standing there.

He surveyed the damaged room, his face troubled. He caught the manager's eye and promised to reimburse him for all breakages and to pay for a professional cleaning service. He pledged to foot the bill for any individual's dry cleaning. He made a joke about needing to be made partner to pay for it all and a few people politely chuckled.

He raised his hand. "Please could I ask you all to move to the yard temporarily while this mess gets sorted and I take Alexandra home?" He flashed a golden smile at the manager. "Any chance of getting the heaters on outside? And more champagne for everyone?"

Oh, their sympathetic faces as they began to gather their belongings. They spoke softly among themselves, pretending it was all fine, nothing to look at, everything perfectly normal for a Saturday night.

I felt desperate, heavy and hurting. I looked for my tribe—but the women were pulling on their coats, collecting their bags, looking resigned and sorry. Mom was sitting at a table with Meryam, dabbing at her face with a tissue. Cerys and Iris were nowhere to be seen. Only Ben dared to look at me, his gaze steady as he mouthed, "I believe you."

Weeks ago, he'd stood in his kitchen and told me he'd believe every word if I ever dared speak. Now, seeing him there—the one still point in the room—gave me hope.

One person was better than no people. And what did I have to lose?

"You're a liar, John." My voice rang out across the room.

Alarm flashed briefly in his eyes, but he covered it quickly. "Don't start up again."

"I don't have a condition."

"Hush, Alexandra."

"You took me to a doctor to keep me quiet. You drugged me to shut me up."

"I said, hush. No one wants to listen to this."

Everything was so private behind closed doors. Even if it was only Ben who believed me, I wanted to drag it into the open—like turning a stone and watching all the furtive creatures hidden underneath being dazzled by light.

I filled my lungs with air. "You're a bully."

John held his hands up in horror as if that was the most ridiculous statement he'd ever heard.

"You are," I said. "You're a bully. Who bullies people."

It really was very simple. That's what he was. It sounded so right that I said it again.

"Stop this nonsense." John's eyes flared with anger as he walked toward me—his whole face going from handsome to ugly to mean in a second.

I glanced over at Mom, but she was sitting very still, hunched into Meryam, not looking at anyone. She couldn't take sides, she never could. Ben was still looking right at me. "I believe you."

I stood my ground, raised my voice a notch. "You bully my mom and you bully me and now you've started to bully Iris. What did you say to her earlier? Oh, I know . . ." I adopted his posture from the parking lot—the arrogant chin, the fury in his eyes. "'Put your fucking dress on and stop being a little bitch.'"

"That's enough."

"That's the kind of thing bullies say. And things like, 'You're pathetic and a terrible mom and I don't know why I ever left my wife for you.'"

"I'm taking you home," John spat. "Get your things."

I ducked away and waved at the women, standing with their

coats by the door, and did another of John's poses—the one where he folds his arms and looks at you as if you're nothing. "And apparently you lot are overbearing and drunk," I said. "Did you know? You're embarrassing the other guests and you weren't even invited in the first place."

John's color changed—he looked suddenly pale with a slick of sweat on him. "That's it. That's enough of this madness. You need to stop right now."

But I couldn't. "You're a bully," I said again. "A bully who bullies people." Declaim it. Name him. *Bully, bully, bully.* I said it over and over. It was the deepest truth. And maybe it was like white noise in his head—that one word repeating. *Bully, bully, bully.* It enraged him. Like when the princess guesses Rumpelstiltskin's true name, and hearing it makes the little man so angry he rips his own body in half.

"Would you just shut the fuck up, Alexandra?"

There was a shift in the room. Like a shoal of fish suddenly altering course in a river, the crowd turned their attention to him.

He dismissed them with a wave. "She's going home," he declared.

And a voice cut across the room. "You really are a shit, John." Monika, in her lovely clothes with her pretty young face, stepped forward. "Pick on someone your own size, eh?"

"Stay out of this," he snapped. "It's nothing to do with you."

"Oh, I'd say it is." She raised her glass at him. "I'd say you being a shit is a lot to do with me."

"I suggest you mind your own damn business." His voice was low and deadly.

Monika raised her glass to me now. "What were those rules you were on about earlier? The first rule is to be kind, right?"

I nodded. "And the second and third."

Monika smiled. "Probably the fourth rule too, eh?"

I smiled tentatively back at her. "And the fifth."

John rubbed his head furiously. "Will you two girls shut up with your stupid rules."

Monika laughed. She tinkled with it. She looked at John as if seeing him clearly for the first time and what she saw was a clown with his trousers down. She laughed and laughed.

And for some reason I started laughing too. It seemed so ridiculous that John was raging, and Monika was shining with mirth, and a silent crowd stood around staring. It was beautiful, the sound of us laughing. Not to be afraid! How good it felt! Just for once. Just to taste it.

John loosened his tie. "Pathetic," he said.

Some of the waitresses, standing around the edge of the room, began to giggle.

"Stop it," John said. "Will you just all—"

But we couldn't. His protesting made it worse. "Who's actually in charge here?" he spluttered.

We cackled with laughter.

John's eyes were wild as if he were a trapped creature in a room. I saw a bird like that once, flapping and mad with containment. "Ridiculous," he blustered. "Absurd."

Which made it even funnier.

John slumped in a chair. "Christ, will everyone just give me a fucking break?"

Maybe he gave up because we were laughing. Or because the atmosphere in the room changed—people breaking into excited chatter as if released from an enchantment. Or because the women by the door moved en masse to be at Mom's side. They helped her to her feet and hugged her. They straightened her dress, tidied her hair, and wiped her mascara tears away.

Flanked by her friends, Mom walked toward me, her arms stretched out for a hug. "Come here," she said. "Come to me, baby."

"I'm sorry," I said, collapsing into her. "I wrecked your wedding."

"It's me that's sorry." She kissed me fiercely before pulling me closer. "You have no idea how sorry I am."

Maybe John gave up because I had Mom and Monika and a whole squad of women on my team.

Or because his son left him.

Or because Iris had become badass.

Or because Ben walked over to me and said, "You're a hero," in a particularly loud voice.

Maybe John was exhausted. It must get very tiring being in charge, needing to be right all the time, having to be on high alert in case anyone tries to undermine you.

Maybe he realized there were some things he simply wasn't in control of.

Whatever it was, watching him sag in that chair was like watching a man turn back into a child. Something fell away. Like he could cope with anything except being laughed at.

He said the lights were bothering him. He clutched his belly and curled himself up, then almost immediately uncurled. He had a mild look of panic in his eyes as he sat back up. "Why do I feel like this?"

Someone got him a drink of water. Someone opened a window. Mom went over and reached down to touch him. She said his skin felt clammy.

"Is he asthmatic?" Roger asked.

Monika was looking on with pity. Perhaps she loved him. Perhaps she thought he was faking. Perhaps, like me, it reminded her of Roger collapsed on a chair a few weeks ago. Perhaps this is what powerful men did when they were cornered—they feigned illness? Or perhaps she thought laughter was such a dangerous weapon that John might die?

No one was laughing now.

Someone offered an aspirin, saying maybe he should suck on it, just in case it was a heart attack?

Mom put a hand on his shoulder. "John," she said. "John, you're frightening me. How do you feel? Can you tell me?"

He mumbled something incomprehensible. And because it reminded me of Granddad all over again and because I hated Mom looking scared, I asked Ben if I could borrow his phone and I called an ambulance.

Epilogue

THE WORLD HAD EMPTIED out. Everyone was on vacation. Exams were over and now there was nothing to do except wait for results day. Ben was in Turkey seeing relatives. Kass was still in India. Cerys was off with her friends doing the rounds of music festivals. I spent my days in the yard with Iris—on a blanket sunbathing, in a deck chair reading, or teaching her to climb the tree.

Mom was too busy caring for John to mind what we were up to. She fed him kale soup or broccoli mash or whatever healing recipe she'd dreamed up. The doctor had recommended a complete change of lifestyle—diet, anger management, exercise. It might help with the panic attacks, she said.

On the night of the wedding, the paramedics had helped John out to the ambulance and unbuttoned his shirt and attached sticky pads to the skin of his chest.

"Am I dying?" he'd asked, his eyes full of fear.

I stood there, holding Mom's hand and hoping beyond anything that he lived. Because Iris and Mom loved him. Because, in that moment, he seemed a broken man and not a powerful magician at all. I asked the dead for it. That's how much I wanted it.

The ECG showed no imbalance and his oxygen levels were fine. They told him it was probably a panic attack. But he said it was more than that, he felt dizzy and nauseous and there was something wrong with his heart—a strange pressure in it. They made him put his head down and take deep breaths. They told him he was working himself up, that nothing was wrong, but he begged to go to the hospital and, once he was there, pleaded to be kept in overnight for observation.

Since then, he'd been to a private cardiologist and paid for two more ECGs, blood tests, a chest X-ray, an echocardiogram, and a stress test. They'd all come back fine.

"You need to keep calm," the doctor said. "Give up smoking and maybe take up yoga or meditation? You've been used to being in control, but it's time to ease up now."

"Will he die?" Iris asked me one day. It was hot among the top branches of the ash tree and the sky buzzed with insects. The neighbor's plum tree was brewing with wasps. I could hear them ecstatically vibrating over the fence.

"He won't die," I said.

"He will one day."

"Well, yes—we all will one day."

"And is it OK if I still love him?"

"He's your dad, Iris. You're totally allowed to love him."

"That's good," she said softly. "But I'm not going to marry a man when I grow up. I've changed my mind about all that."

I almost laughed but stopped myself. I looked at her and waited for her to tell me more.

"There is someone I like, though." She said this shyly, her eyes cast down, fiddling with the ragged hem of her shorts.

"Who?"

"Charlie. She's at my school." She looked up at me, clear-eyed. "She's a girl."

"And you like her?"

"I'd rather marry her than anyone else."

"That sounds a sensible plan."

She smiled. I smiled back. She held out her hand and I took it.

She said, "I didn't want Cerys to take me away when you trashed the wedding. I wanted to help."

"We've talked about this, Iris. You're not a monster."

"How come you're allowed?"

"I'm not saying you can't be angry. You're allowed to be mad as hell. But it's not our job to look after Mom. She's supposed to look after us."

"What if Daddy's mean to her?"

"Walk away. Meryam or the others are going to help Mom from now on."

"Where do I walk to?"

I patted the tree. "Here. You've nearly got a handle on climbing it. A couple more lessons and you'll be all set."

I imagined Iris and her friend Charlie up here, cozied together with candy and cans of soda. Maybe they'd bring planks up like

Kass and me used to. And binoculars for spying and blankets for hours of comfort.

Iris said, "Will you show me how to do the wall next—your special way of going along the branch and jumping down the other side?"

"Into the cemetery?"

"You said it's amazing in there. You said there's hours of freedom. You said there's loads of adventures."

I told her of course I'd show her the old paths, the places Kass and I used to go when we wanted to get away. Would Iris need them in the way we had?

In my first message to Kass when I got my new phone, I told him:

YOUR DAD'S LIKE AN OLD BULL ELEPHANT.

Kass messaged straight back:

HE'D HATE THAT! ELEPHANTS ARE MATRIARCHAL.

He messaged me every day after that. He sent WhatsApp and Instagram messages. He told me about Kerala and how he was in a room overlooking a mountain.

SEE, HERE IS THE MOUNTAIN.

He told me how one day he was followed by a snake and two boys chased it off with a stick.

SEE, HERE ARE THE BOYS.

He met a man who played guitar and Kass was swapping English lessons for learning chords, because all girls love a boy who plays guitar. Was that a flirt? Did he mean me?

I sent him pictures of the yard, of the opposite pairs of light green leaflets on the ash tree moving in the direction of sunlight.

REMEMBER THIS, KASS?

He sent a picture of himself sitting on the stone wall of a harbor. Behind him was a stretch of blue ocean dotted with fishing boats. He sent a picture of chickens sunbathing around his feet in the dry dust. He was always alone in the pictures, or with some form of wildlife. He'd shaved his head and looked younger, his ears sticking out.

I described the different ice cream me and Iris bought every day, our trip on the bus to the rowing lake, and how I rowed Iris three times round the island. Once I sent a photo of John sleeping on his back on the sofa with his belly hanging down under his T-shirt. He looked old and his hair was greasy.

Kass messaged back:

IS THAT SERIOUSLY MY FATHER? WHAT HAVE YOU DONE TO HIM?

I texted back:

LAUGHED AT HIM. LOL.

I felt lighter than I had for months, as if a spell had been broken. But I was also scared that everything would go back to how it was. Roger had declared John unsuitable partnership material and said he could choose being demoted, being transferred, or walking away. He walked away and we all pretended it was for health reasons. But seeing John weak didn't mean he'd stay that way.

Over July, Kass's messages came less frequently. I had a rule only to respond and never initiate with Kass. It was to keep my heart safe. Me and Iris had taken cushions up the tree and were sitting reading when I got the picture of Kass outside a little wooden house. There were fishing baskets and piles of rope by the door. But the clue was the pair of girl's sandals on the ground next to him. She would have taken the photo and the smile in his eyes was for her.

Wouldn't you enjoy that, Kass? I thought. A little wooden house and a blue-sky day and a girl who wears slim, white, beaded moccasins.

I showed it to Iris and told her he'd met someone and would probably marry her and never come home.

She shook her head. "He'll be back."

I closed my eyes and imagined him walking across the lawn and gazing up at me through the leaves, his hand shielding his eyes from the glare. "Hey," he'd say, "should I come up?"

And I'd have to say, "Sorry, Kass. No room for a third. These branches are taken."

Iris flipped a page in her book. "Delete the picture," she said.

I opened one eye. "But what will happen then?"

She smiled. "You'll have to wait and see."

✱

"I got you a present," Ben said. He'd only been back five hours and had called asking to meet. We walked to the park and sat by the lake with to-go cups of tea.

The present was in a small paper bag and I was embarrassed it would be jewelry. Kass had given me his coat once, and just last week I'd put it in a carrier bag and taped it up. I planned to take it back to Sophie's soon. It would be interesting to see her again.

I wasn't ready for jewelry from Ben. To distract us from the gift, I pointed out that the lake was covered in green weeds and the ducks had to paddle around in the middle to get clear of it. "It wasn't there last time I came," I said.

"I guess it's the warm weather," Ben said. "It's almost as hot here as it was in Turkey."

He'd spent the last four weeks swimming and playing tennis and lazing around on a beach. At night he'd wander with his mom and aunts to the local café and they'd eat and play cards and Ben would sneak sips of raki and they'd talk until late and then he'd climb the hill back to his aunt's place and lie with the windows open listening to cicadas.

"The best thing," he said, "was the endless time. I've never been on such a long vacation. I took hours of footage. That's got to be a good sign, right?" He turned to me, excited. "I know I've got two years of sixth form to get through first, but I'm definitely applying to film school."

I asked him what classes he'd chosen, and he blushed. In his excitement he'd forgotten that he'd done brilliantly in his exams and I hadn't. He was going to stay on at school for sixth form and I wasn't. It was as simple as that.

I took a sip of tea. He took a sip of his.

"Are you going to open that present, or what?" he said.

I peeled off the tape, unrolled the bag, and opened it up. Inside was a fridge magnet of a woman with wings and a massive smile on her face. I pulled it out and held it in my palm. Her hair streamed behind her. She looked beautiful and murderous all at once. In blue writing across the bottom it said *women fly when men aren't watching*.

"Reminded me of you," Ben said.

"You think I can fly?"

He laughed. "I thought you could stick it on the fridge instead of the rules John's had up there for weeks."

I secretly watched him take another sip of tea and tried to work out what I felt for him. I'd wanted to kiss him at the wedding, but sitting here in daylight, he seemed gangly and strange-looking with his red hair and olive skin and freckles.

He did have a lovely smile, though.

And he was kind.

Why didn't I like him more? Did I find kindness boring? Did that mean I only liked boys who'd end up breaking my heart?

"So," Ben said, "let's talk about the elephant in the room."

I laughed. "We're in a park, Ben."

"I mean sixth form. I mean you not getting in."

"What's the point?"

"The point is you passed four GCSEs under difficult conditions and that has to count for something. They shouldn't throw you out of school because you missed out on one exam."

"You need five to stay on. There are no exceptions, Ben. They've been telling us that for years. And really, I only got media because you attached my name to your movie."

When I'd opened my envelope on results day, I'd shoved it in the trash and skulked back home hoping no one would remember. But John had set a reminder on his phone months ago and was in the living room waiting for me.

The best thing about the lecture that followed (I was a disappointment and had let everyone down) was when Mom came in from the shop and hugged me and said she was sure I'd done my best and that sevens in both drama and media studies was very good indeed and a five in both English papers wasn't to be sniffed at. John said it wasn't good enough to get in to sixth form, though, was it? And Mom said she was sure we could fight for a place. She asked John to phone the school and he said it was nothing to do with him and, in his opinion, I should be sent to a therapeutic facility now that I was refusing to take the meds. Mom folded her arms at him. "Apart from that being a ridiculous idea, how would you propose paying for it now that you're unemployed?"

When I told Ben, he smiled. "Sounds like things are changing at home?"

"She hasn't done anything about it yet and he's still in charge."

Ben said, "She's right, though—you should fight for sixth form. You spent the last few years being told you were crap and the school never did anything. They pride themselves on results and do nothing for kids who are failing. I'll come with you if you like and we can make a case together."

"It's too late. I'll do a pathway course somewhere."

"But they don't do drama."

"I have to give up on the idea of drama."

"About that . . ."

Ben handed me a sheet of paper folded up. "Please don't be mad."

Dear Ben

Thanks for your note. As you guessed, I'm unable to discuss Lex's sixth-form application with you. However, I don't mind sharing that I'd love to have her on the A-level drama program. She's a performer of great sensitivity and courage. Why not ask her to contact me and we can arrange for her to come in for a chat?

Best,

Steven Darby

"You wrote to Mr. Darby about me?"

"See what it says?" Ben stabbed a finger at the paper—"*A performer of great sensitivity and courage.* That's you, Lex. Isn't that amazing? I swear that guy thinks you could make a career of it. He'll do anything to help you."

"Everyone at school thinks I'm crazy. The principal, the receptionists, most of the kids. I threw a chair through a window, Ben."

"Sixth form is a fresh start. You can reinvent yourself." He grinned. "An actor as courageous as you should find that a doddle."

He looked delighted and I couldn't work out how I felt. Was this a guy telling me how to manage my life, or a friend who believed in me?

"John won't like it," I said. "He'll think acting's a waste of time."

"You don't need his permission, Lex." Ben nudged me. "You can fly, remember?"

Ben came home with me to talk to Mom. He stayed all afternoon and Mom fussed around him like she used to with Kass—offering him snacks and drinks every five minutes. Iris climbed all over him. I wanted to take a photo and send it to Kass: *We have a new man in our lives.* But I didn't. Partly because I had to leave Kass alone and partly because I didn't know what I felt for Ben. I found myself secretly studying him. Friend or boyfriend? Handsome or not? Mom invited him to stay for supper and John became the world expert on further education and interrogated him: Wouldn't it be more ambitious to do core subjects for A level? Do colleges even respect media studies? And what exactly do you learn at film school? Surely better to get some real qualifications under your belt because anyone can press play on a camera?

Ben smiled and said it was all in hand and then he asked John some questions. How's the work search going? How's your health? How do you feel about Kass giving up architecture? John deflated in front of us and excused himself. It was odd how that kept happening.

Over the next few days, Mom came around to the idea of

contacting the school without John's support. She told them I'd been anxious and under a great deal of pressure. They said if that was the case, I needed a medical statement from the Child and Adolescent Mental Health Services, because only students with exceptional circumstances would be allowed to stay on at sixth form without the required exam results. Mom said she'd see about that and she wasn't going to let this drop. I hugged her. She reminded me of a mother I used to know.

Every morning, she asked John to help with her plans and every morning he made a face and went off for his morning workout. Round and round the park he went like a hamster. The cardiologist had recommended daily exercise.

Mom asked Dr. Leaman to provide the school with a medical letter saying I'd been incorrectly diagnosed. He refused, so she went to our family GP and got one from her instead. Meryam wrote a supportive statement and Ben emailed more teachers. I don't know if anyone contacted Kass. I wrote a letter under Cerys's guidance entitled "Opening the Forbidden Door," which stated how I'd been "living under a harsh regime and thundering with injustice and now I needed the opportunity to heal by practicing creative arts, which only the sixth form could provide."

Ben thought it was my letter that swung it. But I thought it was the meeting me and Mom went to when the principal of sixth form asked what I meant about living under a harsh regime and Mom said, "My husband is very tough on Lexi."

"What do you mean?" the teacher said gently, handing Mom a tissue.

"He can be a bit of a bully," Mom said.

My word. His name.

Say it loud. Shout it from the rooftops.

The school agreed I could stay on with the understanding that I resat math under their Supported Pathway scheme. I chose drama, film, and media studies for my A levels, and for my extended project qualification I decided to explore fairy tales.

When I told the teacher at my interview, she said that might be a bit childish and perhaps I'd be better off with a different subject?

"Like what?" I said.

"Something you'd like to learn more about? Space travel? The history of the Olympics? British politics? The Kardashians?"

"Do you think I'm an idiot?" I said. "The Kardashians?"

"They're very popular."

I told her that fairy stories are not just for children, that they're all around us in video games, on TV, in movies.

"There's an opera called *Bluebeard's Castle*," I said. "There's a *Cinderella* ballet."

"What exactly is it about fairy tales that intrigues you?" she said.

"They teach you stuff. Like how to fight your way through terrible ordeals and get to a happy ever after."

"Would that be a prince?" said the teacher.

"No way! It's more like when you're lost in a forest and you stumble across a house with a light on and know you're going to be safe."

"So the protagonist has to earn their happy ever after?" said the teacher.

"Yeah—like there's always a way out, but you've got to find it. Fairy tales teach you to have hope while you're looking."

"Well, you sound as if you know what you're talking about." She smiled. "I shall look forward to reading your dissertation."

Her smile reminded me of the ones I used to get in drama—*You are a pleasure to teach. It's wonderful having you in my class.*

✳

Ben propped himself against me and we sat on the grass eating slices of pizza. As sixth formers we had those gate passes I once envied Cerys for and we spent almost every lunchtime in the park.

"So," he said, "how about a film about snow?"

"It's September," I reminded him. "It won't snow for months."

"A film about ice cream. About ice. About drafty houses."

It was so hot we fantasized about cold as if it was something we might never feel again. The heat literally throbbed. But I still wanted Ben to be propped against me.

It was a fragile thing. A friendship growing into something new. I saw less that he was gangly and just a touch nerdy and more that his kindness shone like a light inside him. I never had to think of anything to say; I just said stuff. If we met up, I knew it would be fun. Everything we did felt adventurous. I'd never once felt as if he might snap at me or put me down. He was always interested. He asked good questions and listened to the answers. He didn't do hot and cold. He didn't play those kinds of games. He didn't get me to do stuff he wasn't brave enough to do himself. He didn't hide. His emotions were right there on the surface to see.

He had plenty of irritating habits too. Right now, he was using his hand as a plate and a massive chunk of pizza had fallen on his jeans. He struggled to sit up, leaving a damp patch on my shirt where he'd been pressing against me, and brushed himself down. He had tomato sauce smeared across his right cheek and a piece of pesto on his tooth. I passed him a napkin and he blew his nose on it, which wasn't what I meant at all, but he had hay fever and had been sniffing all day.

"Come on," he said, stuffing the napkin in his pocket. "We must be able to think of something. How about a movie about pizza? We can splurge on taste tests."

We had to pitch an idea to our group by the end of lunchtime. Each group had a budget of a hundred pounds and six weeks to make a film. The others in our group were new students. They didn't know about my monstrous reputation because they'd only joined the school in sixth form. As Ben had said—a fresh start.

"How about a movie about women and work?" I said.

"Because of your mom?"

"Because she still does the cooking and cleaning when she gets home, even though she's been working in a shop all day."

"Stereotyping of gender roles," Ben said.

"What's that?"

"John being an ass. The presence of a capable woman threatens him, so he punishes her."

Mom had gotten more capable, it was true. She left for work in the morning leaving lists and instructions pinned to the fridge. John was expected to put away the breakfast things and get the groceries and prepare a meal and collect Iris from school and take her to the park or on playdates. He always collected Iris, but he mostly refused to do the other things and spent most of the day locked in his study tinkering with his dream house design.

"You think he's depressed?" I asked Ben.

"I think he's in shock."

"You think she'll kick him out?"

"Sadly not. She loves him, and for some inexplicable reason she needs him."

It was because she believed in soul mates. But I didn't want to tell Ben that in case he thought I was flirting.

We'd been on a few walks on weekends. Not date walks, but friend walks—getting-away-from-the-apartment walks. We walked the cast-iron tunnel stretching beneath the Thames, descending beside the *Cutty Sark* in Greenwich, and emerging at the Island Gardens on the other side of the river. We found a plague pit in a churchyard and a pub with an antique hangman's noose outside the window. One day we filmed butterflies and herons in the Ecology Park and had a picnic in the meadow. Another day we got a boat from Westminster pier to the Thames Barrier. We watched the sun go down over Parliament Hill and ate french fries from a van on the way back to the tube station. And everywhere we went, we took snippets of film. Ben was making a montage of London as part of his portfolio for film school.

"How about a film about an upside-down world?" Ben said.

"There's a French movie where a guy hits his head and wakes up in a matriarchal society. We could do something like that. You can play a girl who wakes up one morning and discovers she's the power holder."

"In charge of her controlling stepfather?"

"In charge of the world."

"Can I fly?"

Ben smiled his lovely tilting smile. "Sure, but you really have to do it. Special effects are beyond the budget."

I stood up and flapped my arms. Ben hid behind his fingers. "I'm not looking."

"You're allowed to look. Now I'm the power holder, women can fly even when men *are* watching." I clambered onto a bench and flapped my arms some more. Ben lay on his back on the grass and grinned up at me. I stood on the metal armrest at the end of the bench and launched myself, leaping up as high as I could and beating my arms. For a millisecond I imagined lifting, air flowing under and over my wings like water in a river. But it was only a millisecond. I landed squarely on the grass and sank down cross-legged next to Ben. "I need a bit more practice."

He laughed. "We'll practice every day."

It was the "we" that let me notice the gap between his T-shirt and the top of his jeans. It was the "we" that let my eyes linger there, that allowed my gaze to travel up and meet his.

"What?" he said, smiling. "Why are you looking at me like that?"

I smiled back at him, gentle and slow. The sunbaked grass beneath us radiated heat.

"Let's make a movie about happiness, Ben."

"Seriously?"

"We can blow the budget doing stuff we like."

"What kind of stuff?"

I reached for my bag and pulled out my notebook. I headed a page: *What brings you joy?* I flashed the header at Ben.

"You're asking me?"

I nodded.

Our eyes met. That tilting smile again. "Making a movie with you."

"Well, yours is an easy fix." I scribbled it down, laughing.

"It goes well with our movie about fear," Ben said. "You're aware of that?"

"*Our* movie?"

"It had your name attached, right? So I'd say it was ours." He tapped the paper. "It's a good question. Would you interview people?"

"Me?"

"You'd be great at getting to the core of things. I bet people say one thing first and then, when persuaded by an intrepid reporter, they say other stuff—deep stuff, you know? It could be a real tearjerker."

"It's supposed to be about joy!" But I loved how he took me seriously, was prepared to accept my idea as worthwhile, didn't try and argue me down or stamp his own vision on top. I imagined interviewing people I knew.

What brings you joy?

Iris would say giving up ballet (who knew she hated it after all these years?). Kass would say discovering himself. Cerys would say embracing chaos—her law degree was forcing her to find balance with a hectic new social life. And Mom? She'd say John. Over and over like an incantation. Although there'd been some days lately, when she might say me and Iris. Or even her new job.

And John? Would I dare ask him?

He was mostly snappish and irritable. He was unemployed and pissed off. But every now and then he smiled that golden smile and it wasn't fake or manipulative, but genuine. Had losing power made him happier?

"We could mix interviews with the group doing fun stuff," I said. "We can hang out in cool places and take footage of beautiful things."

"How about an interwoven narrative?" Ben tapped his fingers on the pad. "How about—alien girl interviews humans to try and gain secrets of happiness for her own sad race? You play the girl, of course."

"Ah, but can I fly?"

"That's a given."

We were both laughing as we heard the distant bell. Ben glanced at his phone. "We're going to be late, but you feel like pitching this to the group when we get back?"

We scrambled up, grabbed our bags, and started back across the park toward school. I was feverish with ideas. What brought me joy? Rushing to a lesson, half-dizzy with heat while buzzing with thoughts for a movie. Knowing that in ten minutes I'd pitch it and feel the wonderful tug of an audience. I'd want to bring them close, to tell them a story that grabbed them and pulled them in.

It was hot now, but soon autumn would kick in and we'd wake to mist hanging in the air and go to sleep to the smell of wood smoke. The cycle of things made me happy. The ash tree beginning to lose its leaves again. Iris and her new mate Charlie fending off wasps from their jam sandwiches with a fishing net and hooting with laughter like a pair of tree sprites. Mom watching a program about ten items that make up the perfect working wardrobe. Ben's smile. Meryam taking Mom out for regular girls' nights and John staying in to look after Iris. Ben's smile again, because he was still doing it, even though we were breathless and late for class.

Our fingers brushed, and it was like something electric between us. Like we were alight with possibility.

Stories are about transformation, about starting as one thing and ending as another. And in the middle, when you don't know what's going to happen, all you have is hope. It's the thing fairy tales teach us.

But by the end, when you've fought hard and faced all the challenges, you'll discover something amazing—that joy exists in the world.

And you deserve it.

Acknowledgments

Thanks to Nathalie Abi-Ezzi, Katherine Davey, Patrice Lawrence, Anna Owen, and Elly Shepherd for asking difficult questions, pointing out new pathways, and energetically cheering me on.

Thanks to Marion Scott for early reading and long walks rammed with good talks.

Thanks to Louis and Archie Hill, for their radiant brilliance in all things.

Thanks to the awesome Bella Pearson for hours spent exploring narrative.

Thanks to David Fickling for his continued faith. And to all the splendid people who work with him at DFB. You lot are family.

Thanks to Catherine Clarke—always kind and often fierce. This is the best combination in an agent and I am so very glad you're on my team. Also, thanks to the marvelous women at Felicity Bryan Associates.

Thanks to Andrew St. John for inventing long-papering! And for walking the worlds with me.

Finally, thanks to my tribe—the wonderful women in my life. You know who you are. I hope I tell you enough how much I value you.